A BROTHER AT MY BACK

SACRED HEARTS MC
BOOK 13

A.J. DOWNEY

COPYRIGHT

~

Edited by Barbara J. Bailey

Book design by Maggie Kern

Cover art by Dar Albert at Wicked Smart Designs

DEDICATION

To Dr. Christy Sim. Your work is so very important. Keep doing what you're doing to help abuse victims rise and the rest of humanity help them do it. Wonder Woman, indeed.

PROLOGUE

Lawless & Lost
A Dragon Short Story

One
Dragon...

1992

I counted through the bills as I strode into the bank on old Main St. I didn't have much in the way of a need for banks, but I wasn't keen on handing the dealership so much cash. It was a good way to get on law enforcement's radar. Especially for the likes of me. Nope, they wanted me to buy it, a cashier's check would have to do. I didn't pay no mind to the openly-curious stares or the looks of outright disgust. I just stood in line and counted my money and waited for the dude in front of me to get the fuck out the way.

"Next!" the woman called, and I walked up to the counter. I looked up into the prettiest goddamned face I'd ever seen. Pale, perfect skin, smooth the likes of a porcelain doll. And wide, big brown eyes. Her hair was neat and perfect, framing her face and brushing the tops of a pair of perfect fucking tits that were, unfortunately, covered in an ugly-ass blouse that belonged on some librarian twice this angel's age. It was a-cryin' fuckin' shame too.

"Can I help you, or are you just going to stand there drooling all day?" she demanded quietly, and those eyes of hers sparked fire.

Well, I'll be fuckin' damned.

I glanced at the little plaque declaring her name by her window, "Seriously? A pretty girl like you, and they name you Matilda?" I asked. She looked nonplussed and I grinned.

"Can I help you?" she repeated pointedly.

"Need a cashier's check."

"And for how much?"

"Ten-thousand, five hundred ought to do it," I said and she blinked once, slowly.

"Seriously?" she asked looking me up and down and I admit, I didn't look like much. Grease stained jeans, beat-to-shit riding boots, equally-stained grey tee with a red, white, and black flannel tied around my waist. My jacket was showing some wear, but my cut? It was relatively new. I'd just started my club a few months back with six buddies of mine.

One of 'em had a connection with a guy who was in it with a cartel, and we were making it huge running coke up the east coast. The shit came out of Bogota and across the border. My guy's guy picked it up there and met up with us, and we ran it up north to NYC from there. We were raking in the cash hand over fist and the bike I was currently on, God love her, was about done for. I couldn't afford to break down on a run, so I needed something new. The trick was skating under the radar when it came to making a big purchase like this. I still held down a part-time job as a mechanic and had been living on one of my guy's couches for the better part of the last six or seven months to make this look good. First, a bike, then me and my boys had our sights set on picking ourselves up a clubhouse, solidifying our power base, and making it damned clear The Sacred Hearts ruled this area.

"You got a problem, Sweetheart?" I asked, and she looked me over one more time.

"Do you have an account with us, sir?" she asked and shifted uncomfortably the more those lovely brown eyes roved over me. Couldn't blame her. I worked my ass off to be this cut and I knew my faded tee hugged my chest to show it off. I was just vain enough. And the way she was looking at me right then, a faint little blush across her pale skin, my dick was getting hard just thinking about it.

"No, that a problem?"

"Not if you don't mind the fee associated with a non-member transaction." She leaned closer, which gave me a view and a half down her ugly-ass blouse. "It's free to open a new account and it'd save you a few bucks."

"You want to see me again?" I asked, grinning, and she smiled a secret little smile.

"Not particularly." Damn. "But any chance I have to cost my dad a few bucks, I'll take it." She leaned back and raised her eyebrows, smiling conspiratorially with me. Fucking little minx!

"Alright, how do I open a new account then?"

"I'll get Brad, the branch manager for you..."

"Dragon," I told her.

"Oh, come on, that can't be your real name," she scoffed.

"It's not, but it's the only one that counts in my world, Sweetheart."

. . .

Two

"Oooh, here comes trouble, and it looks like it's got its sights locked on you, D!"

I looked up from the bottle of beer in my hand and glowered at my buddy, Unkind. "The fuck you talking about?" I demanded. He pointed with his own bottle of Bud before swilling some down. I turned and raised an eyebrow. Fuck. Me.

It was the girl from the bank a few days back, the one with the old woman's name. Mildred... no, Matilda! That's right. She stopped next to me and trailed fingertips over the seat to my new ride.

"So this is what you were after, then?" she asked, lightly.

"Yeah, you like it?" I asked, and the two brothers I was with started laughing at me.

We were at a house party, the yard strung up with lights between the trees, some of that modern hip-hop rap shit blaring out of the house. I was a classic rock man myself, and whatever this black bastard was hopped up on, he was fucking annoying as shit. Kept going on about baby got back. Of course, I couldn't complain too much, I did enjoy some of the shit I grew up listening to sometimes, which included Mariachi. I was proud of my wet-back beaner heritage.

"It's nice," she said, and she was standing real close-like, looking up at me. I sort of remembered her being taller at the bank.

She was a pint-sized thing in a white peasant blouse and cut-offs that didn't leave a fuck of a lot to the imagination. She had shapely legs despite being such a short shit, and I wouldn't mind too terribly much gettin' between 'em. Shit, the girl had it going on.

"Matilda, right?" I asked, taking a drink of my beer, playing it cool in front of my Bros who were each watching me, grossly fascinated. She made a face like she'd tasted something bad and looked down at the bike.

4

"I hate that name. My mom and dad are German, they thought it was great. My friends call me Tilly."

She looked up at me again and damn, those big brown eyes slayed me. I was getting hard in my jeans and it was getting a mite uncomfortable. Didn't help that the little minx wasn't wearing a bra under the thin rag she had on, her nipples pert and pressing against the thin fabric. Fuck me swingin'! I loved me a nice pair of titties and Tilly had a gorgeous pair.

"That what we are, Sweetheart? Friends?" I said with a reckless grin.

"Depends, Dragon," she said slowly with a smartass little smile, she opened her mouth to say more but was cut off by a shrill voice from across the yard.

"Matilda! Oh my god, Matilda! What are you doing!?"

Tilly looked up at me with the fire of mischief in her dark eyes and said, "Oh, we are definitely friends, if you get me away from her," she said.

I handed my beer across my bike to Unkind, "Say no more, Sweetheart. Climb on." I got on my bike and she got up after me, her lithe form snug against my back. The woman who had been striding across the yard in our direction shrieked in protest, which I cut off real damned quick by starting up the bike. She was coming across the yard at a full tilt as I pulled us out and onto the road. The high, wild laughter that poured out of Tilly over my shoulder was a fucking turn-on for sure. I was so getting into that pussy if I could help it. God damn!

Three

I drove us out of town and up to the overlook. It was a clear, warm summer night and I figured being up a little higher and out by the river, it might be a little cooler. It damned sure would be a little more private. I pulled into the gravel lot and kicked the stand down on the bike, leaning her onto it.

5

I got up, stretching a bit, and took a bit to admire the stars. It was beautiful up here, but I was more interested in the beauty on the back of my bike. I turned to catch her sitting cross-legged, her wedge sandals dangling near but carefully away from the hot pipes while the engine and exhaust ticked and cooled.

"So, who was that?" I asked. She made a face and then laughed again. I could easily get addicted to that sound.

"My sister, Margaret. She's a little over a year older than me and thinks it automatically makes her the boss."

"You always get on the back of a bike with strange men?"

"Nope. The first time, actually. I kind of live for adventure like that." She winked at me. Actually winked at me.

"Not afraid I'm going to rape you?" I asked. For some reason, I wanted her safe, and if I had to scare her a little to get her to think twice about pulling this shit with someone else, someone who wasn't me, I could live with that.

"Can't rape the willing," she stated flatly, and gave me a curious look. "You honestly didn't think I would get on the back of the bike with a dude I thought was ugly, did you?"

I laughed outright. Jesus Christ, she was direct! I liked that about a woman. Thought it was sexy as hell when they knew what they wanted and weren't afraid to take it or ask for it.

"You want me to fuck you?" I asked incredulously.

"Well, I was sort of hoping you would talk with me first, then maybe you would kiss me a little before we got to that part." She met my eyes and her own sparkled with laughter. I stepped up to her and she jumped down off my bike and met me halfway.

"You're really serious, aren't you?" I asked her. She raised herself on her tiptoes, her hands against the leathers on my chest.

"Yep. You game?" she asked, her breath warm and gentle against my lips.

Fucking hell yes, I was game! I pulled her tight up against me and holy fuck, it was like she was meant to be there. I crushed her mouth with mine, forcing my way past her lips, and she was sweeter than pure sugar on my tongue. The scent of woman and roses surrounded me and I was drunk on it. Drunk on her. I hauled her up my body and her legs wound around my hips. I marched us to the picnic table nearby and set her on her feet, never giving up on kissing her the whole way.

She cried out in protest, which I swallowed whole when I set her down but there was no fucking way... I shrugged out of my jacket and cut and laid them out on the rough wood surface behind her. She was struggling with my belt and made a happy noise when she got it to release. Holy Christ on high, this was really happening!

As soon as her hand wrapped around me, I groaned. Shit, there was still way too many clothes between me and her. I went for the button and zip on her shorts. As soon as they were free, she gave this sexy little shimmy of her hips and they slid right down her silky legs.

I'd broken the kiss to watch and heard myself moan, "Oh God, yeah," at the sight of her little striptease. I put my hands on her hips, fixated on that barely-there landing strip, inviting my eyes to the apex of her thighs and I lifted her up and she gave a happy squeal along with a little giggle. I planted her ass firmly on the satin lining of my jacket and pulled her forcefully to the very edge of the table so I could get at her.

"Spread those legs for me, Sugar," I murmured, and she gave me a salacious little grin.

"No glove, no love," she taunted, and held a condom out to me. I blinked. Where the hell had that come from!? I didn't care. I tore it open with my teeth, let my pants fall around my thighs, and rolled it on. She wiggled closer to the edge of the table with another sexy little shimmy and I grinned.

"Last chance to say no, Baby," I told her and she smiled up at me with an intense carnal glee.

"You chickening out on me?" she asked, her voice sexy and low.

"Fuck no." I slicked my head against her lips and pushed my way inside. She moaned, deep and throaty, and threw her head back as I pulled myself into her. I closed my eyes and breathed deep, drowning in the smell of roses and sex.

"Goddammit, you're tight," I said between gritted teeth.

"Oh, you feel so good!" she cried, and edged her hips to meet my thrusts.

She was so warm, wet, and alive! This beautiful, writhing creature in my arms... and I didn't know a thing about her. Shit, though, from the moment her lips touched mine, the second my cock slipped inside her, she was mine. This weren't no one-and-done. Mmmm, I liked this bitch and I was determined. I was gonna find out everything there was to her.

"You are so fucking beautiful," I breathed and I tried to hold off for as long as possible before I came... but nothing, nothing ever came close to that first time; to my Tilly.

"Oh, god," she groaned, "yes," as I spilled myself into the condom inside her.

I drew back and gave Tiffany a sad little smile.

"Mm, you are entirely too fucking good at that," she said. "No wonder half the bitches up in here want to do you or say not to say no." She gave me a smile that was miles sadder than I'd given her.

I pulled out and tucked myself back into my pants, condom and all, and wouldn't look at her. I wanted to hold on to the vision of my wife, of that first time, for just a little bit longer before the guilt and the fractured heartache crept in. The close quarters of Sugars' back room pulled me completely from the memory of that long-ago night, that first time, way sooner than I was ever ready to let it go. It was the way of things now. My punishment. My cross to bear. My fault, for letting it happen and for getting her killed.

"And who you calling beautiful? Sure as hell didn't sound like you meant me," Tiff said lightly, voice edged with forced sarcasm. I traced a gentle finger down the scar along the side of her face, the reason she would say that to me. Tiff wore a Venetian mask when she danced or she hid behind her long brown hair that was so like Tilly's. Almost nobody got close enough to see the scar, let alone touch her. I felt privileged the girl would let me pay her to fuck her. She was that kind of stunning. And to the right kind of man, the scar only added to that beauty; it didn't detract.

"You are beautiful," I said and I meant it. "You're just not her."

Tiff was young and had a story, it just wasn't none of my business. We kept it to sucking and fucking every once in a while when she was short on rent. I tried to treat her right, I definitely overpaid her, but there was only so much my broken heart had to give and money wasn't going to buy her happiness. Just her body from time to time.

"Hey, don't." She touched the side of my face and regarded me with sad blue eyes. "You do that and this won't work for either of us anymore and I need the money," she said softly. She moved her barely-there scrap of panties back over her puss and slid off the backroom's counter.

"You're good to me, Dragon. I can't do this if you feel guilty for it. I can't..."

"Sorry, Darlin'," I stopped her soothingly with a crooked grin, pulling her short satin robe up onto her lithe shoulders.

"Don't be," she said with a brave little smile and pulled the two sides of her robe together, retying the belt. "Can you do me one favor, though?" she asked quietly.

"Sure," I said, finishing doing up my pants and belt.

"Who was she?" she asked. She was back to hiding the scarred side of her face behind her hair. I brushed it aside and drew her close, laying a line of soft, butterfly kisses along the length of the seam in the side of her beautiful face.

"She was bold, unafraid, an adventurous woman. She was my wife." I told her, leaving off the 'And I killed her.' I handed Tiff a wad of bills, I never paid any of the other girls I did this with. I didn't have to. Most of them were just happy to have the President's cock in 'em. Tiff was special. Tiff was young and didn't need to let me fuck her, but she needed the money. When one of the more seasoned girls had come to me and told me about her, that some of the guys were getting a little rough with her, I had her sent my way.

"Thank you," she said somberly. I hooked a hand around the back of her neck and pulled her forehead to my lips.

"You need to find a different line of work, Baby," I murmured against her hair and she nodded.

I let her go, and went out the back exit into the summer night, intending to head back to the club. I found myself at the overlook instead. Palms flat against the scarred wood of that fucking table. If I closed my eyes and breathed in real slow and deep, I could almost smell it... that hint of roses and sex.

1

Tiffany…

I stared into the mirror of the dressing table I shared with my best friend Delia in the boudoir at our mutual place of employment. Sugars was a seedy little strip-club off the old main drag of town, and popular with the locals. It was also, by all appearances, as low-rent of an establishment as they came, but honestly, the seedier-looking the better. Silas wouldn't look for me here.

I wiped the crimson stain off my lips and stared, all wide brown eyes framed in tatted lace that covered the top of my face and followed the curve of one cheek. It was a gimmick I had adopted to keep me in this line of work. The only thing beautiful about me was my body and the side of my face left unmarred by Silas' handiwork.

I'd been here three years, stripping and even selling my body for sex to try and climb out of the pit of despair that had been that night – the night the good-looking rodeo star had changed everything and turned me all sorts of ugly.

I'd been a runaway at sixteen, had followed the rodeo working the concessions and had fallen squarely into Silas' trap by nineteen. I'd barely gotten my GED and I was working hard to improve my lot in life by taking night courses at the community college. Silas had been everything in the beginning. Another handhold up, someone to look up to and he had made me feel so safe, so long as I had fallen in line and didn't stray. Which I didn't. I never had, and I never would.

It'd been Delia's birthday weekend and she'd begged me to go out dancing with her and the rest of the girls. I'd gone, even though Silas had tried to get me to stay home. He'd shown up at the bar, caught me dancing with another fella. He'd been hopped up on drugs, broke a bottle against the bar, screamed something about making it so only he could love me and he had torn into the side of my face with it.

I peeled off the lace mask, the light theatrical adhesive pulling on my skin. I affixed it to the Styrofoam head and sighed, shoulders drooping under the weight of my pathetic reality.

I didn't usually go down the awful, twisted lane of my memories, but I couldn't help it tonight. The letter that had come in the mail today changed everything. I was supposed to be safe for five years, not three. Silas had been sentenced to five years, screaming about how he was going to kill me as they had bodily dragged him out of his sentencing hearing. Except, according to the trifold slip of single computer printout from the Kentucky Department of Corrections, they were letting him out early.

He's going to kill me had been running through my head nonstop since I'd opened the envelope. I had plucked it from my mailbox on my way in here.

He's going to find me and he's going to kill me... It's only been three years and they're going to let him out and he's going to find me and he's going to make good on his promise. He's going to kill me.

Except as shitty as my life was, I wasn't ready to die. I let out a long drawn out breath and threw down the makeup-removing cloth onto the table scattered with makeup. I stared at the scarred wooden top, at the eyeshadows and lipsticks, the wreckage left behind from wearing the painted mask of a stripper nightly.

I felt frustrated tears well up in my eyes but refused to look at my reflection in the glass. I hated it. Hated what he did to me. Hated that I'd been reduced to stripping and whoring to pay for the medical debt, over a hundred grand! I was so close to digging myself out and they were releasing him early.

The door to the backstage slammed open and my best friend Delia came through. I, of course, jumped and froze staring wide-eyed in her direction before I could even think to fix my hair.

"Ah! God, I am so glad this night is over!" she declared loudly, tipping her head way back and letting out a gusty sigh. She went on to say something else, but she turned to look at me and whatever it was died on her lips. She took a sharp intake of breath and said instead, "Shit, I'm sorry. I didn't mean to scare you."

"I'm not scared," I lied and she gave me a look like, *really bitch?*

"Right, you never leave your face uncovered. I scared the crap out of you."

She was right. I quickly turned back to the mirror and finger-combed my hair over the offending half of my face, covering the wicked, forking seam of scar tissue with a sheet of deep, glossy brown.

"I'll make it quick," she said, striding in her platform stripper heels to the bank of lockers. She pulled on clothes over her bare chest and g-string, and unbuckled her heels to pull on some comfier boots.

I was already dressed in jeans and knee-high leather boots, a soft cotton and rayon long sleeved black shirt that clung to my body with a plunging neck and backline. It was hardly modest, but once I added my scarf and jacket it would be.

"I'm ready to get out of here, too," I said softly, and went back to work on my hair, ensuring it would keep things covered.

Delia, god love her, chattered away about so many things that I just really didn't have the heart to listen to. She knew and didn't press, just went on to fill the silence with her random chatter while I waited for her to finish getting dressed to take us home. She was the only one of us with a car. I shuffled every red cent I had into paying off my debt and for school. Online courses had become a godsend. I was almost done with that, too.

Damn him.

I got up and let Delia take my place at the dressing table so that she could change out her lipstick and touch up her eyeliner, tucking the offending paper into my back pocket and going to my locker for my scarf and my black leather biker jacket. It was really a style-over - function thing when it came to the latter, but I liked it. It made me feel tougher than I actually was.

We cleaned up our mess, stowed our makeup in our lockers, and made sure everything was secure before I followed Delia's bright chatter away from the dim club and pounding music. We moved swiftly through the neon-lit dark of the backstage and both waved bye to Zeke at the back door. A big country boy, he served as our bouncer on the same shift. He swept open the door for us like he always did, Delia and I spilling out into the real dark and nearly empty lot, the crisp night air cold enough to sting our faces. We moved swiftly over to her beat-up Honda and she opened her door, leaning across to open mine.

I got in, clutching my purse in my lap and locking the door behind me, while she started it up. I swept the seatbelt across my chest and clicked it home nervously while she put it in reverse.

He's not even out yet, I told myself, but it didn't matter. The fear that accompanied memory was in full effect.

Delia lived the next town over. It was nicer there, while I lived on the edge of this town on its opposite side in a steal of a rundown studio apartment. Delia lived in a pretty complex, but the nicer part came with a price tag I wasn't willing to pay for in my efforts to get the fuck up out of here.

We were on the two-lane highway headed for home and my mind was on overdrive when I interrupted her shit-talking about one of the other girls, Cherry, by blurting out, "Delia, do me a favor and pull in here up on the right."

She looked over at me, mouth dropped open in surprise and asked, "In there?" with a squeak.

"Yeah, in *there*. Now, Delia! You're going to miss it!"

"Tiff, what in the world do you want to go in here for?" she demanded and I pressed my lips together, trying to think of a reply.

"I know a couple of them, and I want a drink," I lied and got out of the car. I leaned down into the open doorway and said, "Don't wait for me, k?"

"Tiffany!" she called out, as I shut the door soundly. I swallowed hard and walked across the blacktop scattered with gravel to the front of the low, cinder-block building. I dragged open the door, loud music pounding, light spilling out, and without looking back at my best friend, went inside.

My pulse pounded in quick, steady rhythm with the classic rock song while I scanned the crowd, a bunch of surprised and questioning faces turned in my direction. A big man leaned back from the bar and eyed me up and down and asked, "Who you looking for, Sweetheart?" A diminutive woman perched on a barstool in front of him leaned back to look at me from around him. She swept me with a golden gaze, her eyebrows going up.

"Dragon," I called back. "You know him?"

Laughter met me as a reply and another man next to the big blond asked, "Is she for real?"

"Yo, P!" the big blond boomed out over the room and I saw the man I was looking for stand up over a knot of seated people across the room. He scowled and came around the table towards us and I tensed. The man had a habit of moving like a thunderhead across a room. Intimidating.

"You got a minute?" I called out when he was close, and he cocked his head and jerked it past the bar, deeper into the club towards the back. I swallowed hard and nodded, taking a step forward, he held up a hand and halted me mid-step.

"You look like you need a drink, Sweetheart." I nodded and he lifted a chin at the woman behind the bar. She lifted her chin and set two glasses on its polished wood top and a bottle of tequila next to them, her tattooed arms full of flowers.

He picked up the glasses with his thick fingers in the rims, pinching them together, and wrapped his other hand around the neck of the tequila bottle. I shuddered, my eyes fixed on his fingers around the neck of that bottle and felt my mouth go dry.

It wasn't the same grip but that didn't stop the wave of nausea, or the clear glass from turning brown, the silver label turning red and white. I closed my eyes and breathed slow and deep and when the room righted again I opened them. Dragon's eyebrows were raised and he jerked his head. I nodded and followed.

He opened a door just past the archway leading to a branch of hallways and ushered me through. I went in and he flipped on a harsh overhead light. It was a bedroom and of course, he probably thought I was here to line my pockets... shit. *Maybe this was a bad idea.*

I turned and he shut the door, setting the glasses on the scarred dresser top. He poured some alcohol into one and held it out to me.

"Ain't here for that, are ya?" he asked straight-away, jerking his head in the direction of the bed behind me. Dragon was my best, ah, after-hours, client at the strip club. Paid well, was generally quick about it, and was as respectful as a man paying for sex could be.

"No, um…" I downed the tequila in my glass and winced, making a face and held the glass out. I meant to hand it back but he poured some more. I thought about it a second, downed it, too and held out the glass, gasping out around the smooth burn, "No more, please."

He took the glass and set it aside then took a sip of his own. He raised an eyebrow and said, "That there was good sippin' tequila. What's got you so worked up?"

I pulled the letter out of my back pocket and said, "You said if I ever needed anything, I should come to you." I swallowed hard. "I hope you, uh, really meant it, because I'm scared and I, um, I don't know what to do."

I held it out to him and he scowled, set his glass down and unfolded the paper. His jaw clenched, his brows knitting together as his stormy dark eyes skimmed the page.

"Get comfortable," he ordered. "This here is going to be a talk."

I went to sit and he waved me up holding out a hand for my purse. I slipped it over my head and held it out to him and he put it on the coat tree hiding behind the door. He held out a hand for my scarf, and then one for my jacket and, once satisfied, waved me down to sit on the end of the bed.

The letter he set on the edge of the dresser. He came around and dropped heavily onto the end of the bed beside me and looked me over. He reached out and I flinched, knowing what he was going for. He froze mid-motion and said, "Easy, you ain't gotta hide from me, Sweetheart."

I held stock still as he traced along the fall of my hair that hid the ruined side of my face before pushing it back behind my ear. I swallowed hard, feeling more exposed than when he fucked my naked twat in the back room at Sugars.

17

"He how you got that?" he asked.

"Yeah," I answered morosely.

"He's out in a couple of days according to that thing."

I felt my eyes mist and I tipped my head back, staring at the ceiling. "I know."

"He knows where you're at?"

"*That*, I *don't* know."

"Okay." He nodded slowly.

"I don't know what to do," I said frankly.

"You said that," he said with a soft grin and he looked me over.

"Since you're here, you mind?" he asked, quirking a brow and I frowned slightly.

"Will you help me if I do?"

"Shit, I'll get you the help, and I'll pay you for the privilege for right now, too," he said.

I nodded and he did something unprecedented; he drew close and put his lips on mine. In all the times we'd ever fucked or boned, he'd never kissed me. Not once. Partially because I knew I reminded him of his dead wife, and partially because I tore a page out of the *Pretty Woman Art of Hooking* handbook. I didn't kiss my clients. I held that back for myself.

He didn't let his lips linger on mine too long, trailing them in a soft caress along my jaw to where he typically liked them to be, the side of my neck. I closed my eyes and tried to get into it, but it was hard. I wasn't used to there being a bed. This was far and away more of an intimate setting than I was used to. Not to mention, I had on way more clothes as a starting point.

"Last time, Sugar," he breathed in my ear. "Relax a little for once."

I didn't know what he meant by 'last time.' When it came to selling myself for sex, I honestly hoped it wasn't my last time with him. He paid well above what my going rate was, and compared to some of the other guys, he wasn't half bad. He actually cared if it felt good for me, not just whether the show I put on was convincing.

I sighed out and closed my eyes, concentrating on the feel of his mouth against the side of my neck, the tickling sensation of his beard against my skin, the feel of the warmth of his hand against my waist. He pulled my shirt from the waistband of my jeans and slid a hand underneath and I let him.

It was a strange sort of consent, of willingness when it came to sex for money. While your heart rebelled, your mind overrode it. I wanted this with my head, and when it came to Dragon? Easily halfway with my heart. It was frustrating, though, because as much as I wanted it with Dragon, what I really wanted I knew I would never have. Just the illusion of it, and wasn't that what I was selling? Illusions? These men, Dragon included, knew I didn't want them, but I had to pretend that I did.

I needed to go through all of the motions, the sighing, the moaning, the arching and the trembling… except with Dragon, unlike any of the rest, half of it, if not more, was true. He did make me sigh, and he did make me arch, and out of all of them, I did actually let go enough to come from his attention without much accompanying guilt.

This time was different, and it was more than just our surroundings. I couldn't quite pinpoint what it was, maybe it was the buzz kicking in from the good tequila, who knew? But I did manage to let go a little more than usual when he slid a hand down the front of my jeans and teased at my clit. He was the only one of my clients to even pay attention or care that it existed.

"You gonna come for me a few times tonight," he said with assurance.

"I think I'd like that," I murmured back, and I felt him smile on the side of my neck.

"That's a good girl," he whispered, and I closed my eyes and toed off my boots at the same time I lifted my shirt over my head.

"You want me to blow you?" I asked.

"No, I want you to ride my face if you don't mind."

"Not a usual request, but okay." *You're buying,* I added silently. Almost as a way to remind myself that this was business. The alcohol was mellowing me out, my muscles relaxing some, and if I wasn't careful, my guard would slip. I couldn't let that happen, no matter if I held a sort of affection for him.

He pulled back and we both set about stripping down to nothing, quickly and efficiently.

"Boys don't know what they're missing," he said when I straddled his head, hands on the headboard to help support myself. He wrapped strong hands around the tops of my thighs and pulled my bald pussy to his face, licking me in one long stroke from opening to clit.

I closed my eyes and bowed my head, trying to let go enough that I wouldn't focus on the fact that, as attractive as he was, he was old enough to be my dad. So many odd and strange little thoughts went through your head when you took this kind of work, but when you were as broke and as desperate as I had gotten, beggars couldn't be choosers, you know?

He stabbed his tongue into me and I gasped appropriately. It sounded good, but what he was doing wasn't really getting me there, at least, not yet. I needed to let go, and funny enough, I really wanted to let go tonight. I wanted to leave Silas, and all of this fucking bullshit behind for a night. For once, *I* wanted to feel good and hey, if he was offering and I was getting paid besides? *Win/win.*

He slapped my ass and I yelped and looked down at him, offended. He raised his eyebrows and growled out from beneath me, "More tequila."

I laughed and that somehow broke some of the tension. He gave me a nudge and I climbed off of him and went for the bottle. I picked it up by the neck, the glass smooth; the paper label slick against my palm and took a mouthful from the bottle. I held it out to him where he lounged back against the bed, his dick standing at attention, the veins in it nearly pulsing.

He shook his head and I shrugged and took another pull, shaking my head, realizing how this must look from his perspective. Shit, I instantly felt bad. It wasn't like he was unattractive, he actually was pretty much the opposite. He was smokin' hot, for an older guy.

Strong brow, sharp cheekbones, smoldering dark eyes, and super muscular. I mean, he had to be pushing sixty and he still had a six-pack. The epitome of a silver fox. I pushed the thought out of my head when it rose unbidden: *Didn't he just have a grandson?*

"Sorry," I muttered finally after a third pull from the bottle.

"For what?" he asked.

I felt myself blush, which wasn't that rich? The whore, blushing. I bowed my head and let the curtain of my hair hide my face when I said, "I don't want you feeling like I need to be drunk to do you. That's not it, I promise you're hot."

He laughed and said, "Get back up here; bring the bottle if you need it."

I got back up on the bed and moved to the top, setting the bottle on one of the nightstands. He smoothed a hand along my ribs and over the angular curve of one of my narrow hips and sighed.

"What gets you off?" he asked.

"I don't know anymore," I shot back truthfully. I didn't. If it hadn't been sex for money I hadn't had it since before Silas fucked up my face. I couldn't even clearly remember the last time I got off with a partner. I mean, I really had to think about it.

"You like when a man eats your pussy?" he asked. I looked him in the eyes and thought about it.

"I mean, I guess. I never really put much thought into it."

"Close your eyes for me."

I frowned but he gave me a look like I was being kind of silly, one that asked without words, *have I ever hurt you or fucked with you before?* Truth was, he hadn't. If anything he treated me better than any man that had come before which considering you couldn't really treat anyone worse than Silas had treated me, that wasn't saying much.

God, you're a pathetic case, Tiff. I told myself, but I did what he asked. I closed my eyes. I jerked back when his fingertips touched my hair, near my forehead and opened them. He was looking at me and frowned and I instantly felt like a child that'd been caught doing something wrong. I closed my eyes and swallowed hard, reminding myself that he was a paying customer and that he'd always been good to me. It could buy him a little trust here. Not much, but a little.

He traced a fingertip lightly along my hairline, sweeping the long glossy strands of my hair over my ear and away from my scar. I felt the bed shift under me as he leaned forward and kissed my lips lightly. I froze, uncertain, and they lifted, lightly scented from my own essence, and touched down on the corner of my mouth. They lifted again but I jerked back, teeth gritted before they could find their intended target.

His hand tightened into my hair and I froze again, but my gaze fixed on the pillows next to us. I couldn't look at him, not when hot tears threatened. I wasn't up for that. I wasn't up for talking about it, his pity, or his sympathy, or whatever it was he was trying to do. Not when it came to that.

"You want me to fuck you?" he asked. "Bend you over and drive deep, get some of that anger out?"

I felt my pussy throb, giving a long, slow, wanting ache at what he offered.

"*Yes.*" I hissed and he did what I asked, he drew me up by the hold he had in the back of my hair, not hurting, but I either moved with him or it could hurt. He faced me toward the headboard and I grabbed on, offering myself up, bowing my back. He ordered me not to move and went for a condom in the side drawer and put it on.

"You want a good hatefuck? That make you feel better?" he demanded and his voice was low, seductive, and inviting and *yes*, that's exactly what I wanted.

The liquid courage of the tequila swirled in my veins, numbing me just right and I ground out, "Shut up and fuck me already."

He chuckled darkly and said, "You're just like my wife," but he was driving into me. I caught myself and thrust back to meet him and it hurt just right. I felt myself start to grow wet, to open up and I could hear his grin when he hummed out in appreciation. His thick fingers found my hips, his thumbs pressing to either side of my lower back in a smooth, massaging arch and he drew back and it was *on*.

He pounded into my pussy from behind and oh, god, yes, that was precisely what I wanted, precisely what I needed right then. It felt so good. I yowled my anger and pleasure and arched down, facing my ass up so that he could fuck me deeper and harder. Each commanding thrust forced a cry from my throat as he stroked over that spot inside of me.

He kept at it, a punishing rhythm that caused my skin to cool and gooseflesh to break out over my body even as he stoked the embers of my sexuality to life until it was burning bright and cheery and burned all of my uncertainty and misgivings away. I finally, *finally*, let go and it was perfect. Narrowed down from so much anxiety and fear into this perfect being of pleasure and light.

I felt like a woman again. All of a sudden desirable and beautiful for that one shining moment until he reached around to the front of my body, pressed fingertips to my clit and pushed me far too soon into the fall of orgasm.

I cried out and went limp, pressing my face into the pillow and screaming my release into it, but that wasn't enough apparently. He let me calm, let me settle and turned me onto my side. I gasped and tried to catch my breath, but before I could say anything, he had lifted my top leg up, draping it back over his, the arm beneath my body locking me back against his chest. He shoved gently into my pussy with the head of his cock and worked himself in and out of me, his other arm curving over the top of my body, pressing fingers lightly at the top of my sex and teasing the embers of my first release back into flames.

I closed my eyes and let him cradle me against his chest as he fucked me. Too spent to care, my last fleeting thought before I came again, half-drunk on pleasure and fully-drunk on his tequila, was that I was damn sure getting his money's worth this time.

Zeb...

I was tired as fuck and didn't want to ride to the club, but when the Pres asked you to come, you went. I always thought it was kind of funny, Dragon's way. He asked, he didn't order us about like most blokes would if they were in his position. I pulled up outside and backed into my space, the party pretty well over by this time. Usually, everyone was passed out or off fuckin' by now, so you can imagine my surprise when D. met me practically right inside the door.

"Hey, where's the fire at, eh?" I asked and lost my easy smile when his didn't appear right away.

"Asleep in my room. Sit down," he said, and waved me into a chair across from his. "I know you been on your feet all night." I nodded and sank down, wondering what it was he had called me in for. He pushed a folded piece of paper across the table at me and said, "Tell me what you make of that."

"Looks to me like it's a letter," I said, scowling at the typed face of it. "What's it got to do with me?"

"Nothing, yet."

"I'm thankfully not up on the way your prison system works, but I take it this Silas Grable gettin' out early ain't a good thing?"

"Not where Tiffany Dempsey is concerned." I watched Dragon knock back a shot of tequila.

"Who is she?"

"Stripper down at Sugars. A nice girl. I told her if she ever needed anything to look us up, never thought she'd come to me with something like this. Then again, I probably shoulda guessed it was something like this."

"Makes you say that?"

"Come see for yourself, but try not to wake her. She's had a tough night."

He pushed to his feet and I followed him back to his room where he opened the door, a rectangle of light from the hall behind us spilling inside. I moved in and looked down at the girl sleeping in one of his tee shirts. Well, passed out was more like it, judging by the half-empty bottle on the bedside table, but given the wicked nasty scar along her upturned cheek, I couldn't say I blamed her for that.

"He do that?" I asked quiet-like and Dragon nodded.

"When you came here, you said you were down to lead a different kind of life. One where your people could be proud of you again. I think you might be meant for this particular task for a few reasons."

"Yeah?" I asked.

"Yeah. I'll leave you two to get acquainted," he said and finally gave me an order. "Don't wake her up."

I stepped back and dropped into the chair against the wall and he shut us both into the dark. I thought about it, and reached up, pulling on the chain to the lamp over the old recliner. I was in Dragon's reading chair, an old mountain of paperbacks on a low table beside it. I didn't pay the books no mind, wondering instead what the crafty old bastard was up to. I took in her features while she slept.

She was a pretty girl. The ugly that marred her cheek was the kind of flaw that, for some reason, at least to me, made her more beautiful, not less. Like God had made something too perfect, and life or fate or whatever had to mark it, make it just that little bit less so, so that a mere mortal man like me could believe she was real.

Of course, this was all before she opened her mouth. Who knew what she was like personality-wise? Some women were only pretty on the outside and no amount of that pretty could make up for what kind of ugly they had going on their insides. Still, real men didn't treat women this way. Leastways, not the way I'd been raised, no matter if they were good women or not. I also couldn't judge what I didn't know.

The room started to fill with natural light and I sighed and rubbed my eyes. I was tired, it had been a long night, and I could use some sleep myself, but Dragon had had me park it here for a reason. I couldn't deny the view was nice. My eyes kept straying over that lovely face, framed in straight, glossy, dark brown hair, her dark lashes long and forming perfect crescents on her cheeks.

I turned over what Dragon had said in my head and thought that this maybe was some kind of a test. I trusted the man, I trusted all of these men, and if he said the lady needed help, then she needed help. Likewise, I'd been climbing pretty steady out of the hole I'd dug for myself. Granted, I could never go back home to New Zealand, not unless some gang bosses back home died first and even then, I couldn't say my family would welcome me with open arms. I'd fucked that up. Been young and headstrong, and had to come here to my uncle in America, only I fell right back into old habits, had burned that bridge, too. Now I was here with a new family, determined not to fuck up again.

So, with a sigh, I settled in and got comfortable dozing in the chair, resting my eyes and waiting for her to wake up.

3

Tiffany...

I was sore in that delicious way a good fuck left behind when I stirred. It took me a second to remember where I was, and it took two more to realize I wasn't alone in here. That someone was sitting in the old armchair by the bed. It took me only a half a second to realize that someone wasn't the biker president who was my client.

I sucked in a sharp breath and turned away, letting my hair cascade over the scarred side of my face with an equally sharp turn of my head. I had been sleeping on my stomach, so I slid both hands across the crisp sheets beneath me and pushed myself into a sitting position. I was careful turning, giving the man my back, which crawled with nerves set aflame by the action. I don't know why I bothered, but it allowed me to pull the sheet to my chest and cover myself, like the thin gray material would actually do anything to protect me from anything but his gaze. It didn't even register as I did it that I had someone else's, likely Dragon's, tee shirt on.

"Who the hell are you?" I asked sharply, before thinking about it. My voice held far more bravado than I felt and I figured at least that was something. He dropped his booted feet off the ottoman to the wood floor in here and I jumped. He leaned forward, and I cringed back. He froze for half a second and moved slowly, leaning, bracing his forearms on his knees as his gaze swept over me and met mine.

"Name is Nikau, most of my friends call me Nik, the fellas around here call me Zeb," he said and his voice was affable, his accent rich and melodic. It wasn't quite British but it wasn't quite Australian either, although between the two it was closer to the latter. I couldn't place where he was from but I definitely wasn't going to ask.

"What are you doing in here... I'm sorry, I feel like I'm going to butcher your name if I try to say it." I frowned slightly and he smiled, his teeth very white, set in his deeply tan and ethnic skin. I had no idea what he was, but it was some sort of tribal from somewhere if I had to guess. My eyes were fixed on the deep blue-black ink etched into the skin of one side of his face in these intricate lines and whorls.

"Call me Nik or Zeb. Whichever you'd like," he gave a shrug, the leather of his jacket and the vest over it creaking.

"Okay, Nik." I swallowed hard. "What are you doing in here?"

"Dragon asked me to look after yah. Showed me the letter and the like. I reckon you have something to be afraid of with this guy." He raised a hand and halfheartedly gestured to the curtain of my hair. I quailed, but there was something refreshingly forthright and honest about the way he approached the situation.

"So Dragon tells you to babysit a stripper from her completely psycho ex-boyfriend and you just do it?" I asked, mystified.

"Nah, he didn't tell me to do nothin'. He *asked* me."

I blinked slowly, and rolled my lips together. I had to think about this. I didn't know what I had expected Dragon to do, but I sincerely hadn't expected a bodyguard. I let out a breath slowly and I asked, "So, how is this supposed to work, then?"

He gave another shrug that could mean everything and nothing and said, "I reckon we should start with you getting dressed, yeah? Give you a lift back to your flat and see what you've got."

"What I've got?"

"Yeah, locks, chains, you near a busy street? Off in the back? These things can make a difference."

"I didn't really know that and I can't afford to move…"

"No worries, we can work with what you have." He stood up in one fluid motion and I shrank back at the sudden movement. He paused, but only for like a half-second, and gave a nod and said, "Be out here waiting," before sliding out the door and closing it behind him.

I had some mixed feelings about this turn of events. I didn't know this guy. Of course, I didn't really know Dragon all that well either, so I supposed in my case beggars couldn't really be choosers. I got out of bed and slipped out of the tee-shirt I hadn't remembered putting on. That tequila was the shit, but I was certainly paying the price for it now that I was moving around. Queasy, mouth and head full of cotton, muscles tight. I wanted a bottle of water and a couple of Advil something fierce.

As I was lowering my shirt over my torso and back into the waistband of my jeans, the door opened. I jumped and whirled, and as if conjured by magic, Dragon stood there with a bottle of water in one hand, his other curled around what I could only assume was a couple of tablets or something.

"Figured you might could use these," he said, holding out his mitts. I took the water and held out my hand. He dropped a couple of brown round tablets into my upturned palm and I smiled a little one-sided.

"Powered up your extra sensory perception this morning?"

He chuckled darkly and said, "Livin' this life, I've had a hangover or three. How you feel?"

"Like I've been plowed into by a truck."

He nodded, "I've put my man Zeb onto your protective detail until we know if this guy is going to be a problem." He raised an eyebrow and I could hear the question loud and clear, *are* you *going to be a problem?*

"No; yeah, uh, we've met. He seems... nice," I finished lamely. I mean, he did seem nice, problem was that Silas had seemed nice in the beginning, too and trust wasn't something that came naturally or easily, at least not anymore. I did trust Dragon, though. I mean, wasn't that why I was here?

"Give him a chance, kid's got a warrior's spirit. The way I know it, he's descended from a long line of 'em. He's good people and, I think, the right kind of fit for this particular situation."

"You don't need to convince me," I said softly, downing the pills and draining half the water in three long swallows. "I came to you for help." He eyed me critically and nodded once or twice, deciding I was telling the truth about the whole 'convincing me' part.

"I'm grateful," I said, a bit breathless from my hydration binge. "I can't tell you how many times the cops either didn't believe me or didn't care." I dropped my gaze to the plastic bottle in my hands and sighed, the clack of the plastic sharp and loud in the little silence between us as my fingers massaged the bottle nervously. Opening up in any way was hard to do but I felt I sort of owed it to him at this point.

"Yeah, well, we aren't law enforcement, Sugar. We know better." I nodded faintly and finished the water in three or four slightly less greedy gulps. He held out his hands and I gave him the empty bottle and cap. He crushed it down into a round coin with his massive fists and screwed the lid on to keep it from bouncing back. He turned to go and stopped, reached into his back pocket and held out a sheaf of bills. I met his solemn dark eyes and plucked the cash from his fingers.

"Been a pleasure, Sweetheart," he murmured and then he was gone. The way he'd said it, well, it held the distinct flavor of goodbye. Not as in I would never see him again, but definitely that... the professional relationship was done. I looked down at the cool grand between my hands, leafing through the bills, counting it three or four times to make sure I was really seeing it right. By the time I stuffed it into my purse I was definitely sure that it was my severance package and I couldn't say I wasn't a little sad about that.

Dragon, by far and most certainly, had been my best client. Respectful, and gentle for the most part, just an all-around nice guy. I couldn't say I blamed him for wanting the distance, though. My situation was complicated and messy, and by coming to him for help had definitely blurred the set lines we had both abided by up to this point, unspoken as they may have been.

I sat on the edge of the bed and pulled on my socks and boots, getting dressed mechanically as I pondered where things were going to go from here. It was the worst sort of feeling, knowing something bad was on the horizon but not knowing what shape it would take. This wasn't like a storm you could prepare for. There was no telling what kind of crazy Silas was capable of at this point. He'd had three years to think about all sorts of inventive things to do by way of revenge for having him locked up. I had thought I had about five to finish paying for things and to get away from him.

I should have known better. The system had only ever been good at one thing where I was concerned and that one thing had been to fail me. I stood up with a harsh, angry sigh and tried to shake the emotion off. It hadn't done me any good before and being angry would just turn me into the same damn thing I was running from. Silas was always angry.

Silas is just a dick. I thought bitterly and yeah, he was that too. A dick with a less than impressive one at that.

I let myself out into the hall and looked around. It was a bit of a ghost town and I was okay with that. Somehow me slinking out of Dragon's room felt like it should be a walk of shame, but fuck that. I wasn't ashamed of getting what I had honestly come here for in the first place. I was used to the judgment that came along with the job and that was when people only thought I was a stripper. If they knew I was an actual whore? I didn't want to think about that so much. Not here in the Bible Belt of good ol' Kentucky. Hell, the bible-thumpers would have my ass branded a harlot in nothing flat.

People here just didn't know how to mind their own business; it was like it was impossible for them to stay in their own goddamn lane. It's what I liked about Dragon. He never tried to pry, he minded his own business and let me keep mine to myself. I could and did respect that.

I found his man in the barroom, sitting at a table with a cup of coffee in front of him that was mostly empty. He looked up and stood up as I came into the room and said, "Cuppa?"

I think he was asking if I wanted a cup of coffee myself but it was a weird way of doing it. Probably from where he was originally from. I shook my head and said, "No, thanks, I can make fresh when I get home; which I would really like to do."

"Ah, yeah, this way, then."

He led me out into the sunshine and I winced as it sent a railroad spike through my eye and up into my brain. I fished a pair of large, bug-eyed sunglasses out of my purse and shoved them onto my face the same time he slid a pair of wraparounds of his own out of the inside pocket of his cut. He walked up to a battered old Harley in the line of bikes and I blinked, waiting for him to say 'just kidding' and move to one of the other bikes.

Instead, he dropped onto the seat and gave a twist to the bars, kicking up the stand it had been leaning heavily on and thumbing the switch.

"You're joking, right?" I asked and I immediately winced and apologized. "Sorry, didn't mean for that to come out so bitchy."

"Hangover's got you good, eh?"

"Something like that," I agreed. Really, it was starting to hit me that I'd lost my best damn client and I was starting to worry about cash flow some. Not to mention I was really starting to realize that it sort of hurt that Dragon had taken a walk on me. I hadn't expected that, like at all. I mean it made all sorts of sense, and I didn't know how I had convinced myself that nothing was going to change. I mean… *really.* Still, I felt myself going into an almost mourning phase. Like you do after a breakup, which was just goddamn ridiculous.

"Go on, then," he said, in that rich accent.

"What?" I asked.

"Get it out of your system, eh," he said affably, sort-of smiling and I couldn't help but smile a little myself, though I tried not to.

I mean, I was serious when I asked, "Does it even run?"

He grinned and fired it up and oh god, I wished he hadn't. The angry, protesting growl the bike let out thrummed through my whole abused, aching body that I had so thoroughly poisoned with that fine tequila and punishing fuck-fest last night and my body was letting me know All. About. It.

My head throbbed, my face felt as if it was going to slide off and I swear every joint creaked like his leather jacket had inside the closed space of Dragon's room. My teeth were set on edge, and I gritted them and waited for some nausea to pass before I put one hand on his offered arm and swung a protesting leg over the seat behind him.

Good gracious, that hurt. Dragon had done a great job of getting between my legs the night before, and given my 'day job,' you would think I would be limber enough that I wouldn't hurt where my legs met my body, but nope. I'd overdone everything to excess, apparently, and my body was pissed and just letting me know about it at every turn.

"You good?" he asked, over the loud chugging of the beast beneath us.

"As I'll ever be!"

"Right, where you live then?"

"Oh! Shit, sorry…" I gave him the address and he thrust a helmet back at me. I put it on, even as he shook out his shaggy hair and wrapped a bandana around his head, tight to his skull.

He dropped another half-helmet-looking thing onto his own head and without even bothering with the straps, said to me, "Hang on, then!"

I did, because honestly, I expected the bike to fall apart beneath us at any moment; it looked that bad. To be honest, it rode even worse – the vibrations were terrible. I don't know that I could entirely chalk that up to the miserable hangover, either.

4

Z eb...

She was miserable for the ride and I wanted to feel bad for her and I guess I did, even though I knew she'd done it to herself. That tequila she'd drunk was wicked stuff, and I'd been at its mercy a time or two. I could sympathize, or was it empathize? I reckon it could even be a cross between the two.

She lived out the other side of town. The flat she was in wasn't the best. She was on the second floor of a double-decker building. One of those open-air sorts of deals leading up to the door. Only one stairwell up, no back exit or escape route. Her flat was the last one in the row of four on the end of the building, furthest from the car park and backed up to nature. Woods out the windows on the side and the river a short drop down past the back porch, if it had a back porch; I hadn't seen yet. There wasn't really a front where she was at, all that long walk from the stairs at the other end. The fire escape was a rusted, spindly ladder by her front door that didn't look like it'd hold a five-year-old, let alone a grown woman like her.

It wasn't a good defensible position and it wasn't grand for an escape, either. The door, at least, was a solid wood one, painted a peeling forest-green. There were a lot of locks, so she had that going for her.

A gray-and-dark striped tabby cat leaped up and put its paws against the door frame, letting out a howl of protest. It reminded me of my mum back home, when I came home late after bein' up to no good.

"Hey, you," the beauty declared and she picked the cat up and said to me, "This is Mad Max."

"Cute fella," I remarked, and she smiled a genuine one that made me smile too.

"Max is short for Maxine, she's a girl."

"Ah, yeah, never woulda guessed that." I sniffed and reached out to pet the cat's head and she immediately flattened her ears and hissed, swiping at my hand with her claws. I jerked back and Tiffany laughed.

"And now you know why she's called Mad Max." She set her down and, keys chiming softly, started unlocking her door. I shook my head at the fifth lock.

"First off, only lock one or two when you're gone. It's taking you too long to get inside. Your things are just that, things. You're irreplaceable, so you should be the focus. Only lock all of them when you're inside."

She paused and listened to me and finally gave a nod, pushing open the door. I looked at the jamb and already saw some improvements I could make. It was straight wood she had the locks going into; I could anchor a strip of metal to it, make it take more than one or two swift kicks to knock it in. Buy her some time for another improvement I had in mind.

"You got a taser or a gun?"

"No, I don't know how to shoot."

"I reckon we'll fix that."

"Al - all right…"

The front door opened right into her kitchen and inside was gloomy. She had thick drapes over the insides of the windows which was good for keeping a man on the outside from lookin' in on her. She stood aside and let me through and I quickly assessed. No back porch, no bedroom either; Americans called it a studio flat. Just the kitchen and bathroom with her bed set up in the main area out here.

"Nice place," I said, and compared to my regular flat, it was. Of course, I hadn't really even tried with mine. I'd been such a fuck-up I hadn't put down too many roots. Not yet. While I'd felt more permanence here than anywhere else since comin' to the States, I wasn't to that point of commitment yet, I reckon.

She snorted as if she didn't believe I'd meant the compliment and I let it go. No sense in arguing the point. She tossed her keys on the cracked kitchen bench and they clacked loud in the small room, sliding slightly before coming to rest with a metal-on-metal click against the edge of the tired, old, gas stove.

"It's cheap, which I like, and they didn't ask a whole lot of questions when I moved in, which I liked even better."

"Heh, fair enough."

"Can I fix you some coffee or breakfast or something for the ride home?"

"Ah, nah, yeah," I said, not thinking, and a silence stretched between us some.

She just stood there halfway in her kitchen and looked at me, waiting. Finally, giving me a long slow blink she asked, "So, um, which is it?"

I cracked a grin and sheepishly said, "That'd be great."

"All I have are eggs and toast," she said quietly, moving further into the aisle of the kitchen, going to the fridge.

"Sweet as."

She paused, closed her eyes and gave a deep sigh, her shoulders lifting and dropping. She turned around and said squarely, "I'm going to need you to finish the sentence," she said. "Clear communication is important to me."

"Sorry, eh. I don't mean it. I'm just tired-like and my words are gettin' away from me."

She nodded and pursed her lips, "It's fine, just don't get mad at me when I keep asking you what you just said or telling you I don't know what that means because I don't know what that means... at least not the way you just said it. Are you unhappy with toast and eggs, or is it okay? I mean, this is typically how I managed to get my ass beat. Non-committal grunts or incomplete sentences that I would have to interpret with a fifty-fifty shot of getting it right or wrong. I don't want to live like that again."

"My bad, eh. 'Sweet as' means, uh, like *cool*, in American. Eggs and toast are 'sweet as' or 'cool' with me."

She nodded and rolled her lips together indecisively. She was thinking awful hard and finally said, "Thank you. I'm sorry for snapping."

"No worries."

I dropped into a seat at the little two-person table scattered with papers and school books and folded my hands on the top. I could watch her move in the small space and she was even more lithe and gorgeous when she moved. She had a way about her, you know?

I diverted my attention, let my eyes wander over her learning materials and gathered it was for some kind of social work.

"So what you want to do when you graduate, eh?" I asked and she looked up from the stove, where she'd cracked some eggs into a skillet.

"I don't know yet; I thought about working with abused women and kids but it might be too hard. I'm trying hard not to think about it too much until I get to the point where I have to make a decision. Too many things are going on at once, you know?"

"Yeah, I reckon." I scratched an itch on my forehead and took my eyes off her for a minute. I didn't want to come across an awkward bloke that couldn't keep his eyes to himself.

"What about this?" she asked. "I mean, how is this all supposed to work?"

"What, your ex-man? A piece of piss."

"I don't disagree with that," she said and stirred the hissing eggs in the pan.

I smiled, "Nah, well, he's that too, really, but in Kiwi, that means he's easy. Or the problem with him is, anyhow."

"Nothing with Silas is easy," she said and I almost barely heard her over the popping and sizzling in the pan in front of her.

"We'll start now to get into a routine. I'll pick you up tonight and take you into work; you got security there, yeah?"

"Yeah, we do."

"Good deal. I'll pick you up at three and drive you home, check and make sure all is good here, have you lock me out, and then I'll be just a phone call away if you need me."

"Sounds reasonable," she said carefully.

"No worries, girl. Everything is gonna be good as gold, now. You come to the right place for help."

She stared at me for a long minute, one dark eye glittering through the long chestnut fall of her hair. She did that, hid behind her hair to cover the ugly mark he left on her face. She didn't see she was a warrior to survive a thing like that. I hesitated, had a thought, and planted it so it had some time to grow. I wouldn't bring it up now. Not yet, the girl was still too raw, too afraid. Made me afraid she'd just dismiss it.

41

"I really hope that's true," she murmured, then plated some eggs just as the toast popped from the toaster.

I smiled, "It's true, and it looks like you've done this a time or two." She set the plate in front of me and handed me some flatware.

"Maybe," she murmured with a wry smile.

She drifted back and forth between the table and the kitchen getting other things, like salt and pepper, hot sauce, butter, and jam. She finally took a seat across from me and sighed.

"You eat, you'll feel better," I said around a mouthful of my own.

"I know, but it's tough when the mere thought of food makes you queasy."

I knew that was right. I also knew the stress wasn't helping. We would see what we could do about that.

5

T iffany...

I wasn't resistant to any of the suggestions he made about changing how I did things for my safety. The schedule was an easy enough fix, and so were the regular texts and calls checking in.

That morning, he'd eaten, said his thanks, and told me he'd be back later after some sleep. We'd traded numbers and he'd gone. I'd locked the door behind him, done the dishes, taken a long, hot shower, and had, by some miracle, gotten some more sleep of my own.

I woke up to a knock at my door and a quick look out the peephole had revealed his frightening tattooed face. I felt muscles I hadn't realized I'd tensed loosen at the sight of him and I wondered at that for a moment, hesitating before I opened the door. His melodic voice floated through the wood asking, "You all right, Girl?"

No, but it would be a waste of breath explaining it, so I went with the polite little lie. "Yeah, I'm okay," I said after opening the portal to the outside world. He gave me a one-sided grin, a dimple creasing on the cheek unadorned by the deep blue whorls of ink and I sort of just knew that he knew exactly what I'd been feeling.

"I'm here now, eh. Nothing's gonna getcha."

I tried a brave smile in return and said, "You're a little early, I just woke up. Let me get dressed and throw some costumes together, come on in."

"Yeah, I wanted to have a look at your door again, take some measurements." He pulled a measuring tape out from his leather jacket's front pocket. Whipping the yellow tape out, he efficiently went about measuring the inside door jamb.

I blinked in surprise and asked, "Oh, yeah? What's that for?"

He pulled a stub of a pencil from one pocket and a little notepad from his other one and marked some things down. Placing the pencil between his teeth, he answered from around it, "Gonna reinforce this with some metal stripping, make it so it takes more than one swift kick to get her open. A few screws and she'll be right."

"Thank you. I thought the more locks the better."

"They don't hurt," he said affably, pulling the pencil from between his teeth as he jotted down another measurement. "This'll be better."

"When can you do it?" I asked and he smiled.

"When I come pick you up tomorrow. Get here a little early, get it done and you'll be good to go, eh?"

"Sounds good," I murmured and laid out a final matching bra and panty set on my bed. I put hands to hips and considered the sets I'd laid out, the masks I had at the club in my locker, and the shoes I had to pair them with under the bed. Makeup ideas were already swirling through my brain as well. The better I looked, the better the tips, the faster I could leave all this bullshit of taking my clothes off and fucking for money behind.

"Costumes, eh?"

I grimaced a little. "Sounds a lot better than underwear or lingerie. Not my first choice in a line of work, but it does pay the best. I was on a tight schedule before to get the fuck up out of this town in five years; it's even worse now they're letting Silas out early."

He nodded and asked, "Where y' headed?"

No one had ever really asked me that before, not even my best friend, Delia, who I still needed to call – Shit!

"Hold that thought?" I asked.

"Sure, what's up?"

"I forgot to call Delia, she's my best friend."

"Best get that done then, yeah?"

"Yeah, I'm sorry, I'll only be a minute."

"Sure, sure."

I went for my cell on the tabletop, the screen lighting up to a dozen missed calls or texts and I phoned her back. She picked up on the first ring and I could hear she was driving.

"Oh, my god, girl! I am totally on my way over and was about to call the police!"

"No, it's okay, I'm fine, Lia."

"Where are you?" she demanded.

"At home, and no need to come get me, I have a ride into the club."

"For real?"

"Yeah, I'll tell you everything when I get there, but right now I sort of have company."

"Jesus Christ, Tiff. What are you doing?"

I looked over at Zeb who was looking me over curiously, I held the phone tight to my ear and turned away from him slightly, "I'll tell you later, Lia. I'll see you at work. Thanks for being my best friend."

"Tiff – of course, I'm your best friend and as your best friend, I'm worried about you. Who's there? Why do you feel like you can't talk to me?"

"I love you, I'll see you in a few," I told her. I didn't want to be rude and talk about Zeb like he wasn't here. I also didn't quite know how to explain everything. So, socially-awkward me, I was going to make my best friend worry for like a half-an-hour more. Still, I didn't quite have his full measure and I didn't want him upset at me, not like Silas would be if he were in his place.

"Everything good, then?"

"Yeah, I just didn't want her showing up here to give me a ride when I already had one." I tried a smile and felt like it came out watered-down at best.

"Ain't gotta worry about me none, I would have followed you and made sure you got where you were going safe."

"Thank you," I murmured and he gave a nod.

"I'll be out here, you take your time getting ready, yeah?"

"Yeah, thanks…"

Not the reaction I had been expecting. Of course, I was quickly learning that I didn't know what to expect when it came to people; the packaging was often a lie and that old adage about judging books by their cover was most definitely true. We did it all the time, it was just how people were, but I needed to curb-stomp the habit and I needed to do it quickly.

I gathered the scraps of lace and satin and tossed them into the bottom of a gym bag, throwing in a few pairs of shoes on top. I'd learned quickly that there were some nasty bitches in stripping and that they wouldn't hesitate to borrow things like somebody else's G-string without permission. It was so beyond gross that I kept everything – costumes, makeup, and any of my masks – on me, or under lock and key at the club, unless I didn't plan on ever using it again.

I ducked into the bathroom with some clothes and got dressed as warmly as my wardrobe would allow for the coming ride. When I stepped out, he was on his phone texting something and I itched to ask what to who, but it wasn't any of my business.

"All set, then?"

"Yeah," I slung my gym bag over my chest and took up my phone, purse, and keys. I motioned for him to go out ahead of me and took on the arduous task of locking up behind me.

"Only one or two when you're gone, remember?" he said gently and I startled.

"Oh, god. I guess it's just a force of habit."

"No worries."

"I'm such an idiot," I said with a nervous laugh and shook my head, undoing all but the two strongest locks.

He didn't say anything, just waited patiently, his squat, beat-up bike seemingly glowering impatiently under the lone light in my apartment's little parking area. I followed him to it and still wondered how the beat-up old thing ran.

The ride to Sugars was a cold one. It was heading into December and the temperatures got downright frigid after dark. I shivered and couldn't wait to get into the club's back door where at least it was warm. Zeb got off the bike with me and turned to eye Zeke up and down. He stood back here at the start and end of his shift to make sure all of the girls got in and out without a hassle. Not every one of our security guys bothered, and I appreciated Zeke more for doing it than he could know.

"Come on, I'll introduce you to Zeke," I said, and Zeb nodded, following me across the cracked and crumbling asphalt of the back lot.

"Zeke," I greeted and he looked up from his phone, frowning.

"Hey, Tiff. This guy bothering you?" he asked and I could see the concern in his blue eyes.

"No, actually, the opposite. My douchebag-ex gets out tomorrow and Zeb is helping me out, watching my ass to make sure everything is gonna be cool. He's going to be dropping me off and picking me up for the foreseeable future, so I thought you guys should meet."

"Eh, nice to meet ya, Bro," Zeb held out his hand and Zeke grasped it. They pulled each other in and tapped shoulders the way guys did as a universal bro-greeting or whatever.

"Nice to meet you, too. Any friend of Tiff's is a friend of mine."

I smiled and said, "Thanks, Zeke. Three-thirty?" I directed the last at Zeb.

"A little earlier if I can manage," he said.

"Okay, later then," I said to them both and with a little wave, I slipped through the back door leaving the two men to chat.

It was dark back here and I let my eyes adjust to it before heading for my locker and groaning, stripping down and pulling out my makeup kit to get the final touches on my face. I was grateful that Alan, the club's owner, kept the heat cranked for us girls back here. It would have been miserable getting ready otherwise.

Delia dropped into the chair at the makeup station I used just as I was putting on a final coat of ruby-red matte lip paint.

"Oh, bitch, you better spill right now," she said, her tone threatening. I turned to her and sighed.

"I had a Sacred Heart in my apartment; I didn't want to talk about him like he wasn't there. That would have been rude!"

"As opposed to letting me freak out the whole way here? That's not rude?"

"You're totally right, it was, but it was the lesser of two evils and you being my BFF, you should totally get that," I shot back.

I turned back to the mirror and she gave a gusty sigh, "You're right, and I do, but that doesn't mean you don't owe me ice cream and a sappy movie that I get to choose this time! Plus, the full story on just what the hell you're doing."

"Deal," I uttered around the lip paint's wand. Anything to appease her, and quickly, because I really did feel bad for making her worry.

"So, the guy with the weird face tattoos outside talking to Zeke?"

"My brand-new bodyguard for the time being, until Silas either makes a move or proves he's going to fuck off."

She gave another gusty sigh and said, "I'm not happy about this."

"Clearly."

"You're going to be okay, Tiff. What are you thinking? I mean, you've kind of overdone it finding someone more badass than Silas could ever be if that's your aim. Shit, the Sacred Hearts? That's like using a thermonuclear device to kill ants!"

"There's no such thing as overkill after what Silas did to me," I said grimly. "Not like I can rely on the cops to protect me." I gave a sour look into the mirror and added, "Obviously," under my breath.

Delia shook her head, "No, I guess not." I could tell by my best friend's expression that this talk was far from over.

We both shared a deep sigh for different reasons and then glanced at each other, smiling for the same one. Lia laughed a little, standing up. "You gotta swap me, I need more time getting ready."

"Let me glue on my mask and I'll get out of your way," I declared, but I couldn't be sure she heard me over the thumping bass through the wall as the next song started up. She must have, as she gave me a wave over her shoulder and went to her locker to change into her costume first.

~

It was a good night in tips and I was rolling on the energy from the crowd. A good ol' boy's bachelor party was in and those always made for good money and even some good times. When I got into my stage persona, I took possession of a power, a sexual energy that my real-life identity of Tiffany had never dreamed of possessing. I separated the two, almost pretended that I was some kind of masked superhero or even, some nights, a villainess. Whatever got me through the shift around here was a good thing. Besides, I was selling fantasy as a way to make a living, why shouldn't I indulge in it myself every once in a while?

I honestly waxed and waned over how I felt about being a sex worker. Some days it was empowering. Hell, to be honest, most days it was. Then there were the days it wore on you and you felt burned out. Those days, you could find yourself erring on the side of the judgmental douchebags of the world that had never even had to worry about where their next meal was coming from, let alone how a poor girl from the foster care system with only her GED was supposed to deal with the soul-crushing debt of what was done to her by somebody else.

I tried to stay focused on the positive, that tonight was a good night. A night where I was feeling the music, a night where I was as into the crowd as it was into me, and instead of feeling objectified, I felt worshiped. A night where the tips were pouring in and I knew I had enough for yet another payment on whichever debt was next in rotation.

"Please welcome to the stage, for her last dance of the evening, the ever-mysterious, totally gorgeous, and completely exotic… *Francesca!*"

The opening notes of Whitney Houston's *Queen of the Night* from the movie *The Bodyguard* came out over the speakers. I straightened my back, and, one foot in front of the other, strutted out onto the stage like the very queen of the song.

Like I said, it was a good night and it was going to be an even better, rockin' last dance.

6

Z eb...

"Back again, huh?" the big bloke with the thatch of blond hair waved me forward and moved the tattered red velvet rope aside to let me in the front door.

"Ah, yeah. Duty calls."

"Hey, man, a friendly, unsolicited piece of advice?"

I paused and looked up at the bulky bouncer for the titty bar and gave a nod. He twisted his mouth as if trying to decide how much or how little to say and finally sighed, saying in a low voice that was just between me and him, "Tiff is too good for this place, always has been. She's meant for way better than this town has to offer. Not many girls in here I can say that about. Don't treat her like a chore, get to know her, you might be surprised."

I raised my eyebrows and nodded, "Good on ya, Bro. Thanks for saying so; I'm glad you have her back."

"No problem."

I thought about what ol' Zeke had to say as I went through the door, his parting shot to me, "Get a seat by the stage, you made it in time for her last dance."

I'd never looked at a protection job as anything but a professional gig before, even if I'd never quite done it professionally, as in been paid for it. I didn't exactly watch big-money types in the traditional sense with their suits and high rises and their expensive gadgets. I'd watched the backs of my bro's, and back home, a high-rolling gang boss or two. Something told me Dragon had other things in mind when he'd put me with the stripper, and I figured I would need to see how it played out. I knew if I asked him about it, he'd just raise his eyebrows and tell me to figure it out for myself.

The heavy electric of the song that was starting pulsed from the speakers and the announcer guy was saying something about some bird named Francesca. I dropped into an empty seat at the end of the stage, glad to take a load off after a night on my feet. Tiffany, all dolled up with a black lace mask covering her survivor's mark, came strutting out onto the stage. I'd wondered how she handled that, and now I knew, but this wasn't the girl with the tight shoulders, high-strung and throwing calculating looks at everything. She wasn't trying to decide if the next thing she did was going to send the person she was around off, packing a sad.

No, this woman strutting out of the dark was the queen the song named her. This woman was *mean as* and I wanted to see her more often. The idea I'd had back at her place took root and started to grow when she started to actually dance, and the girl could dance. She slunk along the brass pole at the end of the stage and her lean body was poetry in motion.

She was fit, everything tight, flat, and toned. Her lightly-tanned body was slightly dewed with sweat. The way she moved had every man here in the bar dying of thirst and wanting to lick the beaded moisture off her skin. She was too much, and I settled back to enjoy the show while still keeping the other blokes around in sight and mind.

My attention to anyone but her kind of went out the window when she laid down on the stage. She arched her back provocatively over the edge and looked square at me. I stared back into her eyes and all I saw was an emptiness. A disconnect, like she was all inside her own head; in her own little world.

The music faded around me, my mind turned to the weeping, so much like singing, of so many of my people's women that had walked this same sort of path back home. It broke my heart some, but then a spark of recognition lit deep in her brown eyes. I had to smile back when a smile curved her red painted lips and she arched further, one hand gripping the lush globe of one breast, the other drifting tantalizingly down her body, as she rocked to the beat.

She knew what she was doing, that one. I slipped my wallet out of my back pocket and held out a twenty; I'd intended to buy her breakfast anyway, on the way out to her place, which was out in the wops on the far edge of town. She rolled over onto all fours and leaned out, capturing the paper between her teeth and drawing back, moving with the music, back on her sharp heels in a flash and writhing elegantly against the pole. She had it. Raw sexuality, a confidence I wished she could wear as easily off the stage as she did on it. I mean, it was just begging to become a permanent thing, it just needed a little help along.

I have to admit, after our little display, the money came pouring in. All from the guys around us hoping for the same kind of attention. She winked over her shoulder at me, gathered her money, blew another guy a kiss, and moved backstage, and I had to grin. She'd pulled off about ten times the sex appeal of any of these other girls and she'd never even taken off her bra or panties.

Zeke was right, the girl was too good for this place, but it wasn't my job to save her from herself. It was just my job to save her from a guy who might not even push it. I got up and drifted toward the back and she reached out from the curtains and caught my hand, drawing me back to the private rooms.

"Ah, what's this?" I asked.

"A twenty buys you a private dance, I thought that's what you wanted."

"Eh, nah, I just wanted to buy you breakfast."

She stopped tugging me along insistently and turned, "A rain check then? Because I'm starving."

I grinned, "Chur, me too."

"You parked out front?" she asked.

"Yeah."

"Okay, meet me around back. I'll be dressed and out there before you know it. I'd rather not run the gauntlet out front if it's all the same." She made a face. "Every one of them would try to take me home like a lost puppy."

"Ah, yeah, they're all having a hell of a piss up out there, ain't they?" She blinked and I smiled harder, "A party, a hard one," I translated.

She smiled and said, "Thanks for remembering," and then she was gone through the curtains at the end of the hall. I went back out front and gave Zeke a nod.

"Headed around back?" he asked.

"Eh, yeah."

He looked at his watch and nodded. "About that time, I'll see her out."

"Appreciate it, bro."

I left him tapping the shoulder of another bouncer who was talking in his cell. The guy nodded and Zeke disappeared inside, through the building.

Nek minute, I was around back, leaning against the bike, expecting to be waiting a bit; most women almost always taking longer than they say. Not her, though. The back door opened, the big blond bouncer holding it open for her. She said her goodnight and he gave her a nod and, fists buried deep in her pockets against the cold, she stepped as lightly across the cracked blacktop of the back lot in her flat boots as she had across the mirrored stage in those killer heels of hers.

"Hi," she said, and while the choice lace mask she'd had on inside was gone, her hair covered and did the job of hiding her warrior's mark, now.

"Hey," I greeted back, and held out a helmet to her.

"So, where did you have in mind to eat?" she asked.

"Know a diner, open twenty-four hours. American food; ain't bad."

"Sounds good; I could use the calories," she declared.

"Too right, must be a workout in there every night, eh?"

"It can be."

She got onto the bike behind me and settled. I started it up and when her arms were firm around my waist, I pulled out of the lot and onto the road.

The ride was brisk, and if I was cold, I sure felt sorry for her. She didn't have the same amount of muscle or mass that I did. I kept thinking about her dance back at the strip club and the more I thought about it, the more that blank look haunted me. It also bothered me that as much as it did, I still couldn't help that my prick stirred every time I pictured her taking my money between her teeth and those rich red lips of hers.

I pulled up to a stoplight a few blocks down from the diner and she called out over the engine, "It's all right, you know!"

"What?"

"That it turned you on. I know I'm good at my job."

"Sounds to me like you maybe put in a little extra effort, eh?" I called back, flirting a bit, sure, but a bit uneasy she read me so well.

"Maybe I did," she agreed and I almost didn't hear her over the chug of my old girl when she added, "Sorry."

The light turned green and I powered through the intersection and down the road, pulling smoothly into the car park of the diner. I cut the engine and didn't say anything. She seemed content to not say anything either, which was alright with me.

I opened the door for her and let her into the warmth of the place first. Hayley looked up from behind the counter.

"Hey, you!" she said brightly.

"Gidday, Cuz."

"Well, good *night*," she said brightly and I smiled. "Two?"

"Eh, yeah." I tried not to blush. I was actually pretty shy around the club when it came to the ladies, and didn't think that Hayley would be here so late. Blue's shift must've changed again.

"Hi, I'm Hayley," she said leaning around me to see Tiff.

"Uh, hi... I'm Tiffany..." she said back and her voice sounded sus, or rather like she found Hayley to be sus.

"Blue, my husband, is one of Zeb's club brother's, are you and Zeb..?" she trailed off and left Tiffany to fill in the blank.

"Ah, don't put her on the spot, Girl!" I cried and Hayley laughed.

"Sorry, curiosity gets the better of me anymore."

It was true, she and Blue were a matched pair and they tended to bring out the best in each other and now that Cell was gone? They thrived. Bugger all, he'd carked it hard. Left Blue and Hayley in a right state but I can't say I was sad to see him go. He was a right bastard more often than not.

Hayley led us to a booth and Tiff, still hiding behind that glossy fall of hair said, "It's okay," but left it to me to elaborate.

"Tiff is a new friend," I said for lack of anything else to come up with. It wasn't no one's business why we were really together, now was it?

"Well, it's nice to meet you, Tiff. I'll be back to take your order in a second."

"Thanks," Tiffany murmured and opened her menu.

I let her hide behind it until some of the tension left the set of her shoulders and she looked like she'd made a decision.

"You knew it was coming, I reckon," I said and she sighed, setting the menu down and looking at me plaintively.

"You want to know everything, I take it?"

"Not everything, just what you want to tell me. I don't need to pry."

Actually, I did want to know everything, but I didn't want to scare her into clamming up. Easy does it, we had time. I didn't know whether this bloke would bother after he got out, but judging by the state of her face, it wasn't likely that he'd ease off and go away. It was personal what he'd done to her, and any man willing to go that far against his woman truly thought that way. That she was his woman, to do with what he pleased. Some blokes just didn't get that wasn't how things worked.

"It was my best friend Delia's birthday, and I wanted to go out but Silas didn't…"

She told me about what he did to her face, but she wouldn't look at me while she did it. I felt angry for her, and it solidified my idea I'd had that morning, the one that'd resurfaced while watching her dance.

"Real piece of work, that one," I said and she nodded, but still wouldn't look at me. Instead, she stared fixedly at some invisible point out in the diner.

Hayley came by and took our order, but it was pretty clear by the brittle, mechanical way that Tiffany put hers in, she didn't have much of an appetite left. I felt bad for that.

"So what happens now?" she asked quietly.

"How do y' mean?"

"Well, he gets out tomorrow, and you can't be my shadow forever."

"Too right, I had a few ideas about that."

"Yeah, like what?"

Hayley drifted over and set down a cup and saucer of hot water and another saucer with a little metal teapot on it with more hot water. Tiffany selected a tea bag from the little box of them at the edge of the table and set about fixing her cup with honey and lemon.

I nodded thanks when Hayley returned in short order to top up my coffee, and with a smile, she left us alone again.

"First thing, we're gonna teach you how to shoot. That's the easiest, but what are you going to do if you can't get to the gun we'll get you?"

"Die, probably. Horribly… painfully." She looked grim, but not at all resigned. Anger painted her pretty face and I smiled.

"Not if I can help it. What are your days off?"

"Today and tomorrow, Monday and Tuesday."

"Sweet as, mine too."

She frowned. "What exactly do you do, anyway?"

"Bouncer at a cowboy bar; took over for one of my bros who started a family. Didn't have time for it anymore."

"Ah," she raised her cup, "To bar workers and strippers, at least the schedules are making it fairly easy for us."

"I'll drink to that," I said with a grin and clicked my coffee mug against hers.

"So, what exactly did you have in mind?" she asked.

"Well, I'd like to get you trained up on how to use a gun, and I think you should be able to defend yourself close-quarters like, in case he comes around wanting a hiding."

"Want to what?" she looked at me wide-eyed and a little stricken.

"Sorry, that means wanting to fight you. This way you can fight back."

"He's a rodeo star, there is no fighting him. He's twice my size, and plus, that is totally not what I thought you meant."

I frowned, "What'd ya think I meant?"

She raised her eyebrows and gave me a flat look and I still wasn't getting it. I shook my head and she sighed.

"Rape is such an ugly word, but it can and does happen even to women like me."

"Oh, no! That's not what I meant at all, eh."

"It's a possibility, though," she said grimly. "There are worse things than dying; for me that's one of them."

"Hey, ain't gonna happen, we'll get you right."

"I hope you're right."

"Nah, I know I am."

"Alright, here's your plates and here's your tab, you guys can settle up any time you'd like." Hayley set down our food silencing any further conversation for the time being. She smiled brightly and whisked a ticket out of her apron pocket, setting it at the edge of the table before heading back into the kitchen. Tiff set a twenty on top of it. A twenty stained with red lipstick.

"Eh, no I got this," I said and she smiled at me and shook her head.

"You said you were buying me dinner with it, remember?"

"Ah, I did, that. Didn't I?"

I let Hayley take it after adding a bit more to it to cover the rest of the tab and a hefty tip.

Tiffany smiled and it held an edge of sadness. We didn't talk much for the rest of the meal. Hayley came by and took the pay with thanks and I honestly had to say that I felt a pang of something, watching that twenty with its bit of red color whisked away. Couldn't stop thinking about it, actually.

When we got out to the bike, I felt a bit bad that it was so cold but I said, "Forgot something, be right back, okay?"

"Sure," Tiff murmured and leaned her shapely butt against the seat of my bike. I ran back inside and fished out my wallet, going to Hayley at the counter.

"What's up?" she asked.

"That twenty we paid you with, I'd like to buy it."

Hayley laughed a little, incredulous. "I put it in the register, how will I know which one it is?"

"No worries," I told her, "I'll know."

She opened up the register and fanned them out and the third bill down I pointed it out and said, "That one." She handed it across to me and I passed her a couple of tens out of my wallet.

"Thanks."

"Sure, no problem," she said, mystified.

I went back out to take Tiff home, her somber yet curious gaze following me from the front door, down the steps, and all the way down the car park to where she sat, patiently waiting.

"All good, then," I said cheerfully and she gave me a nod. She didn't ask and I wasn't volunteering. It was a quiet ride back to her place as far as the conversation went.

7

Tiffany…

"Oh my god, you're kidding me, right? This is going to be an everyday thing?" I looked up at Delia and frowned.

"Why on earth would I joke about something like this?" I asked, handing her the pint of ice cream she'd picked out of the paper grocery sack sitting on my kitchen counter.

"Tiffany Amber Dempsey!" she cried, mouth agape. "I know Dragon is nice to all of us but he's looking to get laid coming around Sugars, of course, he's going to be nice to us. He's still the president of the Sacred Hearts MC, though. They have a reputation around here for a reason. I heard, they once skinned one of their enemies alive and nailed his bloody skin to his family's front door. They are not nice people and they're going to want something from you eventually. Something that you're probably not going to want to give them, and then what?"

"I know they're not nice people, Lia. That's totally why I went to them in the first place. In case you hadn't noticed, Silas isn't a nice person, either and when it comes right down to it, I happen to know for a fact that it is not 'better the devil you know' in this case."

"So, like, this guy with the scary face tattoos is what? Just going to follow you everywhere you go, and you seriously thought that none of them were going to expect anything out of you in return?"

I shifted slightly and gave her a one-shouldered shrug as I tore the top off of my own ice cream pint. I hadn't thought of that actually, but the more I thought about it, I had things to trade them. Sex, for starters, if I had to. I already traded sex for money. After going that low, sex for protection was a much better deal. I just hoped that whoever I had to fuck wasn't into pain. I'd had enough of that for a lifetime, I'll tell you what.

"It looks like it, so far," I said.

"Yeah, so far, being the operative words. You didn't deal with them in explicit terms from the get-go? Girl! Have you not listened to anything I've told you?"

"Desperate times called for desperate measures, Lia. Silas is out now and he's going to come after me. I'm pretty sure he's already looking."

She handed me a spoon, her expression grim, the wheels turning behind her pretty green eyes.

She sighed, "This town isn't that big, but it isn't exactly small either. I mean, sure, you run into a lot of the same faces, but it's not like everybody knows everybody else's name." She rolled her eyes. "I don't think he's going to find you that easy. He's probably not even looking! I mean, he's clean now and he's spent a few years in prison cooling his jets, right?"

I rolled my eyes and took the spoon she held out, cramming it into the top of my ice cream and putting some into my mouth. Speaking around it, I said, "Do you have any idea how far you're reaching with that shit?" I asked, swallowing the sweet, creamy goodness.

"Yeah, no, you're right. Silas was a douche. He's still probably a douche. You know what they say about guys who go to prison." She sighed and her shoulders dropped. She turned lightly and went into the main area of my studio and dropped onto the edge of my bed like a giant sack of potatoes.

I went around the dividing island of my kitchen and dropped down next to her just as heavily.

"Actually, I don't," I said honestly.

She rolled her eyes at me and sucked on the spoonful of ice cream she put in her mouth. I waited for her to finish her mouthful and spill while I ate some more of my own deliciousness. I would need it to sit through the Hallmark channel movie Lia was about to make me suffer through.

"They come out the exact same way they went in, at least personality-wise. It's like prison is some kind of time warp that holds them in stasis. I knew a guy that went in at seventeen for armed robbery, tried as an adult. Do not pass go, no stint in juvie, he went directly to the big boy's prison."

"And?" I asked.

"Spent the entire five years of his sentence inside, came out at something like twenty-three and I swear to god, he didn't mature at all in there. Like he looked older, and fantastic actually. Was ripped all to hell and had a set of abs to die for but he was still a seventeen-year-old kid. He learned nothing in there that he could use out here."

"What happened to him?"

"Rare success story. He started working for a junkyard pulling apart cars, became a mechanic and stayed out of trouble."

I gave her a look and she rolled her eyes at me again, "I didn't say that was going to be Silas!" Her exasperation made me smile, which I hid behind my pint of ice cream as I took another bite.

It totally wouldn't be. It'd be nice, but he was hell-bent on killing me when he got put away and I seriously couldn't picture him doing anything but seething over it for the last three years. I wished they'd kept him for his full sentence. If they had, I would have been long gone, someplace he never would have been able to find me. Probably with a different name, too, though not by marriage. I couldn't picture anybody wanting a washed-up whore.

"Hey, whatever you're thinking, stop it," Lia said gently and I looked over at her.

"What?"

"I hate it when you get that look," she answered.

"What look?"

"Defeated. Like someone just kicked your favorite puppy to death in front of you and there isn't a damn thing you can do about it."

I took a deep breath and let it out harshly, looking at my friend pointedly. She frowned at me and it was her turn to ask, "What?"

"I can do something about this," I said evenly. "And I did."

She scowled at me and said, "And I still think it's a big mistake. You didn't grow up around here, Tiff. You don't know what kind of men they are."

"Sometimes you just have to make a leap of faith," I said with a shrug. "Trust your instincts."

"Like you did when you got involved with Silas in the first place?" she asked me flatly.

Ouch. Low blow. Real low blow.

"I don't want to fight about this," I said and she sighed. She knew she'd fucked up. It was written all over her face.

"I'm sorry," she apologized immediately. "I shouldn't have said that."

"No, you shouldn't have." I picked up the remote and turned on my little TV, picked up the other and switched on the DVD player. "Just watch your movie," I said and tried not to let my anger get the best of me.

It was a tense showing of *The Christmas Wish*, and I couldn't say the mood improved much after.

"I'm really worried about you," she said as her parting shot when she left that night.

"Me, too," was all I could say to the scarred wood of my apartment door as I threw all the bolts and chains along its edge behind her.

We would be okay. Her heart was in the right place. I just needed to be mad for a while until I sorted out some more of the ugly inside my head.

So far neither Dragon nor Zeb had asked anything from me, but that didn't mean I didn't owe them. I was just hoping that when it came time to pay my dues, it wouldn't hurt as much, if not more, than whatever Silas would do to me.

Rock, hi, I'm Tiff. Nice to meet you, too, Hard Place.

8

Zeb...

I lay back in my bed, hands behind my head, and stared at the paper rectangle taped to the wall next to it. The light in here was bad, which was good, considering I slept most of the day, but sunrise hadn't happened yet, and so I could barely make out the crimson stain across the paper's surface. I touched it lightly and figured it wasn't a good thing that I couldn't stop picturing her with it between her lips. She was so beautifully broken. I couldn't help it, though. There was something about her. Something about the way she moved, the look in her eyes, it captivated me.

She had these walls up, so impossibly high and hiding behind them, but at the same time, she was in there screaming for someone to see her. I did, I could hear her, but I didn't think I could do anything about it except what Dragon had asked me to do. I could keep her alive and her ex-man's damn hands off of her.

I sighed and set aside the book by Thompson I had laying on my chest. I tore my gaze from the rumpled twenty I'd done my best to smooth flat and stared at the cracked and water stained ceiling of my flat instead.

She was too primo for the likes of me, anyway. She'd probably get the idea I fancied her and tell me to fuck off. I couldn't say I would blame her. My eyes drifted back to the lippy stained money on the wall. I didn't think I would be sleeping anytime soon, so I sat up and pressed fingertips into my eyes, trying to rub the tired out.

Ever been that way? Tired, but can't sleep, too much on the mind to make drifting off happen. Even if it was something you desperately wanted?

Her friend was supposed to bring her in just a few hours. I wanted to begin training her on how to defend herself if it should come up with her. I was fair certain it wouldn't, but it was better safe than sorry, yeah? I liked the girl, and not just because she was pretty. I'd made a few observations about her in the short time we'd known each other.

She was smart, for one. The textbooks on her table were pretty heavy reading. If I had to guess, she was getting closer to her degree. Maybe the final year of Uni for her. That wasn't what stood out to me the most, though. What stood out to me, what called out the most was her warrior's spirit. She was a fierce one, that girl. I could see it. Wanted to see more of it.

I reached up to my jacket, hanging on the back of a chair by the bed and fished in the pocket for the mint tin in it. I opened it up and fished out a rolling paper, taking a pinch of the weed in it and crumbling along the paper I had folded with my other hand to hold it. I rolled myself a joint and stuck it between my lips, closing up the tin and putting it back, then fishing for my lighter in the same pocket.

I sucked the herb smoke into my lungs and flopped back onto the bed, staring at the rumpled, crimson-stained American money. I exhaled and watched the smoke plume and roil, perfuming the air with its earthy notes. I took another hit and held it, felt muscles start to loosen and my mind begin to slow its roll. I didn't smoke weed often, but I had to admit, it was the best remedy when my nerves started to jangle for whatever reason so I always kept some on me.

I finished the joint and put it out in an empty lemonade can by the bed before flopping back into the mattress. I turned my head and stared at that crimson mark until the drug kicked in and mellowed me out enough to sleep. Still, pretty sure my dreams were haunted by a sinuous dancer with the saddest brown eyes that at the same time, were as empty as a doll's.

9

T iffany…

"Make a fist," he ordered and I did. He shook his head slightly and stepped forward, taking my hand in his gently and untucking my thumb from inside my fingers.

"That's how you get a broken thumb, always keep it on the outside, okay?"

"Okay."

He put up a hand, flat and said, "Punch it and I mean really punch it."

"I don't want to hurt you," I said and kind of cringed at the thought of full-out hitting his hand.

He smiled at me, a broad grin, and said, "That's the whole point. If you throw a punch, you have to mean it, eh."

He took a stance and held up his hand and I took a deep breath and swung. My fist slapped into the center of his palm and I swear I squeaked. He laughed, shook it out and a female voice called across the empty gym, "Not bad, first things first, though. We need to work on her stance."

I took a step back from Nik and turned my head, looking down. He'd managed to convince me to pull my long hair into a ponytail and keep it out of my face for this but he hadn't said anything about anyone else being here. Just when I was warming up to him, too, despite Lia's worried nagging the whole way here.

"Ah, yeah, Tiff I'd like y't' meet Mali, she's my bro's woman and knows a thing or two about a good street fight."

"Yeah, I think the reason he called me down here has more to do with the fact that I'm a woman and most of the fighting I've done my whole life has been against dudes that are usually easily twice my size when it comes to muscle mass." She held out her hand to me and her arms were covered in flower tattoos. I blinked and shook it, still unwilling to meet her eyes, feeling awfully exposed. I recognized her tattoos, though.

"Weren't you serving drinks a few of nights ago at the MC?" I asked.

"Yeah, that would be me. Full-time ink-slinger and part-time drink-slinger. The bartending is a hobby while my man Data is balls deep in his computer systems rather than me." Her voice held the edge of a smile and I glanced up. She leaned around and nodded.

"Zeb."

"Ah, yeah?"

"Please tell me I'm teaching her how to whoop ass so that if whatever douchebag did that to her decides to come around, she has the potential to cave his nuts in."

"Ah, yeah, that would be why, Mali. Just in case whatever reason I'm not there."

"Excellent. Okay, first thing's first, you need to widen your stance; we need to work on your balance and center of gravity." She redirected her attention back to Nik and asked, "You teaching her to shoot?"

"Thought Trigger would be better suited to do that, eh?"

"You're not wrong and good deal. Should get Reaver involved with his knives, later down the line, but a knife is going to be pretty useless if you don't have the basics down."

Finally, she decided to address me, just as I was starting to get irritated about being talked around. Still, annoyance aside, I was rapt on her every word. I shifted and took a deep breath and let it out in a rush. "This is a lot," I said with a nervous laugh. It was a lot, and I wasn't exactly sure I could do what she was expecting of me. I mean, I'd never really been good at the whole hitting another person even if it was in self-defense. My personal superpower had always sort of been that I could take a beating until help arrived. Which, sometimes it did and sometimes it didn't. At least not always on time.

I swallowed hard, mouth suddenly dry and watched the other woman move. Mali pulled her messenger bag off over her head and dropped it over by the wrestling ring. She pulled down the sleeves of her leather jacket from where they were rucked up around her elbows and shrugged out of it completely, hanging it off the corner post.

"It is a lot, but honey, you want to be a victim forever?"

"No," I said quickly. No, I did not. I wanted to have a life. I'd worked too hard to give myself one after Silas, and I didn't want to let him have what I'd managed to build without a fight. I wanted out of this town and I wanted to help people. That was the goal, by any means necessary. *Never give up, never surrender...*

"Cool," she said. "Now that's out of the way, watch me..."

She and Nik went through the proper way to stand, the proper way to punch and then the real work began. She would have Nik go at her, would evade with expert moves and twists and would use his own weight against him. It was fascinating watching Mali, who wasn't built much differently than me, actually throw Nik around.

They would then break apart and run me through exercises and drills of the same thing over and over until we were all panting and sweating. My body was not going to like me, and I worried about it possibly affecting my work, but the sensations wrought by the workout and drills weren't unfamiliar ones. I'd felt the same sort of aches, pains, and fatigue to get where I was when it came to pole dancing.

"Okay, I think that's enough for today," Mali said after what felt like three or four hours of the torturous exercises. I looked across to Nik who was sweating and panting right along with me.

"I don't feel like I am going to make it in time…" I said.

"How d'you mean?" Nik asked.

"Learn all this before he finds me; before he gets to me."

Nik opened his mouth to speak, a frightening scowl on his tattooed face, but Mali beat him to it saying, "That's not the point, honey. You aren't going to learn this shit overnight. That's impossible. All we can do with this is keep at it and give you an inside edge on staying alive if it comes to it." She gave Nik a meaningful look and whatever he was going to say a moment before was gone.

Instead, he gave me a reassuring grin saying, "One step at a time, eh?" He put his hands on his knees, breathing heavy and gave me a nod that I think was meant to be encouraging.

I was beginning to honestly feel like I was right. That the only superpower I possessed, masked or otherwise, was that I really could just take whatever beating I had coming my way until help arrived. Mali laughed and I blinked at her. Had I said that out loud?

"Well, you're ahead of most then. Most bitches crumble into dust and blow away in the face of this shit. You're fighting back, and pretty hardcore at that. It's always better to be proactive rather than reactive."

"Wish I had been from the get-go."

She gave a shrug.

"Meh, we all do stupid shit when we're young, and trust me, you're still young."

I frowned and asked Nik, "The showers work here?"

"Ah, yeah, nah." I was about to ask which it was but Mali interrupted.

"I've gotta go. You're a quick learner, Tiff. I think your dancing is giving you an inside edge on this. I'll do some thinking on how to make it work even further to our advantage."

I nodded and tried valiantly to not feel completely discouraged. I really hadn't thought I'd done well at all. I also didn't know how I was going to fit this in around coming up with and practicing new routines on the regular. Winging it didn't pay out as well as having a set idea of what to do on stage once the music started.

Mali shrugged back into her jacket over her workout clothes and lifted her messenger bag back over her chest crossways.

"Same bat time, same bat channel," she called over her shoulder.

"See yah, Mali. Thanks again," Nik called. I worried my bottom lip between my teeth for a moment, watching her go and turned back to him. He was watching me intently and I sighed.

"Wasn't what I had in mind," I said honestly and he nodded, dragging down a towel from where he'd hung it over the middle rope on the ring. Watching him toss it over his shoulders was a bit of a treat to watch, the muscles moving beneath his skin in his arms and chest as he wiped the sweat he'd worked up away. I swallowed hard, wondering where that had come from, trying to decide if it was getting around to that time of the month and I was just doing my regular hormonal thing or if the sudden appreciation of his physique was a real attraction trying to sneak in the back door. To help me make my decision, I took him in a little more thoroughly.

He wore a pair of cut-off sweatpants and a loose tank top and it gave him a rugged, no-fucks-were-given, look-at-me-wrong-and-I'll-beat-a-man's-ass sort of vibe that was appealing.

I wore my typical dance practice attire of athletic leggings and a sports bra. The only concessions from my usual practice attire were a comfortable pair of socks and sneakers. I tended to practice on the pole with a pair of heels, or if I was just playing around, barefoot.

The gym had working heat, but that didn't stop the cold from outside from swirling in at Mali's departure, gelling the sweat in place on my skin and causing me to start to itch. It didn't help that the cold wanted to linger and I hated being cold for too long. Sometimes it was like the cold wanted to set in and I couldn't stand that. It looked like this was going to be one of those times. Usually, the only cure was a hot shower or a lot of layers and some time by the heater or a fire.

"So, do the showers here work or not?" I asked again.

"Eh, yeah, they work, but nah, we aren't supposed to use 'em. Wasn't part of the deal with me getting us in here after-hours."

"Fair enough. I'm starting to freeze, though, so can we get me home so I can deal?"

"C'mon with me," he said.

I nodded and we gathered our things. He put the hooded sweatshirt he'd had on when he'd let us in here around my shoulders and I followed him out onto the frozen, night-dark street. After locking up the front door of the gym, he waved me after him. I followed him half a block down to the front of this dive bar. He unlocked a door next to it and waved me through into a narrow stairwell. He threw the deadbolt into the locked position behind us and climbed the stairs ahead of me, two at a time. I lightly stepped after him, climbing them deftly without so much as getting even slightly out of breath.

At least the stripping had kicked up my endurance for this new sort of training. If anything, I had cardio covered in this whole endeavor.

Though, I figured, I could stand to spend a little more time on a treadmill. I never knew if it would come down to me legit or straight up running in an encounter with Silas.

Nik stopped at a door at the end of the short hall at the top of the stairs and fished through his keys on the ring, selecting one and sticking it in the top lock. I shivered involuntarily and hated it. Cursing winter out silently inside my head, I followed him into the space beyond the doorway and blinked at the enormity of it.

"Wow, this place is huge..." I said, and it was. A kitchenette was off to my left, a doorway next to it. The place was a huge open floor plan but empty. Devoid of any real furniture except for a mattress on the floor up against one wall in a corner, and a spindly, old and scarred up dining room chair sitting next to it.

"Ah, yeah, the owner of the bar can't rent it. The bar is too loud, comes right through the floor. They used to use it for storage, but the fire department said they couldn't anymore. Seeing as I work there, I said I'd rent it. I'm working during the hours it would be loud anyhow."

"So this is your place?"

"Ah, yeah. You said you wanted a shower, eh?"

"Are you serious? You're cool with me taking one?"

"Yeah, through there. I'll get you a towel." He opened up a closet door on the opposite side of the room and dug through a big, old, green Army duffel bag, pulling a towel free. I blinked and stood still, my own gym bag with clean regular street-clothes dangling off my shoulder and stifled a bit of a laugh when he smelled the towel just to make sure it was a clean one before he brought it to me.

"There you are, fresh from the wash."

"Thank you," I murmured.

"Try to save me some hot, eh."

"I can try."

"One of them wahine, then."

I blinked, "Wah-he-nay?" I said the unfamiliar word, dragging it out slowly.

"Ah, yeah, it means 'woman' in my language."

I believed him, he looked sincere and didn't have any of the usual tells that he might be having a laugh at my expense. I'd seen enough of that type of cruelty, both from Silas and his friends, as well as at Sugars, to know what it looked like.

"I see," I murmured and rolling my lips together, took a step back toward the door he indicated was the bathroom and shut the door behind me.

"Hey, I hate to ask, but can you leave it open just a crack?" he called out.

I opened the door a crack and called back, "Why?"

"No ventilation, the fan doesn't work and it likes to grow things in there fast otherwise."

"Lovely," I said under my breath. "Fine," I said louder, but to make sure that he didn't get any ideas, I said, "Sit down out there against the wall and talk to me."

"Sure thing," I heard his back thump against the wall beside the door and listened as he slid down it to the floor. "What would you like to talk about?"

I swallowed hard and got to work undressing and setting the towel within easy reach for when I got out of the shower.

"How about you tell me what all those markings are on your face?" I said and then grimaced inwardly. "Sorry, I'm just genuinely curious, I didn't mean for that to come out sounding so rude!"

"No worries, and they're specific, you know?"

I laughed slightly and started up the water getting it as hot as I could stand it. "If I knew, I wouldn't be asking now would I?"

"Ah, well, that would mean I'd have to talk about home, wouldn't it?"

His tone gave me pause and made me want to pry, but just a little. I thought carefully for a second on how to approach, and finally asked, "Do you miss it?"

"New Zealand?"

"Yeah."

"I miss it a lot, actually."

"Then why are you here?"

It was a long, pregnant pause before he answered.

"I did some dumb shit and crossed the wrong gang boss and now I'm here. Could be killed if I ever go back."

"Oh... I'm sorry..."

"Eh, there are worse things. I like it here, too... and I got to meet you."

Wow, that was actually a pretty sweet thing to say.

"Are you flirting with me?" I asked, to make sure. I was almost certain he was, but he laughed, nervously dispelling the notion.

"Nah, I didn't mean it like that. I just think you're interesting, Girl."

"Me? Interesting?" I asked over the shower spray. I thrust my face into the water and listened intently for his answer.

"Yeah, you. I wonder a bit, what's *your* story?"

"You know my story, I told you the other night at the diner."

"No, you told me about how you got your warrior's mark. That's something that happened to you, not your whole story. That's just a singular moment in time. A bad one, I reckon, but just a footnote in a chapter. Not the whole book."

"You like to read?" I asked, massaging the soap into my long hair, the question more to buy myself some time to process what he'd just said. I mean, it was awfully profound. I hadn't expected it to come from someone packaged like him. Of course, speaking of books, that whole adage of never judging one by its cover came to mind again.

"Yeah, I think it's where I got such big ideas that I could change things back home. I got myself to thinking that I was smarter than everybody around me."

"So what happened?" I asked, rinsing my head with the shower spray, listening intently for his answer.

"I learned that no matter how smart you think you are, there's always a bloke out there smarter than you."

"That's all?"

"That and it's never a good idea to try and get one over on a gang boss as powerful as the one I tried to fool. There's a reason he's boss. I'd like to think I'm over being that young and dumb."

I wanted to ask him, *what did you do exactly,* but it was none of my business. Just like there were certain things about me that were none of his.

So he'd gone from outsmarting crime bosses to escorting and protecting a whore. I honestly would consider that a downgrade in lifestyle, but thinking on it, whatever he'd done that was viewed as a betrayal, it was probably a downgrade he was more than happy to live with, considering he got to live.

Live and learn. It was honestly all any of us could do.

"So," he called out, interrupting my introspective silence, "What's your story?"

"I'm just a girl trying to crawl out from under the mountain of debt her poor choices left her buried under," I said. Which was true.

"Alright, I'll give you that," he called. "But you know something I like, so what about you? Name something you like."

He liked to read, I liked to read, too but I had a feeling if I said that it would come across as evasive, or like I was trying to purposefully be difficult.

"I... I guess it's been a long time since I thought about what I like, or what makes me happy," I said finally.

"That's a bit depressing, isn't it?" he asked carefully, and I couldn't disagree, but wondered at the change in his tone.

"I like to dance," I said finally. "Delia is the one that convinced me to take pole dancing as a means to stay fit and have fun after..." I trailed off and finished with a bitter, "Well, after Silas."

"You like your job, then? That's good."

"I like parts of my job, not all of it."

"Yeah, I could see that. What parts do you like best?"

"I like the creativity part. I like coming up with new dances and new moves. I like the music and finding the perfect song. That's the fun part."

"I can see it," he said and I smiled.

"I liked today," I said honestly. "Downstairs, the learning new things... I think it was a good idea. I wish I had done it sooner but I never really felt right going to the self-defense classes around here."

"Why not?" he sounded curious.

"I had one of the instructors tell me that because I was a stripper, I was asking for trouble."

He scoffed and declared, "What a tool!"

"Yeah, Lia and I didn't go back after the first class. We went back to her apartment and ate ice cream. Besides, he was less about actually teaching the girls anything and more about feeling them up and fishing for a hookup."

He laughed and I smiled to myself. It was a good sound. I was just finishing up and shut off the water saying, "Don't laugh. I mean, it's my job, I would know."

"Too right, I reckon."

I worked on drying myself off and practically jumped into my street clothes. His apartment wasn't exactly warm, and the heat from the shower was quickly dissipating from the bathroom.

I pulled my hair dryer from my bag and thought better of making him wait to shower until I'd dried it in here. Instead, I stepped out and he stood up. It made me smile how quickly he got to his feet. It reminded me of a bygone era when men leaped up from their seats anytime a lady entered the room. Except I was no lady. I don't think I could ever be considered 'classy' not even by today's standards. Still, there was something about how Nik moved around me that almost made me believe I could be. It was nice.

"I don't want to hold you up, is there someplace I can plug this in out here and dry my hair?" I held up the hair dryer and he smiled.

"Most of the power points out here don't work," he said, "But the one by the bed does, under the chair."

"Thanks," I said and he gave me a nod.

"I'll be out nek minute, no worries."

I started across the open space towards where he said and turned last moment, blurting out, "And thanks for what you said, you know, about my face. Um, I'm not sure why you called it that, though."

"What, yer warrior's mark? Because you are one. You didn't just survive, Girl. You thrived, you made yer own way. That takes courage

82

that a lot of people lack. That's a survivor's mark you can be proud of, eh."

I blinked but he was gone, inside the bathroom, just the thinnest sliver of golden light coming through the crack in the door. I swallowed hard and went over to the chair that seemed to be serving as some sort of an end table more than a chair. It had a bunch of things on it that I didn't want to disturb, so I sat on the edge of the bed and plugged in my drier.

I sat up, and brush in hand switched the loud machine on. The warm air was welcome against my scalp and I worked the heat through my long hair, which was a real bitch to dry. Still, I was so not getting on the back of a motorcycle, in winter, with wet hair, helmet or not. Just the thought gave me a cold shiver. I would never get warm again.

I let my eyes wander, as drying one's hair was typically one of the most boring pastimes on earth. Especially without my setup at home. I'd usually just sit at my little dining room table with a textbook propped on a cookbook stand and read out of my assigned chapters while drying. Don't judge. I liked to be efficient and look good.

Now I just let my gaze roam around Zeb's large, rundown, and mostly empty apartment. I twisted in my seat and nearly singed the top of my ear with the drier, I was so frozen by what captured my gaze.

Taped to the wall beside his bed was a crumpled twenty, a smear of familiar red lipstick across Jackson's face.

Had he gone back to the diner for it? I'd wondered what he was doing, and here it was staring me in the face. Surprising me the most was the fact that my first reaction upon seeing it was that it was a sweet gesture before my general paranoia about everything kicked in.

I went back and forth for several moments wondering about his intent when it came to the bill. Trying to decide whether it was a sordid trophy or whether it was as a sweet gesture that was my initial reaction to seeing it there.

I shut off the hair drier and finger-combed my hair to feel for any excessively damp spots. It took me a full minute to realize I wasn't hearing the shower run. I twisted back around and he was standing there, watching me, barefoot and bare-chested in just a pair of jeans, his longish dark hair pulled into a short ponytail.

"What is this?" I asked softly, pointing to the bill.

"Ah, shit, uh, for me? A good memory."

I frowned, "Explain please?"

"Well, you see I went to this titty bar and there was this dancer there, and she's a pretty thing. Fierce, you know? Out of all the blokes sitting around her stage, she picked me to dance for and I gave her a tip worthy of her show and she made taking it such a part of her performance. It was special. I liked it, and I couldn't stop thinking about how she took the money."

He wouldn't really look me in the eyes and I realized just how shy he was. I studied him carefully and he radiated a certain amount of embarrassment over having been caught with the reminder taped to his wall. I stood up slowly, leaving my hair drier on the small pile of other things on his chair and my brush behind on the floor.

I was firmly on the side of *not creepy but sweet* when I went to him. I carefully hugged him and his hands lightly went to my hips. He smelled good, earthy and like a clean man, which why did 'clean man' smell so damn good?

"I think it's sweet," I whispered and he leaned back so he could look me in the eyes, a small smile playing on his full lips. My gaze wandered the intricate whorls and designs of his tattoo from forehead to chin, but only on the one half of his face. I didn't understand that but I didn't want to ask and possibly offend him.

"But?" he asked softly, his voice strained, swallowing so hard it very nearly clicked.

"But I'm not a good person to get involved with, like, at all," I told him.

I'd looked away, fixing my eyes on a crack in the wall, down by the baseboards. His thick fingers found my chin in a light, gentle touch that brought my eyes back to his.

"Why don't you let me be the judge of that, eh?"

"Because I don't want to hurt you," I said truthfully.

His mouth was coming closer to mine and he whispered just above my lips, "I'm a big boy, I can take it."

"You sure?" I murmured and almost hated how faint my voice was, how much I wanted his lips to touch mine. It'd been so long since anyone who had wanted to kiss me saw me for more than just tits and ass. I knew it down to my very soul that Nik did. That this wasn't the same as the men from the club. There was something far more to this than that, and I was especially surprised to feel that I wanted it, and then his lips touched mine, warm and sensual, and I lost myself for just a moment.

I kissed him back, Pretty Woman Art of Hooking Handbook be damned. For the first time in a long time, I wasn't a hooker. I wasn't a sex worker. I was a woman and I felt like a real one at that. It was amazing, breathtaking, and so beautiful. I hadn't realized how starved I was for it and at the same time, it frightened me so completely to have that strong of a reaction to him, to any man again after what Silas had done.

I pulled away abruptly, my chest heaving, and turned away, pressing my hands to my mouth as much to hold onto the lingering sensation of his kiss as to keep myself from spilling over into heavy sobs. I was so torn between so many emotions. Want, need, and longing warring with the safety, independence and yes, even loneliness. I was lonely, and I hated that about myself, but it was something that I just had to do.

"Hey, hey, none of that," he whispered soothingly, stepping up to my back and wrapping his arms around me. He rested his lips against my shoulder and he swayed gently; soothingly.

I closed my eyes and breathed deep and slowly relaxed, lowering my hands and murmuring, "I'm sorry."

"Don't be, eh… It was nice."

I scoffed, nearly choking on the bitter, mocking sound. He smiled and gave me a gentle squeeze before letting me go.

"Well, it was for me," he said softly, and I immediately felt bad.

"I didn't mean it like that," I said, tone grave. "It was nice for me, too."

And that was the problem, wasn't it?

10

Z eb...

She'd been tense on the way home, the regular text message check-ins had been short but taking her into her work today, she'd seemed fine. I kept to myself, let her sort through her head, and had a pretty good night of my own at the bar. No trouble, which was the way I usually liked it, being hired muscle.

Zeke waved me through the velvet rope, on his phone, exchanging a nod with me and I plunged into the heat and pounding music of the neon-lit dark. I threaded my way through mostly empty tables and ran into Cherry, one of the girls that hung around the MC.

"Looking for Francesca?" she asked, snapping her gum and rolling her eyes. Cherry was a nasty piece of work sometimes, and most of us just ignored her. This was no different, at least when it came to me.

"Yeah, where she at?"

"In back," she said with a smirk.

"Ta," I thanked her and went that way. I didn't like what I found.

She was on a counter, her eyes lifeless and empty while a bloke plowed her but good. I stopped in my tracks and her eyes focused on me. Panic flashed in them, then they flooded with such a deep sorrow.

I'd been about to pull the bloke off her and beat his ass to death but I realized that she wasn't struggling and then it hit me and my stomach nearly dropped out. I put up my hands and shook my head and backed out of the room, the bloke never even realizing I was there.

I went out to the parking lot and pulled the bike around back since she knew I was there, she'd come out when she was ready. I rolled myself a fat one and calmed my nerves some.

I hadn't reckoned it went beyond dancing for her and I was sort of dumbfounded that she was a whore. It didn't sit right with me. Something about it bothered me. The disappointment so strong I could taste it, but something else was there, keeping me from being hot-headed about it.

She came out pretty quickly and I couldn't look at her.

"I'm sorry, I told you –" I waved her off and straddled my bike, firing it up. I didn't want to talk to her, not yet. I was afraid I might say something unfortunate. It was best I take her home and go talk to my bros.

She looked taken aback, then angry, then resigned and got on behind me in short order. I took her home, waved off her next attempt to talk to me, and made sure she went up and locked her doors. I rode out to the club next and found a pretty busy common room.

I spied out Dragon and went over, dropping into a seat at his table.

"I know that look," he declared with a gusty sigh.

"You maybe forgot to mention she was a whore?"

"Didn't figure her line of employment was all that important to the job at hand. Of course, I also figured it weren't none of your business."

"Oh, no. No, no, no. Dragon, you stay in the truck. I think I've got this one."

Shelly dropped into the chair across from Dragon and next to mine, her blue eyes calculating. One of her little ones was under a baby blanket, latched on and having a feed.

"You eavesdropping, Girl?" I asked and she rolled her eyes at me. Dragon's eyebrows went up.

"Always, and for the most part, I stay out of it, but consider me cashing in a year's worth of my get-out-of-jail-free cards because I won't stay quiet about this one. Now you listen here, I want to lay out a story."

Dragon leaned back in his chair grinning and crossed his arms, I leaned back in my own and folded my hands on the table in front of me real proper and let her know with raised eyebrows that I was listening.

"Picture this, you're a pretty girl. Hook up with a nice guy who ends up being a total douche and pretty much wrecks the only thing you've got going for you which is that you are pretty. Still, you manage to work it. Get the best job that a high school dropout with barely her GED can. You need cash and you need a decent amount of it, what else are you going to do, am I right?"

"I reckon."

"So you find out there's even more money to be made and maybe you're pressured into it, maybe you're not, but that doesn't really matter. Sure, it's illegal, technically, but seriously. What the fuck else did you expect her to do? In this piece-of-shit patriarchal society, what else is there for her to do?" Shelly leaned back in her chair and took a second, trying not to raise her voice.

"She's pretty much wrecked by our society's standards as it is and the only thing she's got to sell is herself. Now, I, of all people, get it. If it weren't for the club, I might have ended up like her, and to be honest, I respect the bitch. I can't fucking blame her for having a better business model than me. I was just a slut giving it up for free, she's way smarter. She's getting straight up paid."

"How the hell you know all this?" Dragon asked baffled and Shelly smiled sweetly at him.

"I know everything that goes on around here, that and Cherry works over there. She's got a big fucking mouth. Probably equal to the size of her cunt by now." She made a face like she'd smelled something bad and Dragon let out a laugh that started as one of his characteristically booming ones, but he strangled it at the last minute so as not to wake the baby Shelly had in her arms.

"Still would have been nice to know," I said getting back to the subject and shifting uncomfortably in my seat. Shelly's practical view of things was making me feel like a total asshole.

"How could you not? You seriously thought she and I were just platonic buddies? I'd go for a dance and that was it?" Dragon asked.

Then I did feel like a total asshole, especially when I blurted out, "You?"

"Yeah, me! The fuck you think when you met her in just one of my shirts sleeping in my bed?"

"I didn't think…"

"Ah, but you knew. You always knew," Shelly said knowingly.

"How d' you reckon?"

"Because you're disappointed, but yer not pissed. You ain't come storming in here downing a bottle. Something tipped you off and your back-brain probably caught on but the front, not so much."

I thought back to the vacant look as she danced, a mirror for the vacant look in her eyes as whoever-he-was fucked her in the back of that shit-hole club she worked. I shook my head and sighed. I knew coming here was right, but I also knew I needed to head back to her place and apologize.

I scrubbed my face with my hands, and Dragon said to Shelly, "You said your piece, now kick rocks a minute."

"Sure," she said softly, her expression thoughtful as she looked at me; not unsympathetic. She got up carefully and shuffled away from us bouncing her kid and I stared after her.

"Living proof that there's a life after that kind of life. She's right, you know. If it weren't for Reave or this club, she could have easily ended up like Tiff."

"She shouldn't have to do that," I said.

"Do you really think she wants to?" he shot back.

I made a frustrated noise and leaned back, staring at the ceiling painted black. Dragon shook his head.

"You like her." It wasn't a question, so I didn't answer, I just looked back his way. He nodded and asked, "She like you too?"

"She kissed me back the other day."

He nodded slowly, "She's never let me kiss her. I imagine she doesn't let just anybody."

"I wouldn't say anything to her, I didn't want to upset her more or say something unfortunate."

"She locked in her place?"

"Yeah."

"You headed back over there?"

I wanted to, but I didn't know if it was best. Dragon sighed and said, "I know it ain't going to make you feel better, but as far as someone in her situation goes, I know she's responsible about it."

"How so?"

"Condoms, always. Goes in for regular testing. Real selective about who she'll fuck. She may sell herself for sex, but she at least has enough self-respect that she ain't doin' it cheaply."

I grimaced, "Too right, you ain't makin' me feel better."

"You want I should have someone else help her?"

"No," I said quickly and he sat back.

"Well, I think that's the only answer either you or me need. Now man the fuck up, and go work out your shit."

"That an order, Boss?"

"For once, yeah. Yeah, it is."

I nodded and got up, "Thanks, Bro."

"You're learning," he said with a nod. "I'm proud of you."

That struck me right in the heart. It meant a lot that he would say so.

When I'd come here, I'd been lost without my family, my people, far from home – shit, you name it. Dragon had sat me down and asked me what I wanted most out of life and I'd told him honest; I wanted to be a man. A man my mum and my people could be proud of and he'd told me flat out that only I could make it happen and I needed to figure my shit out.

Part of figuring my shit out had been admitting to myself that it was all right not being the best, the smartest, or the craftiest one of any given bunch. I needed to leave my pride be, and just concentrate on finding myself and that connection to the rest of it.

I'd put in a lot of work on myself since coming here and I had to admit, even to me, that while I didn't like what Tiffany was doing, I hadn't been completely blind to it, even though I didn't want to see it. I also had to admit, that while I could judge her for it, keep things strictly business and try never to think about her like that again, doing that would just make me a bigger asshole.

She hadn't judged me, even though she'd told me her friend had done plenty of it. She'd always been honest about things and while she didn't readily volunteer what she did, I couldn't recall her actually ever hiding it.

At the end of it all, we were just two people stumbling around in life trying to make our way and be better than the people we were the day before and if anything, I could respect that. In part of being a better man than I was yesterday, I wanted to help her be a better woman, but I didn't want to end up with things more munted than they already were, and so Dragon was right.

I needed to go back to her place, even if it was out in the wops, and talk to her. I rode back the entire time, trying to figure out what just to say. Practiced it a few times even, but all the words left me when she opened the door for me, her lashes thick and clumped with a constellation of tears on them.

I felt my shoulders drop and a defeated sigh escape me as I figured the saying about the road to hell being paved with good intentions was true. So instead of saying anything. I just pulled her tight against me and hugged her and I think it was what she needed because she completely fell apart sobbing against me.

I felt like such an asshole, afraid I'd carked it before it could even get started.

Fuck me.

11

T iffany…

He came back.

I don't know what I'd expected, but that certainly hadn't been it. I also hadn't expected him to shut his mouth and to just pull me against him.

His silence had cost me dearly, and I didn't realize how much I had begun to like him back in such a short amount of time until he had refused to even look at me, let alone talk to me.

It wasn't often I felt like a dirty whore, but that had done it for me and I had barely made it into my apartment before the locks had started to blur as I'd twisted them into place. At the last one, the dam had broken completely and I couldn't stop the tears from leaking out of my face.

I'd slid to the floor against my front door and had sworn to myself that I was done with hooking. I just couldn't do it anymore. I needed to stick to dancing and forget about the extra money because there wasn't any amount of money worth the feeling I'd had when Nik had kissed me. That, and I would be damned if I ever wanted to go through the feeling of the look on his face when he'd walked into the back room and seen me with that john.

So I sat on my floor, hugged my knees, and cried it out in my sanctuary, and no sooner had I gotten up to find a damn tissue then here he was, back again, knocking on my door. He had this look on his face when I'd opened it that was better than any 'I'm sorry' any guy had ever invented and then he'd pulled me into his arms and I lost it all over again for a completely different reason.

It was all I had ever wanted any man to do. I think it's what any girl had ever wanted in a man. Someone who could, even without words, sincerely admit when they may have done something wrong – even though he honestly hadn't. I knew I had, and it made me feel miserable.

"I get it," he said quietly, shaking me momentarily from my hamster-wheel of spinning thoughts. "I get it, and I'm sorry I reacted that way, but I hope you'll maybe talk to me."

"What am I supposed to say?" I asked, pitifully.

"What's in your heart," he answered gently. "It's not for any man to tell you what to say or how to act. Only you get to decide how you think or feel. I think that's been taken away from you enough, don't you?"

I pulled back enough to look up at him and he smiled down at me a little sadly, his fingers sweeping my hair out of my face, his thumb gently tracing the curve of scar in my cheek by way of silent emphasis. I closed my eyes and leaned my cheek into the little touch and told the truth.

"I don't know how to do this anymore."

"Do what?"

"Be normal. Be one half of an actual functional relationship with a man. It's all so foreign and I don't know what to do."

"Ain't no rush, but is that your way of saying you like me, too?"

I opened my eyes and fixed him with a look and said, "See, I told you."

He laughed and it was a good sound. I shivered and he swung the door shut behind him. I automatically went to it and threw every one of the locks.

"Guess I'll stay a while, yeah?" I turned, but he wasn't smiling, the look on his face telegraphing loud and clear that he wanted that. That he'd like that very much.

"I was hoping you would," I said, nervously.

"Come here." I went to him and he pulled me close again, holding me, swaying gently. A soothing thing. He had a hint of a smile in his voice when he said, "Got some music?"

"Yeah, why?" I asked.

"Dance with me."

I smiled then, and he let me go just long enough for me to go to my phone and pair it with the little Bluetooth speaker. I turned on something slow. He took my hand and drew me in against the worn leather of his jacket and the newer leather of his vest, which was still pretty worn. We slow-danced in the little space provided in my entryway until my tears finally dried and my heart stopped its racing. As my pulse slowed, so did my rapidly-spiraling thoughts until my mind was a quiet, pleasant, blank.

"Kiss me?" he asked, and I loved that he did. I raised my head from his shoulder and met his mouth with mine. It was the perfect kiss, deep and full of hidden meaning. A treasure I wished I could just run back into the dark with and cherish. It was a slow kiss, full of promise and heat; a heat that shimmered between us with sensual tension, sexual, sure, but so much more than that.

I cradled his face in my hands, the one side raised in lines begging to be traced by my fingertips, his tattoo something more than just ink under his skin. I'd never felt anything like it before. It was as if the lines were carved, etched deeper than that. As if his heritage were more than just displayed but were etched beyond muscle into his very bone, into his soul. I liked that about him. I wanted to know more about it, but I didn't want him to stop kissing me. I didn't want his tongue to stop its seductive sweep against my own or his hands to stop kneading my body through my clothes.

"I don't want to stop," he breathed against my lips.

"I don't either," I confessed and it felt really good that I didn't.

"Got a French letter then, eh?"

"A what?"

He laughed a little and said, "A condom."

"Oh, no."

He made a slightly frustrated growl and breathed along the side of my neck, kissing me at my pulse point in a way that made me shiver.

"It's not like I bring my work home with me," I said half sarcastically, half defensively. "You're the first man I've ever let into my apartment."

He pulled back, dark eyes alight with desire, searching my face. Satisfied with what he saw there, he gave me a reckless grin and said, "I like that, makes a bloke feel special."

I laughed slightly and he touched light fingertips to the corner of my smile, a sweet one echoing on his own full lips.

"Go get a hot shower, find the warmest whatever you have to sleep in. I want to hold you if that's alright?"

"I'd like that," I murmured. "You're seriously okay with just that, though?"

"'Course I am, I suggested it, eh."

I pressed my lips, swollen from his kiss together and gave a short nod. I really liked the sound of what he was offering. There was sex and then there was intimacy. I needed the latter like I needed the sun, like I needed air to breathe, and the sincerity in his gaze as he followed my movements around the room even as he made himself at home, hanging his jacket on the back of one of my little two-seater table's chairs... It was everything I'd longed for.

Maybe I was letting myself be fooled like Delia seemed to think, but the look in his eyes, his easy posture... something told me to follow my heart and my heart was very nearly weeping in relief.

12

Zeb...

She was warm, soft as silk under my fingertips as I played them lightly along her back, under the hem of the little tank top she wore with these stubbies that, I had to admit, did fantastic things for my dick.

She lay on me in her narrow bed, one leg over both my own, ear over my heart and listened to me tell stories about my greenstone pendant, but only after I got done telling her about my tattoos. I liked how she let her fingertips trace the ones in front of her nose, over my shoulder and one pec.

She reminded me of her cat, Max, who was curled with her nose under her tail, tucked between her owner and me where Tiffany had bent herself at the waist to allow room for her. It was an awkward sleeping position for her, but she was sound asleep against me now and made it look easy.

I didn't like that she slept with strange men for money. I liked it even less that even though I said I wasn't, I couldn't help but be unhappy about it and that in turn made me unhappy with me, because it felt like

I was being a judgmental bastard. Of course, the fact that I said I wouldn't judge and then secretly stewed over it like a judgy cunt pissed me off even more because I hated being a hypocrite even more than I hated being a judgy cunt.

So I lay awake, the same thoughts chased by guilt in a circle around the inside of my head while a beautiful woman was sleeping on me, oblivious to it.

We'd talked about it, and she'd told me she didn't want to do it anymore. That the money was good, but the money certainly wasn't buying her any sort of happiness. I'd asked her if I made her happy at all and she'd really thought about it before she'd answered and the answer was unexpectedly raw and honest. She'd said, "I think I've forgotten what happiness is, but when I'm with you, learning or just talking like this, I can almost remember what it was like. Do you make me happy? I don't think anything could make me happy, but you remind me that it's there and when we talk, like this, I can almost believe I can be happy again."

I didn't know what to take away from that, but it made me smile and I had to laugh a little as I said, "Ah, yeah, now I know how you feel, I think."

"Oh? How's that?"

"I dunno whether you just said yes or no."

She'd smiled then and had laughed and it had been a good sound, but I still didn't know if it was a yes or no. She'd helped me understand a bit better by telling me, "I've learned that a lot of things aren't simply black or white, yes or no answers."

That'd been fair enough, and I'd said so. She'd grown solemn then and our conversation had dropped off and then she'd dropped off, too, into sleep.

I tried, and as comfortable as I was, I reckon I was bothered by the fact that she hadn't said she wouldn't do it anymore – that she'd just said she didn't want to. I didn't think I could share a woman with another man, and not even in the practical application of *it was her job.* Stripping I could deal with, but another man inside her? Knowing that it made her sad, that she didn't want to? I couldn't bear the thought. It was so uncomfortable I must've shifted because she jolted awake slightly and asked, "What's wrong?"

I decided she'd been honest with me, so I could be honest with her. That I had to be honest with her.

"I don't want you to sleep with other men anymore if we're gonna give it a go. It bothers me and honestly, it hurts my heart to know you've done it for so long. You're worth much more than that, eh."

"I told you, I don't want to anymore," she said.

"I know, but not wanting to and not doing it are two different things, eh."

She was quiet for several moments and she cuddled closer to me and stroked the top of Max's head between the cat's ears.

"I don't do what I don't want to, not anymore. Still, telling a guy 'no' outright isn't the easiest thing to do when you're a woman and in the line of work I'm in."

"What're you saying?"

"I'm saying the best way for me to go about it is to say I don't want to, and when they push, the only way I really have to push back is with money. I have a better chance of getting out of it by naming an exorbitant price, but Nik," she let out a bit of a hard sigh and said, "everyone has their price."

"Name yours," I said softly. She named a figure and I let out a low whistle. I could see what she meant. "Yeah, at that price, I reckon even I couldn't argue you going for it."

She rested her arm on me and propped her chin on her wrist, staring me in the eye, "Then whoever asks, that's my price. Most, if not all, of the guys around here wouldn't be willing to pay that much to fuck anyone, so it shouldn't be a problem."

"Lucky if one of 'em doesn't try to hit you for even suggesting it," I said carefully.

"I really didn't turn tricks that often, and only for a handful of men. Regular customers that I got to know enough to know if they were that type of guy. Plus, if any of them tried it, that's what Zeke is for. My problem is that I know not even Zeke could stand up to Silas, which is why I went the only place where I knew I could find someone who could." She looked sad again but I was too busy replaying the part where she said she didn't turn tricks often. 'Didn't' as in past tense. She really was out of the game as far as she was concerned and I was well pleased with that.

"How much extra did that kind of thing net you?" I asked.

"Two, sometimes three extra grand a month, but I'm almost done with my debts. It will take me a bit longer with just dancing but like I said, money doesn't buy happiness, and I'm looking at a chance to maybe be happy again; I don't want to screw that up."

She was staring at me, searching my face. I nodded. "A compromise then. You name that price. If someone matches it or offers more, you really think about it and if you can't pass it up you do what you think is right. Not what I think is right or what a citizen might because fuck them – you do you, and we can talk about it, just like we're talking now."

"You wouldn't be mad?"

I lifted one shoulder in a slight shrug and said, "I didn't say that I wouldn't be. Can't say how I would feel until it happened, but I promise I'll never hurt you, or smack you around." I reached up and traced a thumb along her cheek. "What I will promise is to listen to you and talk it out. I can't and won't make decisions for you, Girl. That's not something you should ever sign up for again."

"I won't, believe me, but Nik, I am signing up for taking your feelings, thoughts, and the like into consideration when making my decisions. That's part of a relationship, isn't it? Doing things with your partner in mind?"

"Ah yeah, that's what I reckon."

She laid her head back down and cuddled up to me again. I held her tight and Max stretched between us and reached out a paw, putting it on my stomach. Then her claws came out and she dug in.

"Ay!" I cried and tried not to jerk. "Crazy cat!" She let up and looked at me, green eyes full of feline judgment and I had to smirk. It was like she had spoken, and I was listening. It was a good talk, and I felt better about things and suddenly felt far more tired than I had a moment before.

"So are we okay then?" Tiffany asked, voice small, and I stroked my fingers along her silky skin beneath her tank, along the top of her stubbies.

"We were never *not* okay, Wahine. Go back to sleep, I'm here and I'm not going anywhere, yeah?"

"Yeah," she said and sounded relieved. I could feel good about that, at least. I kissed the top of her head and tried to put thoughts about her going to work that night out of my head. It was easier than I thought, surprising enough. When she fell asleep this time, I went with her and I think we both slept pretty hard.

13

T iff...

"Wait, you like him as in *like him*, like him?" Delia was staring at me, agape.

"Yes."

It had been three days since he'd stayed the day in my apartment the first time and he'd stayed every day since, except we still hadn't had sex. I wanted him, and I knew he wanted me, but what he was giving me was far more important right now. What he was giving me was an intimacy I had craved for a long time, yet hadn't known with the front part of my brain that I'd needed.

He held me. We talked. Sometimes he just listened, sometimes I did, but it was a bonding that I think we both needed. A friendship that was definitely going somewhere, but one of the things I needed was my best friend to accept him and the only way that was going to happen was if she got to know him like I did.

Unfortunately, the closer I was growing to Nik, it felt like the further away I was getting from Lia, and I would be lying if I said that didn't hurt.

"Come meet him," I practically begged and Delia rolled her eyes at me but followed along reluctantly. Of course, that was probably because I had her by the hand and was towing her out the door past Zeke and across the back lot to where Nik sat bundled on the back of his bike.

"Gidday, ladies."

"Hey," I said softly, smiling.

"You must be Delia then?" he asked, and held out his hand to her. She eyed him suspiciously but took it and gave it a solid shake.

"Yep, I'm the best friend," she declared.

"Nice to meet you." He gave her a smile that I increasingly was finding to be disarming and asked, "Join us for a bit of brekkie?"

"A bit of what?" she asked and laughed a little.

"It's what Kiwis call breakfast," I told her.

"Sure, but for us, it's sort of dinner time for us, isn't it?"

"True, but Nik and I have been going to this diner with really good breakfast food that starts up around this time."

"Maybe another time," she said. "I'm meeting someone."

I blinked, taken aback. Delia was my best friend, we shared everything about one another's lives. How did I not know about this until right before? I rocked back on my heels, surprised to feel more hurt well up and I immediately overruled my heart with my head, thinking to myself *Delia is her own person with her own life apart from yours... Besides, you haven't exactly been forthcoming about Nik.* Of course, there was a reason for that. Delia, while having her heart in the right place, was also pretty judgmental about the Sacred Hearts as a whole. It made it hard for me to want to share.

"Don't look at me like that, please?" she asked softly. "It isn't like that."

"Like what?" I asked back, frowning, my sixth sense tingling. Why would she put it that way? She read the look on my face clearly and sighed.

"I didn't tell you because I didn't want you to worry."

Oh, that was rich! Now I really wanted to know just who it was she was meeting up with.

"Why would I worry?" I asked, and now I was like a dog with a bone.

"Cooper called," she hedged and I felt myself scowl.

"You're going to meet up with Cooper Roth?" I demanded.

"Like I said, it's not like that," she said quickly. "I was suspicious, too, but he swears he just wants to catch up."

"Conveniently, after three years and right after Silas is released from prison?" I asked. "Yeah, no. I don't believe that for a minute, and you shouldn't either, Delia."

"I'm with Tiffany on this one, Girl. Sounds sus to me," Nik chimed in.

"Nobody asked you," Delia snapped at him defensively.

"I asked him," I said shortly, suddenly angry and feeling pretty betrayed. "I asked Dragon, and he asked Nik. I went to them and asked for their help. I need them to watch my back and here you are, my best friend, and what do you do?" I demanded, thinking to myself *you stand there and put a knife in it.*

"This is why I didn't tell you!" she said, exasperated. "I knew you'd be upset. You know I like Coop; that I have since like forever. Honestly, I figured it would be a good idea! That I might be able to find out what Silas is thinking or if he really is up to something. I wasn't going to tell Cooper anything! I'm not going to tell him anything. I already told him that you are strictly off-limits as a topic of conversation."

I shifted from foot to foot and shook my head. "Now isn't the time to play super-secret double-agent spy, Lia. Seriously. Leave it alone, don't go. Come with us instead." I could tell by the look on her face that she was going to be stubborn. She had the idea in her head and she was going to do what she was going to do. I hated how it sounded like I was begging when I asked her to come with us instead of meeting up with her long-time, one-time crush, but I couldn't tell you how desperate I was for her not to do this to me.

"It's gonna be fine," she said and she was already walking backward away from me. Emotions churned up from somewhere in my center and I jumped when Nik's hands fell on my shoulders, kneading them reassuringly.

"Lia," I called out and she waved and went around to the driver's side of her car.

"Let it go, she's a stubborn sort."

"Don't I know it?" I asked, unease raking its claws down my insides.

I trusted that she wasn't going to say anything about me, at least not intentionally, but this was a dangerous game. One that I could potentially lose even though I didn't even want to play.

Nik sighed as she drove past us out of the lot, waving through her window, her face set in stubborn lines that were only accentuated by her worry. She was worried that she was hurting our friendship, which she was, but I was worried for a completely different reason. Cooper was Silas' best friend. He also knew that Delia had a crush on him, so he was likely working her for information.

My poor, much-loved but totally-being-an-idiot friend was trapped between her libido and her loyalty, and I knew that she had nothing but the best of intentions… but Jesus! Who was being the naive one, now? It certainly wasn't me.

God, what a mess.

"She's playing with fire, that one," Nik remarked, and I loved that his voice held a similar worry for my friend that I was feeling.

"I know," I said, and the frustration was a palpable thing, rising to choke me. I sniffed and tried to pretend it had nothing to do with the warring emotions in my heart and head but rather had everything to do with the frosty winter air.

"Let's get you home," he murmured and I realized that without knowing exactly what Delia was doing, I didn't really want to go home. I knew she had my back, she'd always had my back, but the 'what if's' were dogging me hard and I would be lying if I said I wasn't just a little bit worried about *what if she slipped... what if she said something without meaning to?*

"Your home or mine?" I asked, staring off, after where her taillights had faded into the dark.

"Mine, if you'd like, or the club. Anyplace that's warmer than out here." His voice was gentle, and I felt the tension in my shoulders ease.

"Kind of can't wait to learn more about that self-defense stuff."

"Tomorrow we teach you to shoot," he reminded and I turned with a sigh. I didn't know how I felt about the whole 'guns' thing. Bitterness and anger aside, I was a lover, not a fighter and I hated that Silas was making me turn to violence as a solution, but sometimes, just sometimes, it was the only one. The practical part of me recognized that, even if I didn't like it.

"Your place, if that's okay." I searched his face and took a half breath before letting it out. I had been about to ask if I could use his bathtub, but I tended not to ask things for myself anymore. I got too used to 'no' from both the way I was raised and Silas to the point I still had a hard time asking for anything.

I think Nik knew that about me, though. His face split into a broad smile as he said, "Go on, ask it."

"Ask what?" I tried playing it cool.

"It was all over your face, Wahine. Ask me what you were gonna ask me, don't ever be afraid of asking me for anything."

"What's the worst that could happen?" I agreed, "You could say 'no?'"

"Too right," he nodded and sat down on his bike, waiting me out, breath pluming the frigid air.

"I was wondering if you'd let me use your bathtub, my apartment doesn't have one, just a shower."

He nodded. "Sounds like a good idea; you need to relax. Come on, let's go."

"Thanks," I murmured but I couldn't be sure he heard me over the bike starting up. I made sure my bag was secure across my chest and got on behind him. The air was so icy I tended to bury my face in his back in an effort to hide from the wind. He stopped at the twenty-four-hour pharmacy on the way to his place and ran in real quick while I stared at my phone in the parking lot, shivering and trying to decide what, if anything, I should text to Lia. I finally decided there wasn't anything I could say that wouldn't make her angry or upset her and as much as I loved her, my trust in her was more than a bit broken right now. The 'what if's' were whispering some pretty awful things from their dark corner of my mind.

If you text her, what if it makes her angry? What if she ratted you out? What if she's sick of you and doing things for you all the time? What if, what if, what if...

The mechanical tones of the doorbell went off signaling Nik's return. He came over to me and asked, "Put this in your bag for the ride, yeah?" and held up a rather doubled up grocery bag with red 'thank you' lettering on it.

"Yes, of course," I said swinging my gym bag around and unzipping the top. He shoved the bag of items away and zipped it closed and got back onto the bike in front of me.

The ride to his place was pretty short but it was freezing. I was so ready to be warm again.

He pulled into the alley behind the bar he worked at and we took the rickety wooden staircase on the outside of the building up to the floor Nik's apartment was on. The door back here opened right into his apartment as he keyed his way into the two locks. It took me a minute to realize we were going in through the fire escape, but it was handy and it got us inside quicker. The problem was, it was just about as cold in here as it was out there.

I pulled his bag out of mine and handed it to him. He thanked me and rooted around in it, setting a couple of big cans of stew on the kitchen counter and handing me first a box of bath stuff and then a plastic wrapped bath bomb.

"I wasn't sure what you liked," he said, and finally added a big bag of lavender Epsom salts to the top of the growing pile in my arms. "So I got it all."

I blinked, surprised, and laughed a little, "You didn't have to do all this," I said softly and sniffed, my nose running from the cold.

"I'll get a fire going in the fireplace and the soup on. Your best bet on getting warm is the hot water from the tank, so, go on." He hooked a hand behind my neck carefully and stepped up to me, pressing a kiss to my forehead, his thumb stroking along the side of my neck. I closed my eyes and sighed, grateful.

"Okay," I murmured and he let me go, moving past me to the cold, dark, fireplace grate set in one wall.

14

Z eb...

I built a fire, put the soup on low and slow to heat and started to make her some hot tea to warm her up from the inside as much as the bath she was running would hopefully do for her frozen fingers and toes from the outside. She was silent, the strong sound of the water pouring into the tub drowning out any noise she might have been making as she moved around my bathroom. She'd left the door open, and more than just a crack this time. Then again, she'd had her clothes off for most of the night and I liked to think she was more comfortable around me even if we hadn't gotten completely naked together yet.

The water shut off and I heard her get in. I steeped her tea and the fruity scent of one of the bath bomb things that girls seemed to go crazy over wafted out of the open doorway and permeated the open space of my flat. I liked it. It was nice having her here and it was more than just having something or someone beautiful here to liven the place up.

It was nice knowing she was safe here. That no one knew where it was, sure, but that she could breathe a bit easier knowing no one could find her here was something precious. That she could be herself and not look over her shoulder was nice.

I fixed up another cup of tea for myself after a second thought and carried both steaming mugs to the golden rectangle of light coming from my bathroom.

"Hey, I'm good to come in, yeah?" I asked before crossing the threshold and into her line of sight.

"Yeah," she said gently. I went in and handed her down one of the steaming cups. She was huddled in the bottom of the bath, hugging her knees, the water pink and swirling with what looked like silver vapor through it.

I sat down on the floor and put my back to the wall, so I could face her. She took a tentative sip of the tea and closed her eyes, savoring it.

"Got some soup on, no worries, though. I don't want you to rush."

"Thank you," she said. "The tea is good."

"You looked frozen," I said, taking a drink of my own.

"Kind of running low on clean laundry," she confessed. "Usually Lia picks me up and I go over to her place with it. She lets me use her washer and dryer while we watch movies and I do some homework."

"Sounds nice, eh."

"Things are kind of all over the place now, though."

I nodded and she looked a little lost, laying her head atop her drawn up knees, one arm around them, the other gripping the handle of her tea mug as it rested on the edge of the tub. I was suddenly more cross with her friend than I'd been before. She had no idea what she was doing with this and needed to leave well enough alone.

"Warm enough?" I asked and she smiled slightly.

"Much better, yeah."

"Good. Did you bring something to sleep in?"

She closed her eyes and her shoulders dropped, "Shit. I hadn't thought much beyond the whole *I don't want to go home,* you know?"

"Yeah, it's no worries. I have a shirt, I'm sure."

"Thanks," she murmured softly and I reached out, stroking some of her long, silky hair out of her eyes, sweeping it behind her ear and away from her scarred cheek. She didn't flinch this time, which made me smile in appreciation. She was learning there was no bad here with me. No judgment or anything like that.

"I honestly don't think I'm going to sleep that well today," she said, and I nodded.

"A lot going on upstairs, eh?"

"That's putting it mildly."

"I get it."

She shifted and the water sloshed in the tub. I always liked the sound of water any way I could get it. Just something nice about it. Soothing and whatnot.

"You want I should read to you?" I asked.

She smiled and even though it held an edge of sadness, it made her go from beautiful to stunning. "Figured out that I like that, huh?"

"Yeah."

I'd always had a habit of reading before falling asleep and even with her in my arms, I'd kept it up. I always had a paperback of some sort tucked into the inside pocket of my jacket or the back pocket of my jeans and the last few nights I'd brought it out to read while she'd rested against me as we'd gone to go to sleep. Two nights ago, she'd asked me to read out loud and I'd done it. It'd been awkward a bit at first, but she'd seemed to like it and now it looked like it was turning into one of our things.

I sat up and pulled the book I'd started at the bar that night out of my back pocket. I liked to read things that were useful to me and she didn't seem to mind listening to anything I'd read so far. She watched me with those deep brown eyes of hers as I opened it to where I'd marked the page.

This book was by an American bloke in the security industry. Data had recommended it, and it'd just been the next one in my pile by the bed. It was about trusting your gut and how to listen to the unspoken little warning signs folks gave off before trying something stupid.

Tiffany closed her eyes and listened, taking the occasional sip of tea. Wrapping both her hands around the mug, before long she unfurled the length of the tub, sinking down into the fruity pink water with its swirling silver cloud of sparkling whatever. She just listened to me, and it took a lot of willpower to keep my eyes on the words and off her face… and yeah, the rest of her too. She was one beautiful lady and it was hard not to stare.

I finished the last of the chapter and closed the book, watching as she thought it over, simply sitting with her and relaxing.

"The water is getting cold," she said finally and I nodded.

"I'll get you a shirt and dish up the food, maybe drag the bed closer to the fire. You take your time."

"Okay, thank you."

"No worries."

And that right there was one of the reasons it felt so good to do things for her. She was appreciative, never missed an opportunity to say a simple thank you, but what's more, it was the look she gave me. Every time I did something sweet for her, she looked at me with this amazed gratitude that did more for me than anything ever had before. I felt needed, not just wanted, and I have to admit it was a serious boost to my manly ego.

I don't think there was anything else that made me feel like half as much of a man as when she looked at me like that. I pushed to my feet and took her nearly empty mug of tea out with me. Refreshing both our cups, I dragged the mattress across the floor closer to the fire as I listened to her climb out of the tub. I couldn't help myself, picturing the water sliding along her perfect skin, but I resisted the temptation to go to the door and actually look.

It was a struggle for me, making sure I was a decent man and not pushing her, but at the same time, not giving her the idea I was disinterested. Her job made things a little complicated for me in that arena. I didn't ever want her to feel like I was one of the men that frequented her club. I wanted her to always know she was more to me than a perfect pair of tits. She was so much more than an object to be ogled.

I went over to the closet and fished through, finding a clean tee of mine and handed it to her as she stepped out of my bathroom wrapped in the towel I'd had in there.

"Here you go," I told her. "Go by the fire and stay warm, eh. I'll get us some food dished up. Got you some more tea already."

"Thank you, I really appreciate this. I know you weren't expecting we'd wind up here and I can't tell you how grateful I am that you're cool with my being here."

"Ah, yeah, nah; don't mention it, eh? I like having you here with me. I just wish I had more to my flat than this." I waved a hand around and she turned and took in the Spartan flat with a charmed half-smile.

"I like the minimalist look and feel," she murmured. I laughed and she moved off toward the fire, sitting down on the edge of the made-up mattress on the floor, wrapped in the towel, setting my tee on the bed by her hip. She fished through her bag coming up with a tube of lotion of some kind and flipped back the cap. I ladled up soup into a couple of bowls and was suddenly mesmerized by her as she smoothed the loose cream onto her long legs.

I confess, I set the bowl down and leaned on the bench, watching her as she completed the simple act of moisturizing her skin, pulled on a pair of hipster panties, and slipping my shirt over her head before letting the towel fall out from underneath it. I bowed my head and closed my eyes nodding to myself, my thoughts leaning towards not being able to hold out much longer. I wanted her, but I also wanted the time to be right, too.

She was staring into the fireplace, transfixed, almost hypnotized, smoothing a different, fragrant hand cream into her hands and wrists, up her arms when I sat down next to her. I handed her one of the bowls when she was done.

"Thanks," she murmured and stirred the soup with her spoon.

"My pleasure, eh."

We ate in a comfortable silence for a while and I liked that she didn't hide the scarred side of her face from me anymore. That she was comfortable enough to leave her hair pulled back into one of those clip things in a messy bun.

She was the first to break the silence by saying, "Italian Wedding is one of my favorites," and I smiled.

"Yeah? Wasn't something I knew about until I came here; Sunshine, Trigger's woman makes a mean one. The canned isn't as good but it's not bad."

"I make a really good homemade vegetable soup."

"Ah, yeah? Where'd you learn that?"

She laughed slightly, "The internet. I taught myself to cook for the most part. It was either that or starve."

"Cooking out of self-defense," I said with a laugh. "I like it."

"I never thought of it that way," she said with a rueful smile, bringing the bowl to her lips and drinking some of the broth. "I like it too," she said after swallowing.

I was mesmerized by just about every movement she made. She had a natural grace that most women didn't possess and it was something else. She sighed a healthy, satisfied sound and rose gracefully to her feet, taking her bowl with her.

"Tea is in the kitchen on the counter, just there."

"Oh, excellent," she remarked. She stood at the sink and washed out her bowl. I stood up with mine and went over to wash it, but she took it from my hands and did it for me.

It gave me idle hands which I put to her slender hips, stepping up to her back and pressing my lips to where her neck met her shoulder where the stretched neckline of my old tee left it bare.

She sighed out, her body relaxing back into mine, her hands covering mine and pressing them to her stomach where they'd ended up. She moaned slightly, one hand disappearing from the top of mine, touching lightly along the side of my neck as she encouraged what I was doing. Turning her head, questing for our mouths to meet.

Her kiss was sweet as, and I felt my desire for her spike, spiraling high and tight, sending me soaring. I spun her in my grasp and kissed her proper and her arms wound around my neck and shoulders, hands pressing gently, cradling the back of my head holding my mouth to hers.

The heat between us was something, really. Enough that I was pretty sure my clothes needed off. She clung to me, making these soft little whimpers of want against my mouth and I lifted her easily. Her long legs wound around my hips and I backed her up, sitting her on the edge of the sink, letting my passion carry us both.

She was into it, and I was so into her but something held her back. She moaned into my mouth and it held that quality of *wait*. I slowed my kiss but didn't want it to end but when she pulled back, I let her.

"Not like this," she gasped, "Not like this."

"Right," I murmured and backed off, letting her go. Chest heaving with the breath she'd stolen, I maintained my self-control – barely. I took myself to the bathroom to regroup and take a cold shower.

15

T iffany...

He walked away so abruptly it felt like a knife driven into my chest. It felt like a very real physical thing, like a small part of me was torn away as I watched his broad back walk away. He went into the bathroom and all but slammed the door.

I climbed down off the kitchen counter and went over to the window, resting my forehead against the glass as the shower started up. I squeezed my eyes shut and concentrated on getting my breathing back to normal, all the while kicking myself.

I hadn't meant stop completely, I had just meant exactly what I'd said... *not like that.* Not on the counter. Not him, not like I serviced all my fucking johns... I wanted better for us. I wanted something real that didn't remind me of work. Instead, I'd done what I always did. Fucked things up six ways to Sunday.

The water shut off and the bathroom door jerked open and I turned, leaning my back against the wall beside the window.

"I didn't mean stop completely," I said, and couldn't hide the hurt. "I just meant not on the counter, not like *that*."

He straightened a bit and understanding dawned on his face which went slack with that classic look which he voiced in the next sentence.

"I'm a right idiot, aren't I?"

I shook my head and said, "No. If anyone is, *I am* for getting into the line of work I do in the first place, but then again, I never counted on someone like you coming along."

He frowned slightly and came over to me, taking my hands in his, the towel sitting tantalizingly low on his hips.

"And what's that supposed to mean, eh?"

"It means I thought this would be a lot different, I suppose. It means I thought that…" my voice trailed off and I looked at the floor. "It means I thought that I would always be alone, I guess."

"Me, too," he said and I looked up sharply into his eyes. "Look at us, eh? Just two lonely souls." He pulled me to him gently and I didn't resist. How could I, when all I wanted was to be in his arms?

"I'm so sorry," I whispered and he brought his mouth down to mine.

"Don't be," he whispered and kissed me.

I closed my eyes and lost myself in it. Wishing ardently that we could just go to bed. Apparently, Nik had the same idea, but not quite.

"Let's go to bed, get some sleep, eh." He smoothed a hand down my hair and cradled my cheek, running a thumb over it in that way that made me feel appreciated and cherished. Except he was pulling back, I had ruined the moment and all I could do now was nod dumbly and drift along beside him over to the made-up mattress on the floor, in front of the fire. He got in first, pulling me down in front of him so that I was closer to the cheery blaze in the grate, tucked back into the larger spoon of his body so that we could both watch the flames.

"I'm so sorry," I murmured and he kissed my shoulder where the neckline of his butter-soft tee gaped.

"Don't be, there's all the time in the world for us and the best things in life shouldn't be rushed."

It was the right thing to say, stripping away some of my guilt and allowing me to relax into him. We didn't really speak after that, just simply stared into the crackling fire. I closed my eyes, warm and safe in his embrace and I felt the spinning hamster-wheel of my thoughts finally begin to slow.

Sleep wasn't long to follow.

～

I twisted under his grasp, hand around his wrist, trying with all my strength to keep his hand and what was in it back away from my face but he was just too strong! The jagged edge of the bottle dragged against my flesh and sharp pain flooded my cheek. I struggled against the weight of him on top of me and opened my mouth to scream...

"Shhh, shhh, shhh, hey! Hey, wake up now, Girl!"

My eyes flew open and I struggled still, but it was the comforting weight of Nik's body over mine replacing Silas' sinister presence from the past, from the flashback or dream.

I whimpered, and Nik's gentle hands smoothed my hair out of my face as he shushed me gently over and over. I sucked in a deep breath that rattled back out of me on a broken half-sob. His lips touched mine and his body pressed mine flat on the bed and I wrapped my arms around his shoulders and clung to him.

"You're all right now, just a bad dream," he soothed.

Except it wasn't a dream, not exactly anyway. It was a memory, and it could be my future too, and I said as much, hating how broken and whiny my voice came out, but the fear was a palpable thing and just not ready to leave me.

So he kissed me, pressing his body against mine and protected me, and I don't know how he did it, because how do you protect someone from something that is inside of them?

I kissed him back and held him tightly to me, running from the tumult of emotions raging inside, right into the stillness, the togetherness that he projected. He was so sure of himself and that everything would be okay and I so wanted to believe him. I wanted to believe him with everything that I was.

I moaned as he ground his lower body into mine. Somehow he'd gotten between my thighs and oh, how I wanted him to be there. I'd been having plenty of sex but I was starved for the attention and affection he was giving to me. I wound my fingers in his long hair and held it back from his face. I couldn't remember when he'd pulled it from his ponytail, but I knew he generally did to sleep.

I kissed him back, wrapped my arms and legs around him and met his grinding with thrusting urgent rising of my hips. Insistent, wanting, desperate to be with him in every way that counted. The floodgates were open, my heart was open, and I wanted to let him in so badly... and for once I wasn't afraid. I knew, instinctively, that Nik would never raise a hand to me. That he would never hurt me intentionally.

I tore my mouth from his and begged him, "Please."

He reached off the side of the bed and came back with a wrapped condom, tearing it open with his teeth, breaths heavy and passionate. He reached between us and rolled it on, shoving his underwear down and off; hands going to the waistband of mine.

He pulled them down my legs, sweeping them off and dropping them somewhere behind him, pulling the blankets up around us to stave off the chill of the apartment. I didn't care about it. I cared about being skin-on-skin with him. I cared about being as close as possible, so I quickly grabbed the hem of his loaned tee and pulled it off over my head.

He dry-humped me, his cock sliding tantalizingly against my pussy and I kissed him, the urgency to have him inside me rising. We kissed, breath heavy and laden with a desire and passion too heavy to hold in our lungs.

He braced his arms to either side of my head, his hands smoothing strands of hair from my face, dark eyes meeting mine, the tenderness in his touch, the look on his face almost had me completely undone and then he slid inside me.

I cried out, it felt so good, and wrapped my legs around him, my hands drifting up and down his back, urging him on, but he took his time, slow and deliberate with every stroke. Every movement was laden with his intention to love me and I died a little death, gladly, in his arms.

It was perfect. Just so perfect and he felt so good. I felt good, and I loved it, needed it, and was so grateful for it.

"Don't stop," I begged breathily, "Please don't stop!"

"Never," he growled lightly against my lips, and I swear it felt like I was falling forever but I wasn't scared. I had no reason to be scared. I knew he would catch me.

16

Z eb…

I made love to her for a couple of hours, our bodies entwined under the covers; warm despite the chill in my flat from the fire going out. We'd gotten decent sleep. Her nightmare at least allowed for that, hitting her close to when we needed to be up anyways.

I was so wrapped up in her that I didn't hear my phone buzzing across the floor by the bed until the second time it went off. I swore and slipped out of her, reaching for it as she covered her mouth with her hands, eyes sparkling with the smile that she hid.

"What is it, bro? I'm kind of busy," is how I answered.

"Yeah, and we're out here freezing our nuts off, wondering where the fuck you're at. Or did you forget we were supposed to be teaching your charge how to shoot today?" Trigger sounded irritated and I felt a bit sheepish.

"Ah, yeah, nah, Bro, I didn't forget. Just got a bit distracted is all."

"Distracted, right, that's great. Will you hurry your ass up and get out here? We ain't got all day, and it's fuckin' cold as shit out here."

"Point Nowhere, yeah?"

"Yeah, ain't got no goddamn heat, so move it, would ya?"

"On our way, sorry again."

I looked down at Tiffany who was smiling at me, her hands moved from her mouth and to my shoulders.

"I take it we missed our appointment?" she said, and I bent my head to kiss her again.

"Yeah, but they're waiting. Bundle up, it's going to be a cold ride and there's no heat where we're going."

"Lovely," she said rolling her eyes and I could tell she was about as done as I was when it came to the cold outside.

"Gives me an excuse to warm you up when we get home," I pointed out.

"You don't need an excuse," she said, and I smiled at her and moved off of her. She sat up and sighed, a contented sound.

We got cleaned up as best we could without taking a shower and got dressed. She layered up and so did I. Winters in this area were no joke and the bitter cold made me miss home and the summertime there.

"Ready?" I asked her and she looked longingly back to the bed for a minute.

"As I'll ever be," she declared and followed me out into the blistering cold.

I'd never wished for a cage as much as I did then. We couldn't get the bike up the long track into point nowhere, so we'd parked it on the side of the road and Reaver had driven his truck down to the bottom to pick us up.

Tiffany sat stiffly between us as he drove us back to the top where

Trigger waited by an old oil drum, hands outstretched to the fire he and Reaver had going in it.

"About fuckin' time you got here," he mumbled around a cigarette. A real one, which told me just how irritated he was.

"Sorry, bro," I said, and he raised an eyebrow and nodded.

Tiffany slid out of the truck behind me and I shut the door. Trigger got a good look at her and his eyebrows went up.

"All's forgiven," he said and gave a nod. Yeah, I figured he'd understand it when he saw her.

"I'm Trigger," he said and took a final drag off the cigarette he shouldn't have been smoking and flicked the butt into the flames licking at the edge of the barrel.

"Tiffany, most people just call me Tiff."

"Nice to meet you, Tiff. That there is Reaver. You ready to learn how to shoot?"

She shifted from foot to foot in the white powder at the top of the drive and let her gaze wander over the sheet metal building and snow-covered hulks of cars scattered at its base.

"Truthfully, no. I've never liked guns. They scare me."

"Humph, ain't nothing to be scared of. C'mere, let's start with the basics."

She swallowed hard and drifted over closer to the fire and stood a good two feet away from Trig. Reaver walked up to me and knocked his shoulder into mine, grinning.

"Banging the stripper, huh?"

"It's not like that," I said and didn't take my eyes off her. His teasing smile melted right off his face, from what I could see out of the corner of my eye.

"No, I can see that now, sorry."

"It's all good, Bro."

"Trig will get her straight," he said with assurance, and I nodded. "That's not what you're worried about, though, is it?"

"Nah, I'm more worried about her learning what you can teach her. This ex of hers – from everything she's told me, he likes to get up close and personal-like."

Reaver nodded. "If she's scared of guns, they aren't going to be much use to her."

"Too right."

"How far have you and Mali gotten?"

"Not far yet."

"When's her next lesson on hand-to-hand?"

"Tomorrow."

He grunted and gave a nod. "I'll be there."

I felt some relief. "Thanks, Bro."

"Any piece of shit that can do that to a woman's face… I'd like him to meet my blade."

"Yeah, me too," I agreed.

"Come on this way, you two," Trigger called out and we trudged over to them through the snow.

"You ready to shoot that thing off?" Reaver asked, grinning.

Tiffany shook her head no but said: "As I'll ever be."

Reaver nodded, laughing, and said, "All right, I like your style."

We went around to the back of the building and Tiffany kept me in her sight. I went to her and pulled her aside. She looked up at me quizzically through the long fall of her hair and I turned her away from my brothers and smoothed it out of her eyes.

"You can trust them," I told her. "Just like you trust me, eh."

"Not like I trust you," she whispered. She chewed her bottom lip lightly in indecision and finally sighed, her breath pluming the frozen air. "I'm trying," she said finally, after a moment of silence and I smiled.

"I know. I know this is hard for you but listen to what Trigger has to say and I promise, she'll be right, okay?"

"Okay." She fixed her hair and went back over to Trigger, who smiled at her patiently.

"You're gonna be holding a gun, Sweetheart. You're gonna be shooting at something." He let out a breath and said, "You're gonna have to get your hair outta your face."

She licked her lips, the way she held herself stiff but finally, she said, "Don't judge, and try not to stare?"

"Not me," he said and held up fingers in what he'd once told me was a boy scout's salute. Meant he couldn't lie.

Tiffany chuckled and moved her hair out of her eyes, hanging it behind her ears saying, "An outlaw biker who's a boy scout. Isn't that some kind of an oxymoron?"

"We didn't all start as outlaws," Reaver said with a reckless grin. Tiffany's eyes dimmed and her expression lost its hard-won smile of the moment before.

"That's a fair point," she said.

"Oh, how the mighty have fallen," Trigger said, and held out a handgun to show her. "Which is all right. A lot of us didn't like it up there anyway."

"Which is why we're slumming it down here," Reaver agreed.

"This here," Trigger indicated a point on the gun, "pops the magazine." He dropped it and caught it with his other hand, handing it to Tiff. She took it and he said, "Now that doesn't mean it's not loaded. You always gotta assume there's one in the chamber." He pulled back the slide to show her. "See there?"

When he said he was going to run her through the basics, he meant it. He educated her from the ground up, and she listened with rapt attention. I'd asked them to meet us out here rather than at the club because the club was always full of people anymore. Brothers, ol' ladies, and a lot of the time their kids were around. I figured out here would be nice and quiet. Much more Tiffany's speed.

She didn't like being around people much, and I couldn't say I blamed her. A lot of the people around here could be right cunts. Staring at her openly like some bug under glass. Some of them would just walk right up to her and ask. Others took one look at me and assumed the worst. I found those citizens to be the most amusing. And they called us the fuckin' animals.

"It's gonna be loud, you're gonna jump, and that's okay. The goal of coming out here on the regular is to get you to where you don't jump so much, as much as it is to improve your shot. You ready?"

"No."

"Shoot it anyways," Trig said, and hand trembling, she held the gun out, sighted down the barrel, let out a breath, and fired. She jumped and nearly dropped the gun. Reaver laughed and I smacked him on the shoulder. She was a nervous thing, and this was way outside her comfort zone.

"Sorry!" she said immediately and Trig shook his head.

"Don't be, just try to hit the target and this time, don't stop until the gun is empty."

She did as she was told and lowered it when it was empty. She let out a shuddering breath and asked, "Okay, how'd I do?"

Reaver squinted across the snow at the paper target tacked to a piece of plywood nailed to a board out there and said, "Ehhhh, we'll get you a shotgun."

Trig sighed and closed his eyes, shaking his head.

"I don't know what that means," she said blankly.

"Means you're kind of a terrible shot and you're gonna need practice," Trig said gently and I could see her shoulders drop slightly. The look on her face was stone, but the flinching in her eyes spelled defeat.

"Rome wasn't built in a day, eh," I said gently.

She looked at me and nodded, standing up a little straighter.

"Again?" she asked. Trigger nodded.

"One more magazine for today. Let's teach you how to properly load it."

"Okay," she agreed but I could tell she wasn't thrilled at emptying another into the paper target across the snow.

Shooting was not my girl's thing.

17

T iff...

"I really hate guns," I said, and looked at him from across my kitchen counter. He was standing in my small studio, hanging his jacket on the back of one of my two chairs at my little table and he nodded.

"I know," he said.

"There's a reason for it, but I don't know if I want to tell you."

"Why not?"

"Because it will just make you mad, and there isn't anything you can do about it. There's nothing anyone can do."

He nodded and pulled the chair out and sat down in it, leaning back and watching me carefully, waiting me out. I moved around my kitchen, setting water on to boil and bringing down two large mugs.

"Try me, eh?" he said finally and I nodded, pulling down two packs of cocoa from another cupboard. I needed the chocolate fix.

I told him the reason why. That one of my foster dads had used to threaten us with one. Put it in our mouth, threatened to pull the trigger. Sometimes he had pulled the trigger, but it was always empty. Still, the mind games… there were more than a few times that I wished it weren't, just so I didn't have to deal with the fear and the terror anymore when he got to drinking.

Nik sat real still, knee bouncing with agitation. It felt good to tell someone else other than Delia about these things. Felt even better that he was mad about them on my behalf, but at the same time? I didn't like talking about it because I didn't like how upset he got. How angry he looked… dark eyes stormy as his expression drew down in a tempestuous scowl. He very nearly hummed with a barely-contained violence but then he would look at me and if I displayed any sort of apprehension, it would melt away, all that anger would drain as if through the floor and would simply be gone as fast as it'd come on.

"You're right, it makes me angry. You're also right that it's not worth going back and shoving that gun up his ass. But I'd very much like to."

I moved around the kitchen counter and he straightened in his seat, putting his hands on top of his denim-clad thighs and looking up at me as I drew near. I straddled his lap and sank down onto it, my arms twining around his neck on the shoulders of his open red and black flannel, the white waffle pattern thermal stretching tantalizingly over his chest.

"I know," I said, voice huskier than a moment before with a deep emotion. "That's one of the things I love about you. You listen, you want to do something, but you're practical. You don't do anything without a deliberateness… it's kind of hot actually."

He smiled up at me, his hands which had found my hips, drifting up to cup my face and finish bringing me down to him for a kiss. "Yeah?" he asked, right before our lips touched and then it was just the warmth of his mouth against mine.

I felt my muscles lose some of the tension they'd been holding and it felt good to relax. I had such a hard time doing it lately, but with Nik, it was easier somehow. I dipped my head and kissed him, fingertips ghosting along his jaw even as his hands gripped me tighter around my back. I scooted closer, even though it really involved being plastered up against him for all I was worth and his tongue teased at the seam of my lips, requesting I deepen it.

I love how he asked, not always with words, but asked none the less. I parted my lips and met his tongue with mine, sighing out in satisfaction.

He pulled back slightly and rested his forehead against mine, eyes closed, but I watched him and I could see there was something he wanted to ask but it had that weight, that feel to it inside my head that it wasn't necessarily something I was going to like.

"What is it?" I whispered and he looked up at me.

He swallowed hard and he said, "I want to ask you…"

Apprehension filled me and I felt myself go really still on his lap. I didn't like the insecurity I heard in his voice but at the same time, whatever he wanted to ask, it sounded like it had the potential to hurt. I steeled myself and said, "Go on. Ask."

"Is there something that you could give me?" he asked. "Something that you don't give the men at the club. Something that you hold back from them but not me?"

He swallowed hard and I felt the tension that had suddenly overwhelmed me loosen to the point that I nearly went liquid with relief.

"I already do," I said shyly and I kissed him. His breath caught and he kissed me back, arms tightening around me like he was afraid I was going to go, like he was going to lose me for asking, but this? This, surprisingly, is something I understood. He needed to know he was special to me, but I didn't know if there was any way possible I could tell him or even show him just how special he was.

"I kiss you," I whispered against his mouth. "I don't kiss anyone else."

"Yeah?" he asked, voice strained.

"Yeah," I murmured softly. "Pretty Woman Art of Hooking Handbook, kissing someone is special. Kissing is intimate. You hold that back for yourself and your partner."

He leaned back and looked at me, a frown on his face and blurted out, "There's an actual handbook for prostitutes?"

I threw back my head and laughed, high and clear; it was so absurd and took me totally off guard. I looked back down and captured his face in my hands, kissing him fiercely. Happy. I was happy and this was too much.

"No!" I declared. "Pretty Woman! You know, Julia Roberts? Richard Gere? The movie?"

"Oh, nah, I've never seen it," he declared.

I blinked in surprise and said, "Oh, no, this is so happening," just as the kettle on the stove began to whistle.

"What is?" he asked as I slipped off his lap.

"Just a minute. I'm gonna call Lia," I declared. "She needs in on this."

I picked up my phone and called her, thinking this might be a good way for her to get to know Nik and a decent peace offering between us, even though I hadn't done anything wrong. I just didn't want to lose my only friend. I moved the kettle off the heat and tore open the packets of cocoa, dumping them each into their respective mugs.

"Hi, you've reached Delia, don't forget to leave a message!"

I didn't. I just hung up, disappointed. I poured the water and stirred the contents of first one mug and then the other, setting the phone on the counter.

"Oh, well, her loss. We're so doing this, though."

"Doing what?" he asked, an eyebrow raised in intrigue.

"Watching this movie."

He looked me up and down, curious, and said, "All right, then," sealing his fate. Then again, with a man as well-read as he seemed to be, and the fact he didn't really seem to give a shit about what other people thought, I didn't think he would find watching a total chick flick with me to be that big of a deal. I could be wrong, though; you never did know what it would be that could hurt a man's fragile masculinity. I'd learned that lesson time and time again.

"I'll go get it, make yourself comfortable?"

"Anything for you," he said and I paused slightly before moving into the main area of my apartment. I handed him his mug while passing and set mine on the side table by my day-bed. I rooted around underneath the bed for my CD binder that I had filled with DVD's and brought it out onto my lap. He got up and wandered over, sitting next to me as I flipped through the pages looking for *Pretty Woman*.

"You know this is a cross between *Pygmalion* and the *Cinderella* story?" I asked casually and Nik turned his head.

"Wasn't Pygmalion the bloke that fell in love with his own statue he carved?"

I smiled and looked up, "Yes, that's right. Not a lot of people know the story."

He gave a shrug with one shoulder, "I read a lot and one of my favorite subjects was the whole Greek myths. I actually did decent in those classes."

"You strike me as someone who did poorly in school not because you're stupid but because you were bored," I said, and continued flipping pages. I really needed to put this damn thing in some kind of order. Like alphabetical by title or by the director or something. Hell, even by color would work better than this mess.

"I think you may be right about that," he said. "My dad always thought I was lazy and stupid, my mum knew different. So did my granddad."

"A mother always knows," I said quietly and slid the disc out of its sleeve. "I never knew mine. I was found in a dumpster on prom night. Classy, right?"

"Tragic, is more like it," he said softly.

"Yeah, well, they never found her and I always wondered growing up if I passed her, or if she would see me and just know, you know?"

He nodded and then shook his head, but I caught his meaning. He understood what I was saying but no, he didn't know. Couldn't imagine growing up like that. It was no picnic that was for sure. I grew up in the system. No one ever adopted me so it was one foster home after another, after another. No roots, no sense of permanence. Which was why, when I hit sixteen, it wasn't hard to bounce. I had no real attachments to the last family and Mike was a douche. I had to get the fuck out of there before he got braver than just fondling me. I had no intentions of losing my virginity to his nasty ass. Nope, that honor, or lack thereof, went to a rodeo clown, of all things. Don't ask me what I'd been thinking.

I slid off the bed and opened up my little DVD player, slipping the disc into the tray. It slid closed and I pushed myself back up onto the bed where Nik was shoving pillows behind his back against the spindly metal of the bed's... sideboard? I don't know what you called it for a daybed. It was less head- and foot-board than it was making it into a couch, kind of.

I settled against him and reached for my cocoa, using the little remote to start the movie. He kept an arm around me and idly smoothed a hand up and down my arm through the long sleeve of my shirt and the simple action set me aglow. I liked it, very much.

"Ha! You weren't joking, she's a streetwalker."

"I told you," I said softly and he kissed the top of my head taking any of the sting out of his words.

It was cozy, watching the movie with him and I enjoyed it. At one point I said, "A lot of the girls at Sugars wish they were her, I think."

"Ah yeah? And what about you?"

I shook my head, "I don't want to be taken care of as much as I want to be able to take care of myself," I said. "But this is nice."

"What is?"

"Having someone to have my back, I mean, it's not like Lia doesn't but someone stronger than that, physically, I mean."

"No, I get you," he said and hugged me to him a little tighter.

I cuddled into his side, head on his chest and laughed a short time later when he muttered, "You're going to regret that, yah fuckin' nob gobbler."

"What!?" I cried. "*Nob gobbler?*"

"What?" he demanded. "She's an asshole for not letting her shop!"

I laughed, I couldn't help myself. It was the funniest thing I think I had ever heard and once I started I couldn't stop. It was an infectious sort of laugh, I think because pretty soon he was chuckling, too. I pushed myself up and kissed him and he kissed me back but it didn't get far, he genuinely wanted to finish the movie and so he backed me off and held me tight and actually rewound what he'd missed.

"Ha! She told them," he declared and I laughed all over again as Viv walked out of the shop with all of her bags on the screen. I wondered idly if watching movies with Nik would be like this all of the time and had to sigh inwardly. I was sure that the novelty of me would wear off before I would have the chance to find out, but this was certainly nice, and I would enjoy it while it lasted.

"Hey." He paused the movie and I looked up.

"Hmm?"

"Why so sad all of a sudden, eh?"

"I'm not sad," I said.

"You know the more a bloke gets to know you, the more he realizes you're a terrible liar."

I choked on a laugh and swatted him lightly on the chest. When the fit had passed, I sighed deeply. "I like this," I said. "Being here, with you. I was thinking it will be sad when it ends… when the novelty of me wears off, you know?" I couldn't look him in the eye when I said the last and I shifted a bit, uncomfortable, when I could feel his scowl like heat from a fire against my face.

"There's no novelty here, eh. I like you, Tiff. You've got a fire inside. You're not like any other girl I've ever met and I won't hear you talk about yourself like that." He shook his head and tipped my chin up with a light touch, I met his eyes reluctantly with mine. He said, "That's the kind of thing I suspect would come out of that Nob's mouth. I don't ever want to hear it come out of yours again."

I swallowed hard and nodded slightly, and he shook his head, pulling my mouth to his as if the force of his kiss would burn any more thoughts like it clean out of my head, and to be honest, it did. He hauled me up tight against his body and I swear, I climbed him like a tree, straddling his hips and thinking wistfully that there were far too many clothes between us.

"Off," I breathed against his mouth and pushed at his flannel shirt. He shrugged out of it, peeling it off and my hands gathered his thermal at the hem. He lifted his arms and let me take it from him, and once it was off, let his fingers slide into the waistband of my jeans and lift my own shirt from it.

I sucked in a breath when his fingers made contact with my skin, a wash of tingles spilling up my back and across my ribs. "Please," I begged breathlessly and it was a frenzy of both of us to see who could get who undressed the fastest.

"Shit," he muttered and left me, and I have to admit, I loved watching his ass walk away from me. He fished around in his jacket and came up with a gold foil wrapped condom and I blinked. I wasn't exactly a size queen, but I hadn't realized from our first time that he was big enough to require a Magnum.

He came back over to me, and the view from the front was even more impressive than the view from behind had been. He knelt next to me and reached for me, but I didn't want to be on the bottom this time, so instead of going to my back, I knelt up as his mouth met mine, and smiling against my lips, he let me have my way, taking a seat and letting me straddle him again.

God, he was so hard and hot against me, and I confess, I dry-humped him, a bit like a horny teenager, but that was part of the effect he had on me. He made me feel young again. Like that teen-aged girl before I'd lost my innocence and had stopped believing there was good in the world.

Maybe that was it, though. Maybe he was, bit by bit, restoring some of the faith I'd lost in humanity. God, I could love him for that if it were true.

He pressed the condom into my hands and whispered, "I want to watch you put it on for me."

It was my turn to smile against his lips and the thought that I could turn him on with something so simple made me all kinds of wet and wanting him inside me. I tore open the packet using one hand and my teeth, the other I used to stroke him. His eyes dark, heavy-lidded with passion, he watched my face and I was sure that the sentiment he showed me was echoed on my own in every way.

I rolled the latex down his length and he reached for me, hands on my hips to steady me as I guided the head of his cock to my entrance and sank down on it slowly. He captured my body, an arm around my back, supporting me, a hand on my chest, over my heart. He looked up at me, and I, down at him, as he slipped into me, impossibly deep at this angle. I sighed out, breath catching and he smiled and rocked his hips, the movement teasing at my walls, causing me to tighten around him.

"God, you feel good," I breathed and he moved his hand so that he could press his lips over my heart.

I tangled my fingers in the wild mane of his dark hair and held him, even as I rolled my hips, the pleasure rolling through me with every slightest motion.

I loved being with him. Nothing rushed, everything drawn out for maximum enjoyment by the both of us. There was no rush, there was no frenzy to how we did things and I realized that I liked that. I liked it almost too much for words... except for one.

"Nik..." his name fell from my lips, breathy, and I was close. So very close. He was wonderful at getting me right along that razor's edge of pleasure and keeping me there, in that state of blissful pleasure for as long as he liked. It was amazing. It was beautiful. It was everything that making love between a man and a woman should be and I couldn't get enough.

Our breaths came in long, passionate gasps and moans. Our mouths tangled more often than not. I rode him gently, and no matter how I rocked or shifted, it just wasn't quite enough, but it was. I couldn't come, and it was a sweet torture that I couldn't get enough of, and neither, apparently, could he.

We stayed like that for hours and hours, and I don't think either of us wanted it to end. Still, my body craved release and I know his did too, and eventually, he sat up straighter, capturing me with his arms and laying me back on the bed.

"Harder," I begged and he thrust deep. As deep as he could go, bottoming out in that sweet place between pleasure and pain. He gave it to me harder, but not faster, which is exactly what I wanted, that heavy glow beginning to overtake me, building higher and harder than before until I almost couldn't take it anymore.

Just when I thought I might break, he helped me. Sitting up and looking down at me with kindness, even as he found that kernel of nerves at the top of my sex with the pad of his thumb. He teased it, slick with my own wetness, and the cauldron tipped and I spilled out, all over. Out from the edges of my body which couldn't seem to hold me in anymore. I was formless, weightless, and completely, madly, and inescapably falling in love.

18

Z eb...

She leaned back as she rode me, her eyes hooded with that look every man craves from his woman. The one that says she looks up to you, that she trusts you, and yes, even that she loves you. It made me want to try harder with her, made me want to be a better man than I had ever been before. That look made me want to step up and be everything that she thought I was just so I would never disappoint her. She was my incentive for everything now, and it was pretty far out. I'd never had such a connection with a woman before and the look she gave me drove me absolutely wild.

I sat up and grabbed her, pressing her to me and got up, laying her on her back and pressing myself deep between her thighs. She wrapped her legs around my hips and begged, breathless with desire, "Harder."

I pressed deep, thrusting harder like she'd asked me and she cried out in that way that said I was doing everything right. I drove into her, over and over, each thrust deliberate and precisely what she asked for but I couldn't take much more. I wasn't about to come before my lady, so I sat up and, gazing down at her, found that delicate little flower bud of nerve endings and teased it with my thumb.

She arched, a throaty moan escaping between her lips, swollen with my kiss. Her pussy gripped my shaft impossibly tight. I changed the motion of my thrusts, seating my cock as deep as it would go and making them shorter and tighter. She cried out, voice getting higher, choking off as she struggled to remember to breathe and for one split second I watched her lose all control as she crashed back to the bed and writhed uncontrollably beneath me.

Her pussy milked me, her cry deep and full to the brim with satisfaction as her whole body seemed to short-circuit underneath mine. I lay on top of her, pressing her to the bed as she shuddered beneath me and worked back and forth inside her, closing my eyes and taking my own pleasure.

I came, spilling deep inside the Frenchie on my cock, and reveled in the fact that I really came buried deeper still inside of her.

She was unreal. Unlike anyone I had ever been with before. Magnetic and electric, I had never gone as long with anyone as I had with her, and I loved that we could do this for hours, even though I was pretty sure my legs would pay for it in the morning.

She lay serene, eyes closed beneath me, chest rising and falling dramatically as she tried to catch her breath. I made to pull out and she shuddered and shook her head.

"Mm-mm, not yet," she murmured and I smiled, stilling for the moment.

"Too much?" I asked and she nodded and shuddered with a little aftershock. I chuckled and leaned down, as much to keep her warm as it was so I could kiss her.

"Hmm, okay," she whispered and I reached between us to hold the Frenchie on as I slipped out.

"Be right back," I told her and went to her little bathroom. I flushed the used French letter and turned on the tap for hot, letting the water get warm while I rooted around the little cabinets she had in here, looking for a facecloth. I found a stack of them under the sink, and wet one, cleaning myself up while I listened for her out in the other room. She was quiet, and a quick glance out the door showed she was resting, basking in the afterglow.

I rinsed the facecloth good and made sure it was nice and warm before returning to the bed to clean her up. The best sex was messy sex, which we seemed to accomplish. She shivered as I took care of her and I tossed the facecloth from halfway across the room back into the bathroom sink. I got back into the bed behind her and picked up the remote, restarting the movie with her cuddled back against my chest. She chuckled lightly and asked, "Going to finish it?"

"Well, yeah. I have to see how it ends."

"Hmm, do you want me to tell you? Spare you the pain?"

"What pain?" I asked. "I like this, being here with you, watching something you enjoy. This ain't a hardship, Wahine. You're never that."

She made a happy noise and turned over, kissing me soundly.

"Thank you," she murmured and I smiled down at her.

"Hush," I said with a smile. "You're making me miss the movie."

She grinned broadly and cuddled into my arms and closed her eyes. I could tell she was listening, but by the time the bloke Edward took Viviane to the opera, she was sound asleep. I liked that she could sleep so easy around me, so I made sure the blankets were up around her and she was warm, holding her close as the rest of the story played out on the screen, all the while what she'd said echoing in my mind.

"I don't want to be taken care of as much as I want to be able to take care of myself..."

She really had no idea how strong she was for even thinking along those lines. Still, a person couldn't do it all. Part of taking care of yourself was admitting when you needed help, but then again, she knew. That was how I ended up here in the first place, wasn't it?

She was a marvel, that one; and I was honored to help her on this particular journey.

"So what did you think?" she mumbled and I smiled, laughing a little. Not asleep after all.

"I think you and Viv are two very different people, and I think I like your plan best."

"What plan is that?"

"Teaching you to save yourself rather than doing any kind of saving."

"Mm, it's nice too, though."

"What's that?"

"You being around doing some saving. Not every danger is a physical threat."

"Too right, Wahine. Too, right."

19

T iffany…

"He scares the shit out of me," I confessed in a whisper and Nik glanced over my shoulder at Reaver who was striding through the door of the gym. He stopped by Mali and they bumped fists.

"Ah, yeah, he's half-cracked, that one, but you don't have anything to worry about. I promise you that. He keeps his crazy pretty well contained when it comes to it."

"Good to know *I'm* not crazy," I muttered.

"Nah, but I wouldn't go trying to psychoanalyze him either. He'd pick up on it and probably wouldn't be too happy."

"Noted," I said quickly under my breath as he and Mali came this way.

"Now is when this shit gets fun!" Mali declared and I straightened.

"You don't like guns," Reaver said, "So I'm here to show you a thing or two about knives."

I shuddered inwardly at how his eyes lit up when he said the word 'knives.'

"Okay," I said cautiously, and Mali stepped in front of him.

"First we're going to go through some of the drills we went through last week, though. Then, when Reaver has a grasp on how much you know, he'll introduce the sharp shiny objects and how to deal with them in the same sort of scenarios. Sound good?"

No. It sounded really fucking overwhelming, actually. What I said out loud, however, was: "Sounds great."

We went through everything we'd already been through and I was super glad that Nik and I had practiced an hour or so the day before after our sex and a movie date and a couple of days before that after work.

Mali seemed pleased we had too and I can't tell you how grateful I was when the 'sharp shiny objects' that came into play weren't, in fact, the real thing but rather were rubber variations for practice purposes.

"I think you're right, Mali," Reaver said, after the third or fourth go at a particular scenario. "Her dancing is helping her out by, like, a lot."

"I can't tell you how much I hate that I'm over here panting and dying while you're standing there cool as a cucumber and haven't even broken a sweat," I said between gasping breaths.

"I'm used to these moves and cardio, cardio, cardio," he said with a grin.

"I do cardio all night every night five nights a fucking week!" I cried and he laughed. "I'ma punch you," I muttered flippantly and he laughed harder.

"So much for being a pacifist," he teased, and I was beginning to like him.

I took a drink of water and shrugged, "I wouldn't call myself a pacifist," I said. "Granted I don't like violence, especially when there are other options, but when you run out of those options and it's the last resort…"

"You find yourself here, with us, busting your ass to make sure it's covered," Mali said and nodded. "Trust me, Sweetheart, I get you. I'm just a little more proactive than reactive, if you catch my drift."

I nodded, I understood her. She probably would have handed Silas his ass before he ever got the chance to use a broken beer bottle on her face. I was young and dumb, though, and had thought that I could still change him. Trust me, all those stitches and the lesson on how stupid that viewpoint had been had been sewn into my very being with every single one of them.

"I really hope he just fucks off, but I just know it from the bottom of my soul that he's out there looking for me and to cause trouble." I scowled. Men like Silas didn't quit. It hadn't been in his nature when it came to riding bulls and with something that was so fundamentally a part of someone, well, it was likely something that hadn't changed.

"Okay, explain that look," Reaver demanded, scowling. I shifted from foot to foot.

"I still haven't heard from Delia and she's not answering her phone."

"That the best friend?" Reaver asked, but he wasn't looking at me, he was looking over my shoulder at Nik who was leaned up against the wall. Nik nodded.

"She ever did anything like this?" Mali asked.

"Gone off with a guy for a few days without so much as a text?" I asked.

"Yeah," Reaver looked me over.

I nodded. "Not totally unusual for her," I said. She would typically let me know she was off for a couple of days and that would be it. She always showed up to take me to work and I would always bitch her out for making me worry, but this time was different. This time there was like a one-hundred-percent chance there were ulterior motives at play. I said as much.

"Cops won't listen," Mali said with derision.

"Which is why we should," Reaver said. "Pigs are good for nothing and once again, reaction versus pro-action."

"I think the word you're looking for is pro*active*," Mali said dryly.

"Yeah, that," he said with a cheesy grin. I laughed, and so did Nik.

"What? Out of all of y'all, I'm just a po' dumb country boy. Y'all motherfuckers are much more well-read than me."

"No one's arguing that, Bro."

"Yeah, fuck you," Reaver said, grinning.

"Ah, yeah, nah!"

"I don't know, Zeb, that sounded a little indecisive if I've got my Kiwi translation right," Mali joked, tone sly.

I shifted slightly and wanted to scream, *'What about Delia!? Can we get back to that, please?'*

Reaver looked me over, "Try your friend now," he suggested. "Shoot her a text, though. Don't call."

I did as he asked, and we all stood around waiting for something – anything – to come through in return, but after a couple of minutes went by with nothing, he frowned.

"Whereabout does she live?" he asked.

"Other side of town, in the Maple Green apartments," I said.

He frowned, "I don't know where that is, but at the same time, I probably know where that is."

"As in been past it like a thousand times, but never really put the name to it?" Mali guessed with a raised eyebrow.

"That would be it, yes. You interpret my crazy so well, young Padawan."

"Fuck you, who schooled who that one time?"

He rolled his eyes and I met Nik's gaze as they bickered. He frowned and said, "Guys!" They stopped and looked over at me.

"Look, I may not be happy with Lia right now, but her heart is and always has been in the right place where I'm concerned. She did a lot for me after…" I pursed my lips and rolled them together. "After Silas."

Mali snorted and said, "Like turned you into a stripper who's a prostitute on the side?" she asked. It stung but her next words cut even deeper and made me want to stand up for my friend. "With friends like that who needs enemies?"

"Mali," Reaver scolded, and she had the grace to look embarrassed.

"Look, I get how it looks to someone like you –"

Mali scowled, "Someone like me? What's that supposed to mean?"

"Nothing," I said. "Just someone who hasn't had to make any really hard decisions, I guess it what I meant."

She laughed a bitter barking sound. "Oh, oh. That's rich, but fair. Definitely fair, that was a shit thing for me to say." She swallowed hard and looked me in the eyes. "I'm sorry, but please don't think I haven't had to make any tough decisions. I definitely shouldn't be one to judge or poke holes. I'm sorry for being a dick."

I wanted to give her the finger, I mean I was mad, but I really needed to keep learning from her, and she was teaching me and teaching me pretty well, and asking nothing in return. Plus, she had just apologized, even if it looked like she'd sucked on a lemon as she'd done it. So, I swallowed my anger for the time being and grated out, "It's okay, I'm used to it."

"Ouch, and now I feel like an even bigger asshole," she declared and sighed, scrubbing her face with her hands.

"If you two were dudes, I'd tell you to beat the shit out of each other and go have a couple of brews already, but when it comes to bitches, I'm at a loss for how you all handle this kind of shit," Reaver declared.

"Ask your wife," Mali said darkly. "Because I'm too much of a dude on the inside to have a clue, either."

"Good idea," he answered, then added, "And yeah, you are."

I glanced at Nik who I expected to be laughing but nope, he was looking at me, his eyes clouded with concern. He didn't look at all happy with Mali.

"Maybe it would help if I explained from the beginning…" I said.

"It's really none of my business," Mali said. "Especially after the crack I just made, but yeah, if you want to talk, I'd listen. I at least owe you that."

I sighed and leaned my butt against the stairs leading up to the boxing ring in the center of the gym.

"I was just a dumb-ass runaway when I met Lia. We worked the concessions stand together at the rodeo and she was just so much more down-to-earth than me, you know? She really took me under her wing and kept me out of trouble. She was taking pole dancing classes and got the idea to strip from another girl, one of the other cowboy's girlfriends who was bringing in over two grand a week. When she heard the money was that good stripping it was too much to pass up for a girl who had been as broke as her all of her life. We both had grown up poor, and I have to tell you, money may not buy happiness but it definitely does buy security. It's really nice not having to worry about where you're going to sleep every night or where your next meal is going to come from. She was all for stripping, had always been a wild child that way and the bolder of the two of us, but back then she was waiting to turn eighteen so she actually could, you know?"

I sighed, "She was my only friend before and after Silas… I stayed working the concession stands and then eventually didn't even do that because he didn't want me to, but Lia stuck to her plan. She blazed her own trail and ended up at Sugars. She and I never lost touch, even though I kept traveling with Silas and the rodeo. We, I mean Silas and me, happened to be in town with it on Delia's birthday weekend. He didn't want me to go out, but Lia talked me into it, and I wanted to spend my best friend's birthday with her, you know? Then this happened," I drew a finger along the curve of my cheek and sighed again, sniffing as tears threatened to spill over. I always got emotional talking about how Lia saved my ass.

"Delia stuck by me, let me stay with her at her place, rent free, I might add. She was at the hospital every day, went to every court date with me, and kept me from letting the depression swallow me whole. She got me into pole dancing with her as a means to stay fit and really just as a way to get me out of the apartment at first, but then she was the one who came up with the whole 'Francesca' persona and the mask idea. She's the one that got me into this life, sure, but more importantly, she's the one who got me out of my old one and kept me from giving up on life altogether. At the time, she gave me a life back when I thought it was over. I can never repay her for all that she's done for me. Never in a million years."

Silence fell over the four of us and Mali finally let out a gusty sigh of her own, "Well, shit," she said on the tail end of it. "Now I really feel like an asshole. Me and my fucking mouth."

"Pretty sure we keep warning you about that, just sayin'," Reaver sort of sang out and she scowled at him.

"Shut the fuck up," she snapped.

"Case in point," he said and hung his head.

"Yeah, yeah, tell me something I don't know."

"Well —"

She cut him off with, "That was rhetorical, Jackass!"

He laughed and I did too, jumping slightly when Nik pressed himself to my back, hands on my hips.

"I get that you're worried, but you said yourself this isn't out of the ordinary, eh?"

"I did say that, and it's not... I just can't shake the feeling something bad has happened."

Reaver shrugged and said, "You got a lot going on with your douchebag-ex getting out of the slammer. You sure it's not just that."

I shook my head, "That's just it. I can't be sure that it's not just that. Still, I feel better for having said something and I'll keep trying tonight."

"That's all you can do," Mali said, and she and Reaver exchanged a significant look.

"You have her actual address?" he asked, scrolling through his phone and I swear my insides went liquid with relief – but I didn't want to get my hopes up just yet.

"Yes," I said.

"What is it?" he asked and I told him, holding my breath, waiting for him to confirm what I pretty much already knew he was committing to.

"It's on my way home; I'll swing by and check things out and call Zeb with what I find out. You guys will be hanging together after this for a while, right?" he asked, an innocent look that wasn't fooling anyone plastered to his face. He didn't lie exceptionally well. Either that, or he didn't care about keeping up appearances, at least not about Nik and I spending time together beyond the scope of him having my back and looking out for Silas.

"Yes," I said but it was hesitant; suspicious as to why he would even be fishing. I mean, were Nik and I the subject of gossip? Was Nik getting a hard time about me? I mean, going by Mali's judgment call about me and

Lia, it wasn't a stretch of the imagination to think that he was. I felt bad about that. I felt bad about so many things and was seriously beginning to wonder if there was anything left to feel good about myself for…

"Excellent," Reaver said and sighed. "I think we've done enough for today. Next week?" he asked Nik.

"Same time, same place, thanks, Bro."

"No problem, keep working on your form and your speed, you need to be faster. You don't have the size advantage, but no one should be able to top you for speed. Especially judging by the pictures of this asshole."

"Pictures?" I echoed, surprised.

"Yep." Mali popped the 'p' a little and winked at me. "It's what my man does best. Digs up all the dirt. If there's records or pictures, he'll find them. Speaking of which, if there was any record of you or your current whereabouts on the net? He wiped it before your ex even got out of prison. If he's looking, he's hitting nothing but big roadblocks full of a whole lot of nothing on you."

"Really?" I asked. "How did I not know about this?"

"Ah, I guess I forgot to mention it," Nik said.

Mali rolled her eyes and lifted her jacket off the corner of the ring. "Way to go, Romeo. Probably could have saved her a little anxiety, don't 'cha think?"

Nik colored and I blinked. It took a lot for a man with his dusky skin tone, not unlike Mali's, to visibly blush even though he wasn't especially dark.

"I'll call you," Reaver said, buried in his phone and heading for the door.

"Thanks, Bro!" Nik called after him.

"Later, you two," Mali said walking backward at first, before turning and following Reaver out.

I turned to Nik and felt my shoulders drop. He pulled me into his arms and wrapped them around me, holding me tight, chin on one of my shoulders before pressing his lips to the top of it.

"Thank you," I murmured.

"For what?"

"Getting me wiped off the internet, I guess? She's right. That takes a load off."

"Ah, yeah, I can't take credit for that. That's all Data, and, I'm betting, Dragon."

I closed my eyes and nodded. "I don't know if I should feel guilty, I mean, I haven't exactly thanked him lately."

"Haven't seen him, have you?"

"No. No, he hasn't been into the club," I said, meaning Sugars. "Not since I went to see him, but that isn't exactly unusual."

"You could text him, eh."

I shook my head. "Never did get his number. Our, ah, arrangement, wasn't like that. That's why I went to the motorcycle club in person in the first place. I didn't know how else to get a hold of him without waiting for him to come into Sugars." Which could have been any time, and at the time, I didn't think it could wait... I still didn't. I couldn't tell Nik or Reaver, or any of the MC just how grateful I was for their help and if Delia was okay, it was seriously worth any price they wanted me to pay down the line.

"Talk to me," he said softly, and I sighed and held him tighter.

"A lot of judging going on," I said.

"Eh, yeah, Mali was out of line. I'm sorry about that."

"Don't be, and I didn't just mean Mali just now. Delia has had some pretty harsh judgments about you all. Honestly, I was afraid if any of you knew, none of you would be as willing to help me or her."

He leaned back and cocked his head and said, "What she thinks doesn't have a lot to do with you. What you think is what's important, isn't it?"

"True, and what I think is that you all are far kinder than anyone gives you credit for and at this point, I will gladly pay any price for the kindness you all have shown me."

He smiled a little and shook his head, "If it comes at a price, it isn't kindness, now is it?"

"No, I suppose not," I murmured.

"Is that what she thinks? That you're going to somehow owe us for what we're doing?"

I nodded and sighed, "I know, it sounds awful –"

"It does," he said, cutting me off.

"But?"

"But I'm not surprised. Citizens oftentimes think the worst of us and typically we wear it like the badge of honor that it is." He sighed and went on, saying, "We came by our reputation honestly; we aren't nice men, once someone gives us a reason not to be. That's just it, though. You have to give us a reason not to be."

"Like what?"

He smiled and said, "Not even worth talking about, Girl. You're not the kind of person that would ever give us that kind of a reason."

"I hope not," I said softly and he bowed his head, pressing his lips to mine. I kissed him back, a little thrill of fear trickling down my spine. The cold calculation in his eyes during the short conversation told me that I really never wanted to give any of these guys a reason to be upset with me, but that was a scary prospect when you didn't know what it would take to upset them.

"Come on, a hot bath awaits," he whispered and I nodded carefully.

"That sounds good."

"Good, after that, I'll cook."

I had to smile then. "That sounds even better."

He laughed and we gathered our things so that he could lock up and we could go upstairs.

20

Z eb...

Tiffany was in my bathroom, soaking in the tub when Reaver rang me up. I was glad my phone's ringer was off and it was buzzing across my kitchen bench when I grabbed it. I wanted her to relax some.

"Yeah, Bro. What's good?" I asked in greeting.

"Nothing here," he said and I frowned.

"What's that supposed to mean?"

"It means she ain't home. Her car is in the lot. I asked Data to look up her info. Nothing is out of place, but that makes it out of place, you know what I mean?"

"Ah, yeah. Are you in her apartment then?"

"Yup. Picked the lock. It was a little too easy. Everything looks normal, I guess. I mean shit ain't knocked over or anything. No signs of a struggle. She's kind of a messy person, though. Bras and panties *everywhere*. She even has a set hanging off a lamp."

I laughed a bit and nodded, "Definitely fits what my Tiff has said about her."

"Yeah? What's that?"

I shrugged even though he couldn't see it and said, "That they couldn't be more different. Opposites attract and all of that. My Tiff is a neat person, likes to keep things clean. Stands to reason her opposite friend would be a bit messy."

"Yeah, more than a bit. I'm gonna bounce before I accidentally touch something and bring it home to Hayden."

"Hey, now!" I said and he laughed.

"I didn't mean it that way; I just mean I have no way of telling what's growing in here in the dark."

"Heh, I'm not there, so I can't declare if that's fair or not."

"Wow, rhyme a little more there, buddy."

"Fuck you."

"That's not a haiku."

I laughed, "They don't rhyme."

"Meh, I'm a basic guy. Gimme a limerick over that fancy Japanese shit any day... wait, haikus are Japanese, right?"

"Yeah man, they're Japanese."

"Good, I got that right. Okay, then."

"I'll talk to her when she's out of her bath."

"Dude! Why aren't you in there with her?"

"Nah, that's her time for her – she doesn't get a lot of it."

"Yeah, I know what you mean. I'm just blessed with my Doll who doesn't want a lot of it. Time for just her. She just about always wants me there."

"She thought you were dead for almost a year, Bro."

"Yeah, that probably has something to do with it," and he didn't sound too happy about the reminder.

"Go home, make it up to her some more."

"There are some things in life you can *never* make up for, man. That would definitely top the list."

"Just because you can't make up for it don't mean you ever stop trying."

"Now, that, I am on board with. You're absolutely right. I'm going home and fucking my wife, now."

"You do that."

"Just you try and stop me," he said, and his voice was as cold as the winter pressing against the dark window glass up here.

"Nah, wouldn't dream of it," I said and hung up.

I set the phone down and heard Tiff call out, "Hey, Nik?"

"Yeah?" I called back.

"Was that Reaver?" she called and I smiled a little to myself, a smile that held a bitter edge at the strain of worry in her voice. I loved that she worried so much about her friend but at the same time, I hated that she had cause to worry at all.

I went around from the kitchen to the bathroom door and pushed in. She lay back in the tub, scented milky water steaming, covering all the important bits except the perfect peaks of her breasts. I went over and sat on the edge of the tub, trailing fingertips beneath the warm, almost-too-hot water, from her ankle, up her shin, to her knee, and back.

"Yeah, that was Reaver. He said her car is in the lot, but she's not home."

"Damn it, Delia!" she swore under her breath. She closed her eyes and banged her head lightly on the tile wall behind her head, sighing. Her hands raising from the water so she could press fingertips to her eyes and cover her face.

She took several deep breaths and shuddered and I slid my hand up higher, just holding the inside of her thigh.

"God*dammit*, Lia!" she cried and let out a harsh breath. She didn't cry but it was a near thing and my heart went out to her.

"I don't know what to say or do to fix it," I confessed and she shook her head.

"Nothing, there's nothing you can say or do to fix it. At best, you can just distract me and you are so very good and such a pleasant distraction," she said and I smiled.

I slid my hand higher and she parted her knees so my fingertips could graze her silky sex beneath the water.

"I aim to please," I said with a chuckle and she sucked in a sharp breath when I slid a finger inside her.

I held her, cupped in my hand, my middle finger deep inside her, my thumb pressed against her clit and my eyes glued to her perfect, beautiful face. I swear to you, on the souls of my ancestors, I didn't even see the scar when I looked at her anymore. She was just beautiful, just perfect, from the way she came to me the day I met her all the way up until now. Actually, that was sort of a lie. I didn't think such a thing was possible, but I believe she grew *more* beautiful to me every day.

She sucked in a breath and gripped the edge of the tub with a white-knuckled grip, her other hand gripping the top of her thigh over by the wall. She gasped and her hips gave a little jerk, the lavender-colored water swirling with flashes of silver glitter in it in little eddies around her body.

I bit my bottom lip and concentrated on giving her the distraction she'd asked for, playing my thumb in little circles over her clit, working my finger in a come-hither motion over the roof of her pussy, teasing reactions from her.

Her eyes closed, she bit her bottom lip and turned her head to the side, so into what I was doing, she didn't even realize she turned the unmarked side away from me, putting her warrior's mark on full display. I rewarded that bit of trust by teasing at her clit a little more, her pussy clenching tight, her mouth falling open and a little breathy moan falling from her sweet lips even as she fought not to ride my hand, her hips lifting and falling rhythmically just below the water's surface, the sparkles suspended in it dancing and swirling, accentuating her curves, and making me wish more than just my hand was between her thighs.

I tried to tell myself to be patient and that I'd be there soon enough. We had all the rest of tonight and into part of the day tomorrow if we wanted before either of us had to go to work.

"Nik!" she gasped and her voice was like angel song to my ears.

She closed her eyes and shuddered in her warm bath as I made her come and it was beautiful. Like she shattered into many points of sparkling light and dissolved into the glitter in the tub before rising back up whole and new. She practically leaped up, her warm, wet hands grabbing my face to either side as she crushed her mouth to mine. Off-balance, I practically fell on her, half into the water. She exclaimed, a surprised, light sound, into my mouth and laughed against it, even as the warm bathwater soaked into my clothes.

"Guess these are going to have to come off, eh."

"I guess so," she murmured demurely.

I peeled back the flannel I was wearing as she helped pull the black thermal undershirt from the waistband of my jeans. We made some quick work of undressing and discovered with some maneuvering, that it was a tight fit but that we both fit and we learned a bit of a science lesson on displacement while we were at it.

"I love this," she murmured and pulled my arms around her where she rested back against my chest.

"I do, too," I confessed and we silently enjoyed the warmth and closeness until the bathwater grew too tepid to stay.

"You think everything is okay?" she asked as I dried her through a towel and she sounded both fragile and hopeful.

I lied to her, and it killed me to do it, but I couldn't tell her the truth. She didn't need the truth right now, she needed to believe. "I think everything's fine and she's off getting her rocks off with that bloke."

"I hope you're right," she said and she sounded like she didn't believe me. She leaned up and kissed me softly and said, "You're a terrible liar, but thank you. You're right for doing it."

I smiled and said, "Guilty, but then again, I hate to see you hurt."

"I love that about you, too."

I felt a sudden warmth radiate out from my center at her words.

"The more I get to know you, the more time I spend with you... I really think I'm starting to love everything about you," I said evenly.

"Except my job," she murmured and I smiled.

"Hard to love that," I said.

She nodded and looked a little sad, "There are some days I loved my job, but they haven't come in a while."

"So why don't you quit?" I asked, and held her close. She looked up at me and her expression was sad and a little bit torn.

"The money, for one. Honestly, I don't know what else I would do."

"Well," I said and kissed her softly, "Nothing has to change right now, or even soon."

"Seriously?" she asked and bit her bottom lip, giving me a skeptical look.

"Truly," I told her.

She hugged me close, resting her head on my shoulder and I held her back, smoothing a hand over the towel over her lower back and her bum.

"Thank you," she whispered.

"For what?"

"For not lying, but for not forcing me to choose or make a change right now."

"I will never force you to do anything you don't want to. That's not how I want any of this to work."

"But you want it to work?" she asked and that fragile hope was back in her voice.

I didn't lie one bit when I said, "More than anything, Wahine. More than anything I've ever wanted before."

21

T iffany…

"What's that now?"

Shit, we had a bad connection and the fact that I was in my g-string, barely-there bra and nothing else had kept me inside the club, rather than let me be outside where the signal was both better and there wasn't pounding music to contend with.

"Delia!" I cried. "I'm worried about her, Nik; she didn't show up for work."

"Shit, yeah, alright. Let me make some calls and I'll call you right back, yeah?"

"Hold on," I said. I turned and blinked at Alan, the club's owner who had touched me on the shoulder.

"I'm sorry," I said immediately, "I thought I had longer before my next dance."

"You're fine," he said. "Cherry is going on for you, right now. Take the back stair up to my office, there's a..." he paused and groped for the right word, "Situation at the front Zeke has alerted me to."

"Tiffany, what's wrong?" I heard Nik say distantly, but my adrenaline was spiking and I was already moving.

"I'll call you back, I think he's here."

"What?" Nik demanded sharply.

"Go now, Tiff, my office," Alan said gently and I went.

"Alan's sending me to his office, Zeke's handling it at the front. I'm okay for now," I told Nik. Despite Alan trying to keep me calm, my heart was pounding. I almost didn't register what Nik said.

"I'm on my way, just do what your boss says."

"I am," I told him, but I was talking to the empty air, Nik was already gone.

I clattered up the back stairs in my stripper heels and kicked the door to Alan's office closed and turned the lock. I figured it was his office and he had the key. The space was small, and a bank of windows overlooked the floor below. It was all right, though. They were mirrors on the outside and you could only see inside at very specific angles. If I sat at the desk in front of the windows and ducked down a bit behind the monitors, I would be invisible so that's precisely what I did. I sat at Alan's desk, heart pounding, stomach curdling, and kept bouncing my gaze back and forth between the cameras on the monitors and out the window at the floor below.

Zeke was on camera, out front, hands raised and pushing down in his classic 'calm the fuck down, I'm trying to explain something to you' pose. Alan stood back, beside the bar, his cell phone pressed to his ear, nodding and speaking occasionally into it.

My heart thudded painfully in my chest as someone outside the camera's range swung on Zeke, in a flash, out of nowhere, and Zeke went crashing to the ground out like a light. Silas strode forward into the camera's view and then, through the front door, larger than life and screaming at the top of his lungs. Dancers stopped, patrons stood up, and Alan walked calmly forward.

I couldn't hear anything. There was nothing to hear, the office up here was so well insulated and soundproofed only the dullest thumping of the music's bass beat made it through. I swallowed hard as Silas stopped just outside Alan's reach and Alan waved him forward with a broad sweep of his arm.

"What are you *doing?*" I asked, and realized he was taking Silas on a tour, either to get him out or to buy time for whoever he had been on the phone with to get here. I knew Nik would make it. I knew he would be here, I just didn't know when, and with how fast and how hard Silas had knocked Zeke out? I didn't know if I wanted Nik to square off with him.

I was suddenly very afraid for my lover and biker bodyguard.

I followed Silas and Alan from camera to camera but kept glancing back to Zeke who was sitting up now and rubbing his jaw. My chest loosened with a bit of relief at that and I still couldn't believe that Silas had gotten the drop on him like that. Zeke was good at his job and I'd seen him handle himself in more than a few fights before.

The phone in my hand buzzed and I answered it without looking, "Hello?"

Indistinct club noise came through the line and voices, hard to make out. I looked at the screen and realized Alan had dialed me.

"What's up there?" I heard Silas demand.

"My office."

Shit!

I got up and looked around and finally had to settle for ducking into his bathroom up here. I stepped into the shower and pulled the curtain, holding the phone to my chest as I heard the door being messed with out front.

I held my breath and ended the call, fighting with the phone to silence the ringer just in case.

"I told you, there's no one up here," I heard Alan declare. "We have no dancer by that name at this club. Now, as I told you downstairs, the police have been notified about you striking my bouncer. You can clearly see there is no one up here, so please leave."

I heard the bathroom door swing wide and bounce against the wall and the fear swarmed over my skin, sweat standing out along my spine under the short, light silk robe Alan had gifted me after my first year here. He did things like that on all of the girls' anniversaries.

"Fine," Silas grated. "But I don't believe you. What is it? Her night off or something?"

"I swear to you, there's no 'Tiffany' here." Alan maintained.

"I find out you're lying to me, I'm coming back here and burning this place to the fucking ground with you in it."

Their voices receded and I squeezed my eyes shut, hot tears tracking down my face. All he'd needed to do to find me had been to pull back the curtain. He just hadn't thought to do it. Dumb luck on my part? Who knew? All I did know was that he was going or gone and I found myself choking on a silent scream that I would not let out from behind my teeth.

I slid down the wall onto my butt against the cold tile and shuddered, sweat slick against my palms where I clutched my phone with both of them over my heart, like it would protect me or something. The blood rushed in my ears and when the curtain jerked back I screamed and cringed but it was Zeke that knelt down, a purple knot swelling on his jawline. He put his hands on mine and said, "Easy, Tiff! Easy it's just me."

"Is he gone?" I cried and a hand fell onto Zeke's shoulder. Zeke jumped and turned but immediately relaxed and got out of the way of our boss who knelt down in front of me.

"He's gone," Alan assured me.

"Are you sure?"

"I'm sure, I'm so sorry. I had to get him out of here. You did great." He patted my cheek, the side without the mask, and he looked sorry.

It was something we had discussed before, but it was a long time ago. Alan knew everything about Silas and had given me a chance but only because Delia had practically begged. He really was a nice guy. In his late thirties, maybe early forties, just beginning to go slightly grey at the temples.

He looked me over with light colored eyes and sighed, saying, "It's okay now," and "I think you should take her home."

I looked up past him to Nik who was standing hands at his sides, fingers flexing with a want to do something with them, the look on his face scarily cold.

"I think that's a fine idea, Cuz," he said, and I pushed my way up and past Alan and flung myself into Nik's arms. They automatically went around me and he held me tight.

"I'm sorry I couldn't get here any faster," he breathed into my hair and I sniffed.

"It's alright, you're here now."

"Police are here," Zeke called from out in the office and Alan excused himself and slipped back out the bathroom door.

"Roll back the footage and save it to a flash drive for them. Tiffany, I believe they are going to want to speak to you."

"Bloody hell," Nik muttered and I was with him. I'd talked to the cops countless times about Silas, yet here he'd been, again.

169

Nik led me out of the bathroom and to the black leather couch in Alan's office. I couldn't stop shaking. He sat me down next to him and ran his hands over my shoulders and arms, finally putting a hand over my heart against my chest, leaning in and putting his forehead to mine, his jaw clenching, his eyes closing as he willed me silently to be calm.

His quiet strength calmed me. Allowed me to close my eyes and echo his slow, even breaths with my own which in turn slowed my racing heart. I was vaguely aware of Alan watching us while Zeke clicked around through screens and on the mouse and keyboard of the security systems.

"I have you, Girl," Nik whispered and I nodded, which was awkward with our foreheads pressed like they were.

"She okay?" Zeke asked.

"She'll be right," Nik told him.

"Good, because the cops are here," Zeke said dispassionately.

"A lot of good they'll do," I said and let out a shuddering sigh.

"I know that, and *you* know that," Alan said and sighed, "But we all know the right man for this particular job has already shown up." He cast a meaningful look at Nik and Nik pulled back from me to give him a nod.

"Too right, Brother," Nik said and the men left it at that. Alan nodding once and dropping his arms from where he had them crossed.

He turned and gave Zeke a meaningful look and said, "I'll go fetch our guests."

"I'm sorry, Alan," I called after him and he raised his hand and waved me off over his shoulder. My heart sank.

"He's not mad at you, Tiff. He just wants the cops the fuck up out of here. We don't want them sniffing around for any reason."

"I know," I said gently and felt guilty as hell. Alan had always been good to his girls. He'd never expected a cut of our extracurriculars, just the ten percent house's cut of whatever we walked off stage with. He knew this life was hard for a lot of us, and while Sugars looked shabby and careworn, the rest of us understood this was the isle of lost toys. For some of us, like me, it was the only place left to go.

Alan was a decent guy, his only major rules were that we had to practice safe sex if we decided that the extracurriculars were for us. None of us were required to turn tricks to be here, although most of us did. Alan simply looked the other way, for the most part, on that. He didn't condone it, for plausible deniability where the legalities or lack thereof were involved.

The other rule was his cardinal rule: none of us could be on drugs. If he found us on something, or we brought anything into his establishment? That was it. There were no second chances for that one. Still, there was always one or two that were dumber than a box of rocks on that one and would test the theory. Those of us loyal to Alan, who understood just how much he did for us, didn't hesitate to dime a stupid bitch out to him when it came to either of those rules.

He ran a clean place, both figuratively and literally, despite the flesh-peddling that went on here.

"What are you doing?" Nik asked and I sighed, slightly frustrated at the pulling I was doing on the skin of my face.

"Getting the mask off," Zeke said. "More sympathetic. You only got a couple more seconds, babes, and they're gonna be at the back stair. Looks like Alan's taking them the long ways."

"Okay, okay, okay!" I hissed through gritted teeth and got the lace the rest of the way off, working my jaw and scrunching my eyes, resisting the urge to rub it.

Nik was frowning at me and tipped my chin, whisking a thumb over some of the hurt with a super light, almost-not-even-there touch.

"Usually I have a solution to help me get that off," I explained and he opened his mouth to say something but was cut off by the door opening, and Alan escorting a couple of uniformed officers into the office.

"You the bouncer?" one asked Zeke and Zeke scowled.

"How could you tell?" he asked wincing and moved his jaw back and forth with his hand to it. He didn't have to pretend much to look pained.

"Who are you?" the second cop demanded of Nik and I tried not to roll my eyes or throw up my hands. It was typical that they would ignore the woman in the room. I'd dealt with it more than a few times before with the local police. This was good ol' boy country and as sexist as it got.

"I'm her boyfriend," Nik answered them and any irritation I felt completely fled.

I settled in for the slow grind of their 'procedures' and the fact that they weren't really going to want to get involved with the trash essentially taking itself out. That was how they always treated these kinds of situations with people like us. From the cop's perspective, it wasn't the first time they'd had trouble with a dancer's ex-boyfriend showing up, nor was it the first time they'd responded to one of our bouncers getting into a scrap with one of our patrons. It didn't happen super often, but it happened often enough to be considered 'normal' for an establishment like this one.

Of course, all it took was the stereotype to get something like that labeled as 'normal' for a place like this, which was sad because even though it was rundown, it was rundown because Alan made sure we got our fair share which left little to actually do any renovations with. Really, it was barely enough to keep up with necessary repairs.

"You have a restraining order against this guy?"

I missed the question, or really that they were finally addressing me and it took Nik shaking me a little for me to come back to the room from inside my head.

"I'm sorry, what?"

"Restraining order? You got one?"

"Yes, I'm sorry. They gave me a five-year one, it doesn't expire until next year." Which, honestly, he would have still been in prison had the system kept him in but that had been a bridge I was going to cross when I came to it.

"You wouldn't happen to have a copy of that protective order handy, would you?" the other officer asked, bored.

"Actually, I do. It's in my purse downstairs."

Both cops exchanged a look and then really seemed to look at me for the first time. I turned my face into the light a little better and one of them frowned.

"Could you go get it for me?" he asked and I swallowed hard and nodded.

"I'll come with you," Nik said and the first cop, who was being an asshole, frowned and said, "You'll stay right there."

"Why?" Nik asked. "I didn't even get here until after the nob was gone."

"Because I said so, and I'm not done talking to you yet," the cop snapped.

"I'll go with you, ma'am," the second, nicer, cop said.

"Thank you," I murmured. Nik didn't look at all happy to let me go, and it was a sentiment echoed in my own heart. Still, I did as the officer bid and went to get the envelope of paperwork that I carried in my purse, always.

We went downstairs, the officer ghosting along behind me a respectful distance away. I immediately went to my locker, twisting the dial on the combination lock while the officer stood close by.

"He do that to your face?" he asked and I nodded. He didn't know. I tossed my lace mask into the bottom of my locker and pulled out my gym bag and purse.

"Can I get dressed while we're down here?" I asked.

"Um, sure, I don't see why not."

I hauled out my leggings and jeans as soon as I was done fishing out the restraining order for him. He opened the envelope and pulled out the sheaf of papers, reading through them while I pulled on first my leggings, then my jeans over them, right on over my dance costume. They weren't the most comfortable underwear on the planet, but I didn't care about that right now.

I sat down on the bench and pulled first a stretchy camisole over my head, tucking it into the jeans, following it up with a printed, form-fitting thermal. Black with roses and angel wings. Another piece of clothing that was biker-ish when I stopped to think about it.

He was on the third or fourth page, eyes scanning back and forth when I pulled on my boots and zipped them. I shoved my gym bag back into the locker and took my coat down off the hook, shrugging into it, and pulling my hair from the collar just as he finished the last page.

"You're fast at that," he said and I sighed.

"Years of practice."

He chuckled a little darkly and sighed, "You know he's going to have a warrant issued for his arrest, but manpower-wise, we won't be actively looking for him."

"No humans involved, right?" I asked and he scowled at me.

"How did you know about that?" he demanded.

"That I'm one of the inhumans by the boys in blue's standard?" I said and sighed. "I heard one of you say it two years ago. One of the dancers here was killed by her boyfriend. When the detectives came and investigated, I overheard one of them say it. I asked Alan about it later."

"Alan being your boss upstairs?"

"Yeah."

"I'm really sorry you had to hear that. I hope you know not all cops think that way."

I gave him a sad sort of smile, "Not enough of you don't think that way, honey. I know which ways the scales tip. I also remember one of the cops that responded when this happened told me that if I'd listened the last time Silas had hit me, and if I'd left, I wouldn't be in that position and that I'd pretty much done it to myself. So, sorry if I don't have a whole lot of faith in the system anymore. Once you're branded a "professional victim," I made air quotes with my fingers around the phrase, "You don't have a whole lot of faith left that anyone cares enough to actually help you."

"I'm really sorry that any of that was said or happened to you," he said, and he genuinely looked upset.

I shrugged. I was used to it by now, which is why I'd gone to find help on my own. It was hard to care about the system when the system didn't care about you.

"We'll get him," he said.

"Don't make promises you can't keep," I replied, but I said it gently.

"We always get them eventually," he said.

I shook my head and sighed, "Problem is what they get away with in the meantime, though. Isn't it?"

"You have me there."

"Are you done with that?" I asked and gestured to the piece of paper that was basically my only shield, and as we all know, a piece of paper makes a really shitty shield.

"Not yet," he said holding out a hand indicating I should proceed him. I headed back upstairs and he followed, both of us trapped in an uneasy silence. On the same side but the opposite end of the spectrum, as it were.

"Took you long enough," his partner, who was slightly older than him, said dispassionately on our return.

"Ah, good, you're going home. I was going to insist," Alan said.

I went over and gave him a hug and said, "I figured. It's one of the reasons you're a good boss."

"You can't perform your best after something like that," he declared.

Nik made to get up and the older cop who was being a dick barked at him, "Sit down!"

"Myers, easy!" The younger cop, the one who'd gone downstairs with me, handed his partner the restraining order while I slipped over to Nik and tucked myself into his front. He remained standing, defiant, and I know that he made Myers nervous.

"She'll be right," Nik muttered softly to me and I lost some of the tension that was riding me. It was a Kiwi thing to say. It pretty much meant that everything would be okay, meaning that he wouldn't go full metal idiot when it came to the cop and his ridiculous amount of disrespect. To a certain extent, it was to be expected. Cop and outlaw biker in the same room together was like mixing oil and water in the same Mason jar. I think it said something that the biker was the cooler head, though.

"Alright, so we have everyone's statement but yours," Myers declared, and his partner nodded to me behind his partner. Despite the fact that I knew it wouldn't do any good, I started from the beginning.

22

Zeb...

"Right pain in the ass, that one," I murmured to Tiff as the two cops got into their patrol car to leave. She shivered and nodded slightly, staring after them.

"The young one wasn't so bad," she said with a heavy sigh. "The shiny 'defender of the world' hasn't quite worn off him yet."

"You alright?" I asked and she nodded, somber. She paused for a moment, pressed her lips together, and as soon as the patrol car turned out of the lot, shook her head.

"I fell apart. The second I knew he was there, I just... I froze. I couldn't do anything except hide and be afraid."

"You did good," I told her. "You did exactly what you were supposed to do, eh. You called me."

She rolled her beautiful eyes at me and let out a plume of her breath into the icy air saying, "I was already on the phone with you."

"Yeah, true, but you thought on your feet, hid, kept yourself safe. That's what we want you to do. Just be safe. You brought us, me and my bros, in to handle the rest."

"Yeah, well, it's up to the cops now," she said and her expression was as dispassionate as they got as she stared after where they'd been.

"Yeah, nah –" I'd been about to say the cops weren't going to do anything but my mobile rang. I pulled it, vibrating, out of my jacket pocket and answered it with, "Yeah, Bro, what's up?"

"Your lady friend's missing bestie… I think I've got her in my ER," Doc said by way of greeting and I felt my heart sink.

"How bad?" I asked, taking a few steps from Tiffany, which of course, tipped her off that something was wrong.

"If you're with her, I'd get her here five minutes ago. It's bad, Zeb. I don't know that she's going to make the night."

"Shit," I said low and with feeling. "We're on our way."

"Meet me at the ER main entrance. I'll be waiting."

"Right." I hung up and Tiffany narrowed her eyes at me.

"What's wrong?"

"We have to go," I told her and got on my bike, dropping my skid lid on my head. She didn't hesitate and got on behind me. I started it up and turned it 'round to head out of the lot before she even had her skid lid fastened beneath her chin.

"Nik, you're scaring me!" she cried as I drove like a hoon through town to get to Doc's hospital. She hung onto me for dear life, but I didn't think she would want to miss any time with her friend that she could have. I knew they were close and it broke my heart what I raced her toward. Still, I could never forgive myself if we didn't make it and a grim sort of resignation took hold.

I went flat tack down the main drag that'd been salted and it was scary even for me, but I had to get her there. Doc had sounded grim and he didn't sound that way for nothing unless it was something. Dire, yeah, that was a good word for it.

I pulled up in the ambulance bay and off onto the sidewalk in front of a bench, making my own parking. I shut off my motorbike and heeled down the stand for it, leaning it over. She jumped off, her chest heaving and stared at me with real fear in her deep, dark eyes.

"Why'd you bring me here?" she demanded and I felt my shoulders drop. I took a breath to tell her when the doors whooshed open and Doc strode out in his white lab coat and pressed Dockers. He turned his bald head in Tiffany's direction.

"I could get in a lot of trouble for this," he said going to her. "Anyone asks you, you're her emergency contact and that's how we called and got a hold of you. Her mother isn't answering her phone."

"I don't understand," she said hollowly, but she did. It was written all over her face that she knew exactly why we were here now. She just didn't want to know and I couldn't say I blamed her.

"You have her info?" Doc asked me.

"Yeah."

"Call Data so he can get to work and cover my ass. Come on, sweetheart, your friend is waiting and she's in really bad shape."

"Delia?" she asked and I could see the devastation in her eyes. Fuck me. I phoned Data but followed them up the hallway.

"Yeah, Zeb, I'm already in. Just give me her name, address, phone number."

"Right," I murmured and stood outside the hospital room door as Doc led her through.

Tiffany leaned over the bed, her shoulders hitching, a broken cry coming from her at the sight of her friend. Doc backed out and stood with me as I finished giving Data what he needed.

"Dragon there?" I asked.

"Nope, already here," he said from beside me and I said into the mobile, "Never mind."

"Later," Data said. "I gotta go to work."

I lowered the phone and shoved it into my pocket. Doc sighed.

"Beaten, raped, there's too much damage. Even if we got her into surgery it's a lost cause, but they're prepping now," he said low and soft so Tiff couldn't hear.

"Jesus Christ," Dragon muttered, tapping the filter of a cigarette on the web of his hand between index and thumb. "Couldn't find her so went after her friend," he muttered and sniffed.

I looked back into the room and relayed what had happened at the strip club.

"It's on, now," I said. "I'm going to kill him."

"We are going to kill him," Dragon corrected and I nodded, staring into the dimly lit hospital room at my girl, sobbing next to her dying friend.

23

Tiffany…

I stepped into the dimly lit hospital room; a fluorescent light, barely enough to cast a halo on the head of the bed, was lit, harsh, blue-white light falling on the still figure in it. Lia's face was so swollen and purple, it was grotesque. I couldn't even recognize her. I wouldn't have recognized her at all had it not been for her familiar wheat-blonde hair and the birthmark on her wrist.

I leaned down, shoulders shaking with sobs as I choked them down and tried not to wake her. Her eyes were so swollen, I couldn't believe she could see out of them but she did, she hadn't been sleeping at all. She turned her head in my direction, choking out my name pitifully, "Tiffany?"

"I'm here, Lia. I'm right here," I said and smoothed back some of her hair. She winced and coughed weakly.

"Silas," she rasped. "Cooper and Silas…"

"He came to the club, but its okay, I'm okay. He hit Zeke, but Alan hid me."

"You have to go, you have to run..." she made a choked, strangled noise and tears seeped from her eyes, slicking down her temples into her hair.

"Shh, don't try to talk, okay? You're in the hospital, they're going to take care of you, alright? I'm going to take care of you like you took care of me."

She shook her head back and forth and gasped, "Run, Tiffy. Get away. Go far away. Take my car, just go. Promise me you'll go!" She wept, her voice broken and pleading, the more I looked at her, the more bruises I was able to pick out on her fair skin.

I shook my head, "I'm not leaving you!" I cried, and stuffed my hand into my mouth to try and curb the broken sound that followed. She squeezed my other hand where I'd wrapped it around her fingers. She was gasping, having a hard time breathing and I looked back over my shoulder. The doctor who had brought me in here craned his neck in our direction and I turned back to Lia but she was still. So still.

"Lia?" I asked and when she didn't answer, I cried louder, "Lia!?"

The monitors began screaming, there was a shout out in the hallway, and the doctor had me by the shoulders, moving me out of his way. A nurse rushed in and shoved me out and two more people barreled into the room past me. I stumbled backward, the scene in front of me blurring and large hands grasped me by the arms, pulling me back against a hard chest.

"Lia!" I screamed and my knees gave way. I sank towards the floor, Nik trying to hold me up. They had her gown open, were charging paddles. The curtain whisked along its track cutting off my view.

A high pitched sound, just like in the movies and her prone silhouette bounced and shuddered. I screamed, long and loud and wordless my pain and my rage but I knew. I knew they wouldn't get her back.

I knew my best friend was gone.

I sat on my butt on the cold tile floor of the emergency department's floor and howled my rage and pain to the sterile ceiling tiles.

24

Z eb...

She was a right mess. Completely munted on her sorrow and I didn't blame her one bit. She sat on the floor in the middle of the bustling hallway and screamed and I just went to the floor with her, wrapped my arms and legs around her and held her. I let her have her total meltdown and waited for her to finish, more than a little brassed off at the whole situation.

She wept bitterly against me and I looked up at the ceiling, glancing at Dragon who stood near us to fend off anyone that might try to make us move or have something to say about my girl's apparently packing a sad in the middle of the hospital hallway. *Fuck them, anyhow.*

He put his mobile to his ear and said into it, "Yeah, Doll, get me Reaver on the line."

It was all I needed to hear. This would be taken care of, and my brothers and I would see it through, but right now my girl needed tending and that was something only *I* could do. It hit me then, that I had completely fallen in love with her. Not only that, I realized that I was it, now. The only other person she really had in this sad, lonely little life she led had just completely carked it.

Bugger all.

"Take my truck, take her home to get some of her shit, and take her to the club," Dragon ordered and handed me down a set of keys. I handed up my own in trade.

"Motorbike is by the front doors."

"Yeah, I saw it. Damn rat bike of yours," he frowned but gave me a wink.

"Ain't got to be flash, just has to run, eh."

"Get you gone, motherfucker. Take care of your woman."

"On it, boss." I got up and picked Tiffany up completely, one arm behind her back, the other beneath her knees. She let me, face buried in the side of my neck, arms around it, clinging to me tightly.

I went out and found Dragon's old truck, which was just as beat-up and sad-looking as my bike was, and unlocked the passenger door, opening her up. I tucked Tiffany in and pulled back, cupping her face with one hand.

"I don't know what to do from here," she said, her face red and tear-stained. I'd never seen her cry like this before. A few stray tears here and there, but this desperate and devastated weeping scared me a bit.

"You leave that to me, eh? She'll come right."

She visibly crumbled, everything about her expression screaming that she wanted to believe me but that she just couldn't right now. I can't say I blamed her for the notion, either.

"What do I do?" she cried, panic making her eyes go wide, her voice rising, and tears spilling. "What do I do?"

"Shhh, shhh," I leaned forward and pressed my lips to hers. She quieted, freezing and her eyes drifted shut. When I knew she had a bit more of a grip, I drew back and said, "You trust me, that's what you do."

She nodded and pressed her lips, biting them together. I gave her a nod and shut the door on her, quickly jogging around the bonnet and getting in on the other side. It felt wrong, still. Driving on the wrong side of the road I'd grown used to, but on the wrong side of a cage, I still had issues. I wasn't used to shifting with my right hand, still.

"Have to forgive me, I'm still not used to driving a cage in America," I told her, firing up the truck.

She huddled miserably on the seat and said, voice far away as she stared at the hospital through the windscreen, "I'll forgive you on account of being warm."

"Thanks," I said, and ground gears, working the unfamiliar pedals to get us out of there on our way out to the wops where she lived. It'd been too long since I'd driven a cage. It'd like to make me crazy.

I drove us in silence. To be honest, I didn't know what to say and she wasn't talking and that was okay. Sometimes words weren't needed. Sometimes you just needed to be there. When I wasn't shifting gears, she held my hand tight on the seat between us.

I didn't like driving the truck. I kept sliding and was so used to the motorbike that I didn't feel like I had the right amount of control on four wheels that I had on two. Funny that, eh?

I made the turn into Tiffany's lot and cut the engine, turning to look at her. I sighed and told her the truth.

"The rules of the game have changed, you get that, right?"

"Yeah, yeah it's kind of hard not to get it," she said back and looked so tired, so miserable, so completely wrung out and brittle, I was afraid my strong brave girl was going to give up on me.

"We're gonna take as much as we can, throw it in trash bags if we have to and right into the back of the truck."

"Okay," she agreed, nodding somberly. She had to know her place here was compromised for sure.

"Okay, come on, then."

I went around and took her hand and we went up the stairs. I stayed out in front and couldn't help but swear when we got to her door, "Aw, shit, no." He'd nailed her cat, fur slick and dark with blood, to her door, guts spilling out onto the ground.

I heard her gasp and I turned right around, pulling her into my chest, pressing her face into my shoulder as she shuddered and hushing her. "Shh, don't look," I said. "I'm so sorry, Wahine. Don't look."

She was trying so hard not to fly apart, she was being so brave, but this? I don't know how she did it. How she held it together.

"Let's just go inside!" she cried and I nodded.

"Gimme your keys." She fished them blindly out of her purse at her side and shoved them into my hand. I turned around and she hid against my back as I worked the locks and tried not to get anything on me. I opened the door and shoved her through, once I knew there was no one inside and followed her in, shutting the horror back out on the other side.

"Max?" she muttered in disbelief. Her damn cat stretched on the bed, kneading the covers with her paws and meowing quizzically. "Max!" she cried and I felt my muscles loosen.

"Thank fuck," I muttered and set about moving around her kitchen, looking for trash bags.

"Oh my God, thank you," she said, and held the displeased animal tightly to her, kissing her between her ears.

"You got something to carry her in?" I asked.

"Pillowcase if I have to," she said, tears leaking from her eyes.

"Clothes and essentials in here," I said. "I'll take care of out there."

"O-o-kay," she stammered and reluctantly put her cat down. Fuck, I can't say how happy I was to see that insane furball.

We made quick work of her place. I bagged the dead animal, a different stray from the neighborhood, I reckon, and threw it in her apartment's dumpster. We loaded her clothes, Mad Maxine, and her laptop and school books into trash bags, pillowcases, and a knapsack, as much as we could carry in one trip between the both of us.

One trash bag held the cat's food and dishes, another her litter box and such. It was heavy, but we managed it all in one go, which we needed to do. She set the hissing, growling, struggling cat between us on the flat seat of the truck and the rest went in the back.

"Where are we going? Your place?" she asked.

I shook my head and said, "Someplace safer," and headed for the clubhouse.

She was shaking, but not from the cold. She kept murmuring to the damn cat who wasn't having any of it, and it all just broke my damn heart.

25

Tiffany...

I bit my bottom lip when he pulled into the lot at the motorcycle club. I didn't want to be around a whole lot of people. It just wasn't what I needed right now. I felt some of my apprehension ease off when he pulled back, behind the main building, and followed a shoveled asphalt track around to a low, cinder-block outbuilding, beside a much larger, corrugated-steel one.

"Come on, get your stuff and Mad Max together, I have a room back here, no one will bother us."

"Thank you. I just don't think I can handle being around people right now," I said, hitching my purse strap back up on my shoulder and across my chest. I reached for the loop on top of my backpack and wrapped the top of the knotted pillowcase holding Max around my other hand.

"Don't worry about the rest," he said gently. "I'll bring it in, once I get you in there."

"Okay," I said and he got out of the truck, cold air rushing into the cab in his wake, the cat *not* pleased by any of it and growling menacingly, hissing and struggling in the bag. It was the safest way I had to transport her though, and I really really hoped she would forgive me for the rough and just generally shitty and stressful handling. Of course, she didn't know that I thought I had come home to her furry little ass nailed to my door. Just thinking about that made me want to fall apart. The fact she was alive and hissing, god, I was so grateful. So, so, grateful.

She could be mad at me all she wanted. She was alive. We were both alive and someplace safe... but Delia?

Poor Delia...

My door opened and I jumped, a little yelp making it out of my mouth, which Max answered with a hiss and another low, angry growl. She was pissed and I needed to get her out of this damn pillowcase. I was lucky she hadn't pissed everywhere, which is what she had done last time, when she'd come home bitten by something, and Delia and I had raced her to the vet.

A five-hundred-dollar vet bill I couldn't really afford later, she'd been cleaned up, stitched up, and was in one of those cones of shame so she didn't try to lick her wounds. Pilling her had been an absolute joy and it had taken both me and Lia to do it.

What was I going to do without her?

"Hey, come here, hey, hey, hey..." Nik pulled me out of the truck into the snow at the side of the track thing we were on and held me tight, letting me cry into the cool leather encasing his chest.

"Just a little bit longer," he begged. "Just hold it together for Mad Max in there, and then you can scream and cry and do whatever it is you need to do to feel better, eh?"

I nodded. I could do that. I really could. Just a few more feet and we could be inside and Max could be warm. I followed him into one end of the building into a hallway that ran the length to another door at the opposite end like the one we'd just entered. The hall was lined on both sides with doors, and Nik touched the first one on the right.

"Bathroom and toilet here, same at the other end, opposite side of the hall. My room is down here."

I nodded my understanding and followed him almost to the other end of the hall, the last door before the exit on the left-hand side. He hung his head and sighed.

"Bugger all, I gave Dragon my keys." I felt my shoulders drop and he brought out his phone, dialing someone up.

"Yeah, Bro, its Zeb. I'm here and I have a guest, but I gave Dragon my keys, have ya got a spare?" He paused while someone said something on the other end of the line. "That'd be great, thanks. He ended the call and said, "Mali'll be right out with the key. In the meantime, I'll bring more of your stuff in, yeah?"

"Okay," I agreed.

He gave me a nod and went to turn but stopped, took a half-step closer to me and leaned over, pressing his lips to my forehead. I closed my eyes and let the comfort the small gesture was meant to give me wash over me. Too soon, he was gone, striding up the hallway, the logo on the back of his vest over his leather jacket larger than life. I took a deep breath and let it out slowly, closing my eyes and counting the seconds. All the way to sixty and then over again. Just something to do, something small to focus on while I held onto the pillowcase with Maxine in it. She'd gone still and had stopped fighting but her frightened and confused cries had taken over now, and they were a knife to my heart, every single one of them.

The door at the end opened, and my eyes flew open. Nik strode up the hall laden with trash bags full of my shit. He was alone, a set of keys dangling from one hand. He set bags down at my feet and went through three keys before he got the right one.

The door swung in on a dark room. He reached past it and flicked on a light switch on the wall; golden lamplight flooded the space and spilled across the low, industrial-business carpet in the hall.

"After you," he said gently and I went in, blinking in surprise.

It was furnished in here. Furnished far more than his apartment over the bar and gym was.

Bookshelves lined one wall completely, floor to ceiling, all handmade and beautiful. The foot of the bed, beside the closet door, held a dresser of the same wood but the bed is what caught my attention.

It was an actual bed, not just a mattress on the floor. With a hand-carved headboard and footboard that begged to be touched. I wanted to inspect it more thoroughly but I had Max to attend to.

"Is that everything?" I asked about the bags he was picking up, bringing across the threshold, and dropping inside the room.

"Yeah," he said gently.

I nodded and said, "Thank you. I'm going to let her out now if that's okay?"

He closed his bedroom door and said, "No worries, have at it."

I dropped onto the edge of the bed and picked the loose knot out of the top of the pillowcase with my fingers. Max shot out, slinking low to the ground. She sniffed the air, looked left, then right, and immediately did an about-face and shot under the bed. I hung my head and sighed.

"She's going to be under there a while."

"Gives us time to set up her things and put yours away, eh?"

"I guess I'm going to be staying a while?"

"We," he corrected. "We are going to be staying a while, yeah. I wouldn't leave you here alone."

"Thank you," I said again, softly, and he shrugged out of his jacket and vest, hanging it on a hook on the back of the door. He held out his hands to me and I pulled my purse over my head. He took that, and hung it beside his jacket and reached back just in time for me to hand him my jacket. I smoothed my suddenly-damp palms over the denim encasing my hips and ass and asked, "What now?"

"Now we put this stuff away, get Mad Max set up, and then it's whatever you want to do."

"Trying to keep me busy?" I asked.

"The only idea I've got right now and it needs to get done. I know I always seem to think better when things are in order."

I nodded. "Yeah, me too."

He smiled at me and said, "Not trying to be a cheeky bastard, but I know."

I felt like I suddenly had a liquid center. That was so incredibly sweet of him, taking care of me like that, especially at a time like this. I moved around the room, setting up Max's food and water dishes, using a bottle of water he handed me out of the mini-fridge he used as a nightstand. The only things in it seemed to be bottled water and some beers. I didn't want either, even though he offered.

I stood up from filling the little water bowl and he took the empty bottle from me and threw it in the bag of trash he'd collected.

"I'm going to run this out, make yourself at home."

I nodded and hugged myself, going to the bookcases and letting my eyes rove across the spines as he ducked out, shutting the door behind him. I wanted to check on Max, but I resisted the urge. She was stressed out and pissed off and just needed the time to chill.

I didn't read a single spine, nothing that went in through my eyes and into my brain really wanted to compute. I didn't know what to do with any of this. I didn't want to feel anything anymore. Everything was just open, raw and aching. It was wholly awful and I just wanted it to all go away. I wanted to drown myself in something, anything to make it all just go away for a little while.

Nik came back in and I went to him. He didn't even ask, he just put his arms around me and I kissed him, pouring my absolute desperation to concentrate on something, anything but how I should be feeling.

He kissed me back and I bit his lower lip, he jerked at the unexpected and exclaimed "Ow! What was that for, eh?"

"I'm sorry, just… I don't want to feel any of this, you know? All I want right now is to feel you and I really don't want you to be all that nice about it… if you know what I mean?"

He lowered his hand from his bottom lip and gave me a half charmed little smile.

"You want some rough sex, eh?"

I nodded. I liked it rough sometimes and this was definitely one of those times. When everything was all screwed up and turned inside out, that was the perfect time. Just something about being pounded into the damn sheets grounded me, but I'd never really had to ask for it before. I figured the love bite would have been enough but if it was one thing I was learning from a lot of my psych classes, it was the importance of communication and asking for what you needed.

I couldn't tell you how grateful I was that Nik made it easy; to ask, I mean. He didn't judge me. I mean, he had at first, but he'd apologized, we'd talked and things were actually better. It was how I'd always thought a relationship was supposed to work, but up until this point, mine never had.

"You don't have to ask for that," he said softly, hands alighting on my hips, pulling me in.

I put my hands on his shoulders and whispered back, "Clearly, I did," boldly adding, "Now, shut up and fuck me."

He grinned, and it was a happy but savage thing, his mouth crashing down on mine. I wrapped my arms around his neck and bowed my body into the shelter of his and just tried like hell to let all of it, everything around me, just fall away.

26

Z eb...

Her kiss was desperate, but for what I couldn't tell. It wasn't usually like me to hurt a woman, even if she asked for it, even in this context. I was a lover, a man, and not an animal, but I understood exactly what she wanted. I was angry enough, over what was happening to her and what had happened to her friend, that I knew exactly what she meant. With no place else for it to go, I was happy to give her what she seemed to so desperately crave. *Rough sex it is.* I thought to myself, but first things first, I had to get her out of her clothes.

I pulled her shirt over her head and frustratingly, found another layer. I worked my way through them as fast as I could and unhooked and took her flash bra from her.

She had the most glorious pair of natural tits and I wasted no time in palming one, massaging it with a grip a little tighter than necessary while I took the other's nipple into my mouth. She arched, pressing her breast more firmly against my teeth and into my palm and struggled to shove my flannel off my shoulders.

I wasn't as concerned about getting naked myself right this minute as I was about getting her undressed. I wanted her nude and laid out underneath me and I wanted her there now.

I kissed down her body, her fingers winding in my hair, clutching it, which pulled on it giving just that slightest edge of *ow,* which unleashed the beast a bit. I peeled her jeans down her legs and met with the g-string she'd had on at the strip club. I decided I much preferred her cotton hip hugging panties instead. They were more her and I didn't care if I ever saw these fucking things again, so I took them in both hands and snapped them.

Her body jerked and she cried out a little bit, a passionate throaty sound that said she liked everything I was doing but wanted so much more. I gave it to her, cupping her sweet pussy in my hand and massaging her lips, finding her wet with my fingertips and plunging two of them up inside her. Her hands fell away from my hair and just dropped to her sides. I rolled my eyes up to look at her as I kissed her stomach and locked an arm behind her back to keep her from falling.

Her eyes were dark and heavy-lidded with passion and a power she usually didn't robe herself in. A sureness about herself that she usually didn't quite have all the way there. She really had stopped giving a shit. She really wanted this and wasn't going to beat herself up for asking for it, and god it was hot and I was about to give her everything she asked for and then some.

I thrust my middle and ring finger deep inside her hot wetness and teased at her walls. She threw back her head, hissing between her teeth, her voice goddess-like as she said; *"God yes!"*

"You like that, eh?"

"Mm, yes, more," she said with surety.

I stood up, but left my hand against and inside her body, backing her up to the bed and shoving her down on it. I went to my knees between hers and wrapped my arms around her thighs, just above her knees and yanked her across the covers so her ass was at the very edge of the mattress. She had no idea how beautiful she looked with her hair spilled across the deep blue and green bedspread, her hands trailing down her body.

I returned my fingers to her pussy and sealed my mouth over her clit and did everything I was supposed to just to make her fucking come. I wanted to. I wanted to make her come so hard and so many times she forgot her own name, because that was what she had asked for. To forget for a little while. To leave the emotional pain behind by focusing on shit that was purely physical for a while.

She gripped the bedcover with both fists at her hips, her breaths coming in deep, panting gasps while I forced the orgasm out of her. I wanted her to come at least twice before I got my dick involved and oh man, how I wanted to get my dick involved. It was straining at my jeans, pressed so hot and tight to the inside of them and so full and hard it fucking hurt so damn good.

I licked and sucked on her and she tasted fresh and so clean. I don't think I was going to ever get enough of eating her pussy. It also didn't seem like it took any effort at all for me to coax that first orgasm out of her, either. Before I knew it, she was bucking and crying out, and it took me using my free arm to bar across her hips to hold her to the bed. Sensitive or not, I didn't let up, either. Not until she begged me to stop, at which point I sat up amused.

"Just give me a minute," she said between panting breaths and she just laid there, spent. I took the time to get my clothes off a piece at a time, my eyes never leaving hers. She watched me, the fire of her desire stoked and burning, naked in her expression as she watched me strip, piece by piece, layer by layer.

"Fuck, that has to be the hottest thing I've ever seen," she breathed.

"Yeah? You ain't seen nothing yet."

She smiled and it held a wicked glint of laughter even though no laugh came. I didn't know what made me say that, but I buried it pretty quickly – made her forget all about it – when I buried myself in her slick, wet heat, going balls deep in one thrust. She cried out and writhed on the end of my cock and I didn't give her time to adjust any. Instead, I set a punishing cadence, pushing into her hard enough our bodies met with a crack and not letting up until I felt a need for a change in position.

"On your knees," I demanded, pulling from her and giving her a light slap on the outside of her thigh. She rolled onto her stomach lazily and I grabbed her by the hips, pulling her back and up onto her knees when she didn't move fast enough.

I was a man possessed and the only cure was getting back inside of her. She reached out her arms, arching low like her cat, pushing her hips back to meet me stroke for stroke and I couldn't get enough. I just would never be able to get enough, but that wouldn't stop me from trying.

27

T iffany…

Oh, my God, I couldn't get enough. I would never be able to get enough. I arched low to the bed as he grabbed my hips and slammed himself into me, against my body, his cock going impossibly deep and it hurt so good.

I practically yowled like a cat in heat as that heavy, tight sensation started in my pussy, somewhere around where his cock slammed into my cervix. I know most women couldn't stand it, couldn't take it, but when I was in the right mood, like now, I fucking loved it.

"Harder, oh god, please! Right there, oh, right there!" I don't really know how I formed the words, or that I was even saying them, but I could hear them and it was my voice so I must have been.

"You like that?" he asked. "You want it like that?"

"Yes!" I cried and it was as much in answer to his queries as it was an exclamation over the orgasm rippling out from my center. It was probably the most extraordinary sensation I had ever experienced. It was as if the stars had fallen from the heavens and taken up residence in my center, nestling there for just a moment before exploding out along every nerve ending, lighting me up from the inside out, trapped by my skin and stuck, leaving me glowing far past the final wave of beautiful devastation.

He'd parted the red sea of emotional pain for me, just like I'd asked, but as with all things, what goes up must come down and I crashed hard. I couldn't hold it in anymore. Like at all. He leaned over me, gathering me close as I dissolved into raging, wracking sobs.

So what a man wants from a woman while he had yet to go soft inside her, I thought harshly.

"It's okay, I've got you," he murmured and it was exactly what I needed from him when I needed it. I still didn't understand how he did that so well.

He moved from between my legs and lay beside me, pulling me into him, holding me tight while the storm of emotion swept over and through me. I held onto him, and, it was like I clung, not to a man of flesh and bone, but to my very last shred of sanity in the incredibly cruel and twisted drama that my life had become.

I wept until I had absolutely nothing left and he was so patient and so kind, smoothing my hair out of my tears, kissing my forehead, my eyelids, and even the tip of my nose.

"I know it's bad, eh, but I'm not going anywhere," he promised and I realized I was all cried out. I felt my body ease from its stiff posture and he smiled sadly at me and I could read from his expression that he was absolutely miserable for me. That he genuinely lived in my misery right along with me and it was both a comfort and the most distressing thing because I didn't want him to hurt. Not because of me.

"Never because of you," he said and I realized I had said what I'd been thinking out loud. "You make me the happiest I've been in a long time, Wahine."

"I don't understand that," I said, honestly.

"You don't have to understand it, just believe it," he told me and I sniffed. He thumbed some stray tears out from underneath my eyes and smiled saying, "Let's get cleaned up."

"Okay," I murmured. He got up and handed me one of his tees, pulling on a pair of loose shorts. He pulled a couple of towels from the top of the closet and his hair from its loose ponytail, tossing the hair tie on top of the dresser. I hugged myself and he held out a hand to me. I reached out and twined my fingers with his, and stopped for a moment, just staring at our hands.

"What is it?" he asked and I looked up at him, just so overwhelmed by how much I felt for him but now, of all times, was so not the time to say it.

"Nothing," I lied, and he drew me to him.

"Won't make you tell me," he said softly, "But you should know you don't ever have to be afraid to tell me anything."

"I know that," I said quickly, my pulse suddenly quickening in the side of my throat.

"No judgments here," he whispered and I swallowed hard.

"I know that, too," I murmured. He nodded and pressed lips to my forehead and led me across the hall to the bathroom.

It was a locker room, sort of, in here. Tile floors with a bank of three showers, a urinal, and two toilet stalls. A bank of two sinks was right as you walked in, and there was a low bench just outside the shower bay.

"Reminds me of this swimming pool I used to go to when I was a kid. The mom thought it was a good idea all of us kids learned to swim and the lessons were free for kids like me. I liked it there." I closed my eyes and breathed deep, but the smell of chlorine was absent from the room, though the smell of clean was there. Of cleanser and disinfectant, also of new, like this place had barely been used and like it wasn't that old. Not freshly built, the scent of new caulking and sealant was too faint for that.

His hands lightly fell on my shoulders and I jumped, my eyes flicking open to his strong, tattooed face that was somber with an emotion I couldn't readily define.

"What?" I asked.

"Just you," he said back.

"That doesn't tell me anything."

"You're so beautiful to me. Just so sad at the same time. Even before this."

"I'm happiest when I'm with you," I said, and it was true. It was just hard to find any bit of light right now.

"I see that too," he said.

I sniffed and he pulled me close and simply held me for a time.

"Will you read to me before bed?" I asked.

"I'll do whatever you want."

"You sure about that?" I asked and I meant it to sound teasing, but I don't know that it came out that way. He went to his knees, carefully, hands slipping up the hem of his tee to rest along the top of my thighs, just under my ass.

"What are you doing?"

"Well, I figure if I were going to get you to look at me, I needed to come down here."

I blinked and frowned slightly. "I don't understand."

"The floor, Girl. You're always looking at the floor."

"I am?"

"Yeah."

"I hadn't realized," I said and he got back to his feet. He smiled faintly, his fingertips traveling around my legs and up my hips, dragging the tee with it as he stood. I raised my arms and let him drag the soft material over my head. He dropped it, lying beside the towels on the bench.

I was suddenly fascinated, completely mesmerized by his movements as he slipped out of his shorts and went into the shower, turning it on, getting the water warm before reaching out to me. I went to him and he drew me under the spray, tipping my head back and letting my hair soak, the water from the shower-head sluicing it back from my face.

"You're an extraordinary woman," he whispered and I stepped closer to him and pressed my lips to his. I loved that he said these things to me, out of the blue, but at the same time, for reasons I couldn't understand, they embarrassed me and so I kissed him to silence him and his compliments. The only way I knew how to tell him I loved them, but also, that I was uncomfortable hearing them.

He washed me. Carefully, mindful that I might be, and actually was, sore. Of course, it was that delicious kind of soreness that only a really good fuck could provide.

"Just lean against me," he murmured as he washed my hair and I did. Holding him around his waist carefully.

I felt so disconnected from everything. Wrung out and exhausted, but not tired. It was confusing. I couldn't really hold onto a single thought in my head and I didn't know what was wrong with me. So I let him take care of me. I let him do everything and stood in my zombie-like state and fell ever more hopelessly in love with him, which was terrifying to me now.

I mean, what if Silas found out? He would hurt Nik, possibly even kill him, just to hurt me.

I found myself fetched up hard against his chest and trembling, my lips pressed to his shoulder as he held me and soothed me. I hated this. I hated what I'd become, this trembling, anxiety-riddled thing.

Things blurred and the next I knew he was drying me off, but I couldn't remember him turning off the shower. Then we were cuddled in his bed, but I don't remember walking back across the hall.

"You're exhausted," he said. "Just sleep," but I couldn't, not really.

He read to me and I don't know what it was he read from one of his many books off one of his many shelves, but that didn't matter so much. What mattered was I was safe, I felt loved, and I was carefully cradled against his chest as his rich, melodic, accented voice lulled me word by word, minute by minute until I saw, felt, and heard nothing, claimed by sleep.

28

Z eb...

A soft knock at my door, but damn it, Tiff had just fallen asleep not long before. I didn't want to move her so I called out, "Yeah!" and hoped that it wouldn't wake her.

Dragon opened the door and stepped in, swinging it shut behind him and putting his back up against a jutting corner of the wall. He pressed back into it, wincing, and I couldn't tell if he was stretching or scratching his back like a bear against a tree.

"I hate your bike," he said, and I laughed a little, cutting it off and checking on my girl but she was out.

"Keys to your cage are on the dresser, same with the spares for all the club rooms."

"Ah, shit, got locked out huh?"

"Yeah, Data and Mali to the rescue."

Dragon nodded and swapped out the rings of keys.

"Boys are out there, lookin'. I don't reckon it's going to take long to find one or the other of 'em."

"Find one, you find 'em both," I agreed.

"No women, no children," he said softly, and his dark eyes roved over her still form draped over my chest. I felt a spike of jealousy. Knowing that he and she had… Well, it wasn't easy for me, and despite understanding with your head, sometimes your feelings on the matter had other ideas.

"Didn't mean nothin', you know?" he asked and I blinked. I guess my feelings, unlike my thoughts, were being broadcast on my face.

"Ah, nah, yeah, I know that, Bro."

"You better, because I don't think I've ever seen her half so peaceful as she looks right now."

"She's had it rough," I agreed.

"Just keeps on truckin' though, don't she?"

"Starting to realize you might be right, boss."

"Oh yeah? How's that?"

"Strength comes in a lot of different forms, power ain't always about how many blokes you got doing what you say."

"So you were listening, then?" he said with a grin.

I nodded. "May seem a bit thick, eh?" I looked down at the crown of her head, her tangled, glossy dark hair and sighed. "I may be a bit thick yet."

"Nah, I think you're doing fine. Feelings are natural, but you do have to decide. It ain't easy, and life don't come with an instruction manual. The system is a lie, but figuring out your own way ain't easy, either. I think she's learning that just as much as you, huh?"

"Yeah, too right."

"Get some sleep, keep your phone charged. We'll call you with any developments," he said and pushed up off the wall.

I nodded and he went out, shutting the door behind him. I thought about a lot of things before I tried to join her in some good sleep.

When I'd come here, it'd been in a bit of a state of disgrace, personally. It was kind of amazing that Dragon had even taken me on. He'd looked at me point blank and had told me that I couldn't bullshit a bullshitter and to not even try. I'd just come from my granddad's funeral; it was even a miracle my sister had even bargained that for me, my being able to go home to pay my respects.

With Tiffany laying on me now, I didn't even want to think about what my sister had traded up to make it possible.

I don't know what had made me do it, sitting across from Dragon then, but I had come clean. Told him everything about betraying my own gang in a bid to get ahead back in New Zealand. About how I'd come by the Sacred Hearts colors less than honest with my previous chapter and how I was as low as I could go and lookin' for a change.

He should have put me out bad with the club right then and there, but he hadn't. He'd looked me over impassively and had told me every man deserved a second chance in life. That once upon a time he hadn't believed that. That it had always been one and done, but then someone had given him one. One he hadn't deserved, and that not only that but given him more chances after that.

He'd told me he hadn't deserved a one of them, that he'd taken them for granted until he was granted one last final chance but at a terrible cost.

"I'm giving you a chance," he'd said, leaning back in his chair. *"A last chance, because Brother, I do believe you earned your colors with this club despite your having a past. Hell, we* all *got a past; and the way you're spillin' your guts now tells me one of two things – either you're ready for a change, a* real *change or you're fucking suicidal. Either*

one of which means you're ready for something *and this situation right here with the Suicide Kings is gonna give you exactly what you want. It just may be fate which decides for you."*

It'd sounded good, it'd sounded really good, and I'd taken it. I didn't think it was a mistake, him choosing me to relocate that woman Darlene with her sick kid across the country. Dragon was a firm believer in lessons but didn't fancy himself a teacher. He didn't have to, life was there to do it for him. It wasn't a coincidence he chose me to help this betrayer and the circumstances of her betrayal had been heartbreaking, for sure.

Maybe that was why I took Tiffany's line of side work so well. I understood that every man and woman had a story to tell. I also understood that not everything was black and white. The world was full of living color for a reason. There was no sense in dulling it down just to make sense of it. Life was meant to be lived in a riot of sight and sound and feeling.

I set aside the book I'd been reading on top of my mini-fridge and reached up, turning out the lamp I had sitting on top. The room was plunged into darkness and still Tiffany didn't stir, even with all the moving around I did. I smoothed a hand up and down her nude back and closed my eyes, smiling when I felt Mad Max jump up onto the bed.

I woke when Tiffany finally stirred. She pushed up off of me and groaned, dragging her fingers, or trying to, through her tangled hair.

"There's no fixing this," she griped. "I need to start over."

"You know where the bathroom is, yeah?"

"Yeah," she said and sat up completely, stretching luxuriously. I watched her as Max padded across the covers at her.

"Oh, hey, baby girl," Tiff crooned at her and picked her up, snuggling her to her chest.

"She came out last night after you fell asleep," I said, pushing myself up and leaning back against the headboard behind me.

"I still don't understand all this," she said, looking around.

I smiled and shrugged a bit. It had made sense at the time for me but now it seemed silly. I stayed quiet but the truth of it was when you were running around up to all sorts of illegal things, stuck between law enforcement and a rival MC trying to kill you off, you wanted to be comfortable. While the club was on lockdown and all of us were here, I made my surroundings as comfortable as possible. Kept all my favorite things here, the things that reminded me of home.

After, when Rush was looking for new projects to complete, I'd helped him with the bed frame, drawing from everything I missed most about home. I'd figured he could sell it or whatever, but he'd given it to me. Then, I'd felt isolated, homesick, and so I'd kept everything here safe, but had relocated myself closer to my work at the bar. Distancing myself from the memories this room contained.

"Well," she said when I didn't offer up explanation straight away, "I'm going to go get in the shower."

"You hungry?" I asked.

"Yes and no," she said.

"Now I know how that feels," I said with a bit of a grin and though she didn't laugh, she at least cracked a bit of a smile.

"The thought of food is nauseating but my stomach is growling."

"Ah, fair enough."

"I guess I could eat," she said, and it was in a relenting tone of voice.

"I could get us some Makka's," I suggested and her eyes crossed.

"Some what?"

"Sorry, it's what we call McDonald's back home."

"I have no idea how you got that out of Micky D's."

I smiled and Max struggled to get out of Tiff's hold like, *okay mom, enough of this,* so Tiff let her go. She came over to me and got in my lap.

"Yeah, you can stay there," I told her. "But I'm not falling for it for one minute." She looked up at me with golden-green eyes and blinked and I swear it was a trap.

Tiff smiled and said, "I think she's starting to like you."

"Yeah until she hooks teeth and claws into me."

"So melodramatic," she scoffed but she was smiling again, her old smile that held nothing but sadness to it.

I sighed on the inside. She'd come so far and I didn't want to see her go back there. She petted Max one last time where she rested in my lap, dangerously close to my dick, and I hoped that the blankets and sheets between me and the cat would be enough to protect me from her claws if she decided to live up to her name and flip her shit.

"I'll be back," Tiff said, rising and collecting the shirt I'd lent her from the floor.

"Towels are in the top of the closet."

"Okay."

I looked down at Max who looked back at me and I twitched a bit saying, "Go on now, let me get up."

She dropped her chin onto her paws and closed her eyes and I swore softly. I nudged her with my hand and she got up and jumped down. I can't tell you the sigh of relief. I got dressed while Tiff showered again. I didn't really think about it. I just made the bed and laid out some of her warmer clothes that I knew she liked to wear.

When she darted back in, it was with one of those towel turban's on her head, wrapped in another one.

"Oh, wow, thanks," she said, taken aback.

"Just trying to make things easier."

"It was very thoughtful of you," she murmured.

"Come sit," I urged and she drifted over, sitting on the end of the bed. I tossed her head towel into the top of the laundry hamper in the closet and took up her hairbrush off the dresser top.

I knelt up behind her and carefully started to brush her hair. She closed her eyes and bowed her head slightly and let me do it. I was taking a bit of a chance, I reckon. I mean, my granddad used to brush my grandmother's hair. I never understood it, but I remembered it, and I figured it was worth a try.

I took my time with it and she lost some of the rigidity to how she held herself, muscles relaxing the longer I did it. Her hair had started wet, and even though neither of us used a hair dryer on it, by the time I finished brushing her hair, it was barely damp and nearly dry. She sighed and held still for a full minute once I stopped and murmured a quiet thank you.

"Of course," I murmured back and she looked up at me.

"I'll get dressed."

"Sounds good."

It was awful of me I'll admit, but watching her put her clothes on made me just want to take them back off and love her slow.

"Are there going to be people?" she asked softly, as we walked hand in hand along the shoveled and salted track around to the back of the main clubhouse.

"Probably, I reckon."

"Okay." She steeled herself and I held open the back door.

"Even if there are, you're safe here with us. All of us."

"Yeah, I know," she said, "I'm just worried you all aren't safe with me."

29

T iffany...

Nik paused with the door half open and then shut it firmly. He turned and took me by the arms and drew me a little closer. The look on his face was indescribable and totally terrifying but I knew so completely that I had nothing to fear from him.

"Listen to me," he said. "You are safe, everyone in this club is safe, but your ex-man? His buddy? Not so much when we find them."

"You mean if you find them," I said, because I didn't really believe that they would. Silas was slicker than owl shit. Nik shook his head, once left, once right and the look on his face was stone-cold.

"There is no *if* in this scenario, Wahine. It's *when*, and when we do, he's going to have a really bad day."

I sighed and stared off over the freshly fallen snow, so calm and so serene. "I'll believe it when I see it," I said. "I just don't want to go through believing I'm going to be okay when it comes to Silas, only to have it yanked out from under me again."

"That's fair enough," he said softly and sighed himself.

He knew how much and how many times I'd been let down before. We'd talked about it. I hated that I was so damaged, and while I trusted him and he knew I trusted him, there were still just some things I couldn't trust anything about anymore. Silas was a big one of those things. So was law enforcement and the system that had failed me time and time again.

"Come on," he said and reached out, hauling open the door.

I was enveloped in warmth as I went through the door, and he stepped in quickly behind me, shutting it firmly. We wound our way through a dim hall into a wide spot with open doorways leading into bathrooms, but not like the locker-style ones we'd used in the outbuilding. The one or two I could see were more like something in a home.

The other doors, I had to guess, belonged to more bedrooms, except for one large set of double doors. They seemed to lead into some sort of media room with a large couch and recliners in front of a TV bigger than I had ever seen before.

I followed Nik through an open archway and into the more familiar barroom I'd first entered this place through. A few women were sitting around a table, coffee cups steaming in front of them.

"Hey, Zeb." A small woman with dark hair that was in the in-between phase of short and growing it out long smiled at us, her expression as warm as the coffee cup she held steaming between her hands.

Another woman, equally small but more delicate, with long auburn hair, turned around in her seat. She had some expensive-ass contacts in that turned her eyes a bright gold and she looked me over with such an expression of sympathy I shifted on my feet.

"Hayden," Nik nodded to the first woman. "Ashton," he greeted the second. "This is Tiffany." He put his hand on my lower back and gave me a light shove forward. "Tiffany, Hayden is Reaver's woman and Ashton is Trigger's."

"Oh, thanks for letting me borrow your guys," I said and kicked myself immediately for how it came out. "You know, for teaching me self-defense. Sorry, that came out real bad, probably the last thing you want to hear out of a stripper where both of your significant others are concerned."

They both laughed a little and Hayden stared down into her coffee cup, a charmed smile playing on her lips. Ashton stood up and pulled out a chair at the table saying, "Please, come sit with us. I'll get you both some coffee from the kitchen."

"I've got it," Hayden said, standing. "I think you and Tiffany have far more in common and you two should talk."

I took a halting step forward and froze at Hayden's words, asking, "What's that supposed to mean?"

"Please, sit and I'll tell you," Ashton said, smiling.

Nik's hand returned to my lower back beneath my jacket, a warm and heavy comforting presence. He wanted me to sit and I trusted him, but still, I was apprehensive.

"Okay," I said carefully, drawing out the word.

"Boy, we're batting a thousand already," Hayden remarked with humor, her tone light, and made her way behind the bar.

"Sorry, but word has gotten around about your situation with your ex." Ashton put her hand on mine where I rested it on the table and I stiffened. "I'm so sorry to hear about your friend," she said softly and it hit me right in the feels. I averted my eyes and stared at a random point in the room until I was sure I wouldn't cry.

"Me, too," I murmured, choked.

"My ex-husband was a real piece of work," she said and I turned back. "The club fixed the problem for me. They will for you, too."

"You sound awfully sure about that."

"Reeeeally not their first rodeo," Hayden said setting a tray with two coffees, cream, and sugar on the table. I flinched, and she froze, asking, "Shit. What'd I say?"

"He's some sort of rodeo cowboy, her ex," Nik explained. Hayden visibly cringed.

"Like I said, batting a thousand."

"It's okay," I said after clearing my throat. I doctored my coffee after Nik told me to go ahead and go first.

"I'm not really good at being social," I confessed.

"It's okay, we don't have to talk about any of it," Ashton said gently.

"Seriously," Hayden agreed.

I licked my lips and stared into my coffee for a minute, not really sure what to say or even what to talk about. I was so used to not letting people into my life, so used to hiding behind my walls. It wasn't necessarily because I thought that everyone I met was going to hurt me, though, if I were being honest with myself, that was definitely part of it. I think it was more that after so long, I pretty much felt like I was a waste of everyone's time and pretty unworthy of being loved... until Nik.

I looked over at him, pleading with my eyes for him to start the discussion and save me from this situation, too, and he smiled at me.

"Ashton works the front desk at Trigger's tattoo place and Hayden is an interior decorator," he said, and I figured line of work, as long as it wasn't my own we were talking about, was safe enough.

"Stripper sounds way more fun," Hayden said dryly and I shook my head.

"Dealing with a bunch of crabby grabby entitled assholes is not my idea of fun times," I said. "The money is pretty good, though, and it keeps me in pretty good shape. That's how I got into it in the first place. As a means of exercise."

"You pretty much described every single one of my interior decorating clients. Even the grabby part, just usually not me."

"Get some real gems through the shop, too," Ashton agreed.

"People suck," Hayden observed dryly and Ashton laughed.

"People do suck," I sighed heavily.

"There are still some good ones, I reckon," Nik said and we three looked at him. "Sitting with three of the best, right now."

"Oh, please!" Hayden laughed. Ashton blushed and I felt myself smile, I couldn't help it.

"Flirting game is strong with this one," I observed.

"It's strong with all of these guys," Hayden said. Ashton kept watching me, and I tried not to get uncomfortable under the scrutiny.

"The rest of the club should be getting up soon," she said softly.

"Yeah," Hayden nodded then observed, "You guys are up awfully early for living the vampire life."

"Sleep is all screwed up," I said bitterly.

"We called it an early night."

"I bet," Ashton said. "Emotional exhaustion is just as exhausting as any other kind."

I nodded. I couldn't disagree with her there.

"Want to come in the kitchen?" Ashton asked. "We can still talk while I cook."

"Yep, Ashton is head kitchen witch around here and she will conscript you. None of us mind, though. We have a blast in that kitchen." Hayden stood up with her coffee in her hand and I nodded. Food was sounding better by the minute and there was absolutely nothing appetizing to me about McDonald's.

I looked at Nik and nodded and he smiled encouragingly and gave a nod back. Still, I wasn't ready for the training wheels of his presence to come off, so when I got up to follow the women, I reached down and clutched two of his fingers with my hand, dragging him along with me. He, of course, followed. He was so damn patient and good with me like that.

In the kitchen, a big modern stainless steel monstrosity, Ashton pulled an apron off the hook and lifted it over her head, trapping her hair as she tied it around her slender waist. Hayden tossed me another one, a red one with black polka dots on it with ruffled edges.

I put it on, even though it was just a little bit ridiculous. I couldn't argue that it was still kind of retro-cool in that rockabilly sort of way that was popular with a lot of the biker club women.

Ashton asked me, "You know how to make biscuits from scratch?" I shook my head and she smiled. "Well then, come over here, and I'll teach you."

And that, ladies and gentlemen, is how I learned to make authentic, southern-style biscuits and gravy.

Hayden had been right, the kitchen was the central hub for a lot of the women. She and Ashton may have gotten things started, but eventually, other women from the club began to drift in and it would seem that all of them were here. The entire club.

It started with Hayley from the diner and another woman, slender with long dark hair and vivid blue eyes named Dani. Then came Everett and

Mandy. Everett introduced herself as Dray, the vice president's ol' lady and I didn't have the heart to really tell her that I knew who Dray was. He was, after all, Dragon's son. Not to mention, all of the men of the club, at one time or another, had come through Sugars. Usually as a big group, but not always. Sometimes they came in two's or three's together and every once in a while, some of them came alone, like Dragon did for the most part.

After Everett and Mandy came a man named Aaron, who was apparently considered one of the women, which confused me until one of the brothers, a tall, slender man full of vivid tattoos, walked in and kissed Aaron like he wanted to eat him from the mouth down. It was unbelievably hot, and I think I stopped and stared a little too hard because a lot of the women watched me nervously for a reaction. I sighed; we were in the Bible belt, after all.

I didn't want or need them thinking I was one of the narrow-minded cum buckets I was sometimes forced to work with so I told the truth, "Do that again, I'm going to need some alone time," I said. Smiles broke out and the tension drained out of the room like water from a bathtub.

After Aaron came a platinum blonde named Shelly with a kid on her hip, smiling at me in a way that said she knew something and she was pleased by it, which made me slightly uncomfortable.

Right on her heels came Mali, sporting a pair of sunglasses, groaning and saying, "Please, for the love of Christ, tell me there's coffee."

"Out at the bar," Hayden said, grinning.

"Real coffee, or the swill these barbarians claim is coffee?" Everett asked.

"Did you make it?" Shelly asked.

"No," Everett answered.

"Then it's swill," Shelly said with a shrug, and Mandy laughed.

"Good point," Everett said. "You can have swill now or wait like ten minutes and have the good shit."

"Fuck," Mali barked. "Swill now, good shit in ten minutes. I can't handle anything this early without caffeine."

"Come on, I'll see what I can do with what's out there."

They went out and it was just enough people leaving the crowded kitchen that I felt like I could breathe marginally better. I kneaded biscuit dough and flattened it, cutting out rounds and laying them on the industrial cookie sheets lined with parchment paper while I took everything in.

"Anybody know how long we're staying here?" a woman who was new asked

"Bails," Dray's voice called from out front, "Will you let those capable ranch hands take care of shit for you for once in your fucking life, and stop worrying about everything on that farm of yours?"

"Yes, cousin dear!" she called back, rolling her eyes.

"I'm Bailey," she said with a smile.

"Tiffany," I said softly and jumped when someone gathered up my hair from off my face behind me. I froze and yelped, "What are you doing?"

"It's driving me nuts," Hayley said. "You can't cook for people with your hair in your face like that. You'll get it in the food if you're not careful."

"Then I'll be careful. Please, let it go," I said.

"Not gonna happen, not while you're working around food. Besides," Everett called, "You're a hottie."

I blinked gathering tears away and was glad they didn't spill, muttering to myself, "Clearly you haven't gotten a load of my face."

"We have," Shelly said, bouncing her kid on her hip. "And Everett's still right."

I felt my face flame in embarrassment and dusted the flour off my hands, "Did you need anything else?" I asked Ashton.

"You can help me bring out the dishes," a soft voice said. I turned around and a young girl, and I do mean young, smiled at me. "I'm Maren, Nox's Ol' Lady," she said. What I heard was, *I'm Maren, Nox's barely legal teen.* I'd also immediately thought to myself, *who's being the judgy cunt now?*

"Sure, just let me wash my hands," I said.

I did and resisted the urge to immediately pull down my hair before I helped her haul out plates and stack things on a table at one end of the bar. Mandy and Everett were already setting up those metal tub things over warmers, the kind that caterers used, on its top, and I had to admit, when you were feeding this many people it was a good idea and a good investment.

Something crashed and a kid screamed toward the back.

"Here we go," Hayley sang, and she and Shelly both headed in that direction.

"Tell Dante he'd better be behaving himself," Mandy called after them. "And send Melody for some coffee if she needs a break!"

"Will, do!" Shelly called back and disappeared through the archway, calling out, "Hey, hey, hey! What's going on here? You giving your mama trouble?"

"It can be a little bit of a madhouse at times, especially with all the kids," Maren said.

"Who you tellin'?" a moody teen boy sitting at the bar playing a handheld video game muttered.

"Sage!" Maren snapped and I could see the resemblance.

"Little brother?" I asked.

"Yeah," he answered. "What's it to you?"

"Good luck ever getting laid with that attitude, kid." He scowled at me and got up, stalking away like a thunderhead. Maren sighed and I apologized.

"Sorry, I don't relate to kids the best, my filter is kind of out of whack when it comes to them."

"It's fine, he's that age and since my dad died it's just me. Well, me and Nox."

"Which one is Nox?" I asked.

"Shredded guy, tall with dark hair. Um, I know that's like a third of the guys in the club," she laughed, "But they're all in Church or out looking for somebody right now."

"With a name like the Sacred Hearts, I should have guessed there was some sort of religious angle. Catholic, am I right?"

"Oh, these boys don't actually go to church, honey," Everett said.

"That's just what they call it when they do one of their official meetings," Mandy said.

"Oh, should have figured it meant figuratively, not literally."

They shared a laugh that I was comfortable being part of, too.

"So where are they all?" I asked.

"Probably out back around the fire pit. They're planning on building what they call a chapel this spring," Maren said. Everett hissed a little and Maren jumped.

"What?" I asked.

"I might have just overshared," Maren said apologetically.

"Ah, gotcha," I said, adding, "If it makes you feel any better, I know how to keep my mouth shut."

"It does, but still, you're new around here and better safe than sorry," Everett declared. "Club business is just that – club business."

"I understand," I said and leaned back against the bar.

"Good deal," she smiled at me and yelled, "Coffee's up!"

I heard a little laughter and Mali groaned, "Thank fucking God." I turned and found her leaned over a table in the common area.

"Hungover?" I asked.

"Yup."

"Hair of the dog?"

"Fuck no, I really would start puking then."

Everett laughed.

"Anything else I can do?"

"Not really. Many hands make light work," Maren said.

"You've pitched in more than enough," Everett declared.

"Okay." I stepped back in, just inside the door to the kitchen and hung up the apron where Ashton had gotten it from. I stood around for a moment not really knowing what to do with myself, or where Nik had gotten to, though if I had to guess, he was with the rest of the guys. I drifted over and sat across from Mali. She was really the only person familiar to me here and I didn't know what else to do with myself.

"I want to die," she moaned, her voice muffled where it was buried in her arms on the tabletop.

"Tequila?"

"God, no, I really would be dead if it was Dragon's tequila. This is a bourbon hangover."

"Ew, no good." She looked up, propping her chin on top of her folded arms.

"How you been?" she asked, "You know, other than your friend?"

"Heard about that, huh?" I asked softly and stared out the front window.

"Hard not to, Babe. Small town and an even smaller club, plus my man was the one fixing the hospital records to cover Doc's ass."

"Ah, thank him for me, would you? I would hate for that doctor to get in trouble. Delia didn't really have any family worth anything. We, uh, we were sort of each other's family." I choked up and sniffed and Mali nodded.

"Same for me and Kyle now. Um, Data is his road name. If it weren't for the club, we'd be the only family each of us would have."

I nodded. It seemed like a lot of misfits and strays found their way here. Mali smiled and nodded when I said as much, though super quietly.

"We are nothing if not the outcasts of the rest of society," she said with a gusty sigh. "Honestly, fuck them anyhow. They don't know how to really live. These guys?"

"Totally do," I agreed.

I'd noticed that about everyone here. They were all vibrant and full of life. That life may not be easy by most of the rest of society's standards, but in my opinion, the rest of society didn't necessarily know what they were missing.

"Here they come," Mali said, staring behind me.

I turned around to a bunch of boulders in black leather piling through the archway from the back. Some of them were shivering and bouncing in their black motorcycle boots, some of them blowing into their hands.

"We need to get that chapel built," one of them griped. "It's too fuckin' cold to be standing out there jawing like that in this kind of weather." He was tall and had dark hair and I wondered fleetingly if he was Maren's Nox.

"You could always take your happy ass back to Arizona," one of them grated, a man with long brown hair in a loose ponytail down his back, just starting to gray at the temples.

"Shut up, big brother," the dark-haired one muttered.

Nik came in through the back and I felt myself perk up. He didn't see me sitting here with Mali, and instead went into the kitchen first. He scanned the room out here next when he didn't find me in there, and spotting me, lifted his chin. I gave a nod and he headed my way.

"I didn't even see you disappear," I told him, smiling to try and take any perceived accusation out of my comment. I added, "I was so wrapped up in I was doing that when I looked up, I hadn't even noticed you'd gone."

"You know you don't have to do that with him, right?" Mali asked.

"Do what?" I felt my smile falter.

"Stroke my ego," he said. "Craft what you say around my feelings. Only insecure douchebags need that." He pulled a chair from another table and dropped onto it, leaning forward against its back.

"You can have mine," Mali said. "My man's back at the controls." She jutted her chin past Nik and he and I both turned. The black curtains blocking the view inside the little glassed-in fishbowl had been whisked aside, revealing a wall of TV's and monitors, computer towers and keyboards. A man stood inside talking on a cell phone and waved Mali towards him. She went and kissed him decadently, dropping into his lap after he sat in a rolling desk chair.

He kept an arm around her as he typed one-handed, like it was as natural as breathing. I couldn't help but smile at the genuine love between them. They had a partnership and it was easy to see. As effortless as breathing.

"How are you holding up?" Nik asked. "And, sorry I got called away."

"It's fine, really, that's all I meant by saying it the way that I did."

"Yeah?"

"Yeah."

Silence lapsed between us and he studied my face finally saying, "You didn't answer the question."

"I'm doing as well as can be expected, I guess," I said, swallowing hard.

He nodded and reached out, covering my hand with his. I gripped his fingers and drew breath to say something when a female voice from the kitchen shrieked at the top of her lungs, "Breakfast!"

Light chuckling swept through the men and women standing around talking in small knots and people just naturally fell into a single-file line to move along the bar buffet-style.

"Stay here," Nik said, low and soft. "I'll bring you something."

"Thanks," I murmured back and he winked at me.

Before he could get back to me, Trigger and another man I didn't know pulled up a chair each.

"How are you doing?" Trigger asked. I bit my lips together and tried to decide how to answer and he grunted saying, "That good, huh?"

I let out an explosive breath and said, "Yeah, that good," and it sounded miserable even to me.

"I'm Ghost," the other man said, and I looked him over. Compact but well-proportioned, he held himself like a cop or a military guy and shoveled food in his face like a prisoner. If I had to guess, I'd say some flavor of former military and the eating habits could be from the same or because of some kind of ex-con status. Delia had waxed on about the club's reputation in the criminal world so I was betting ex-con, but then again, a lot of these guys were seriously surprising my preconceived notions.

"Tiff," I answered him, and he gave me a nod.

"You're not harassing the woman are you?" The platinum blonde, Shelly, dropped into the chair Mali had vacated and suddenly the two-person table was seating five. Or would be as soon as Nik got back.

"No, wife of mine, I'm not. I just sat down and managed to introduce myself."

"Oh, well, good," she said and winked at me. I pulled the hair tie off the end of the braid Hayley had put in my hair and ran my fingers through it, shaking it out and combing it over the scarred half of my face.

"You got any plans today?" Trigger asked.

"No, not really," I answered.

"Feel like trying some more shooting? We got a range out back. Might be a good distraction for you."

I nodded, "Okay."

"Oi!" Nik cried, "I go to get my lady something to eat and nek minute every one and their dam cuz moves in on her? What the shit is that?" His tone was light and joking, and Trigger and Ghost both laughed quietly and tried not to choke on their food.

"What?" Shelly asked. "She's the new shiny object for this lot of ravens." She winked at me and I smiled back a little nervously. While I was used to being the center of attention at work, I wasn't really equipped to deal with it in my personal life. At work, I wore a persona, slipped on the personality of Francesca like a second skin. Out here I was just plain, old, boring, Tiffany and for the most part, I liked it like that. The extra attention was especially hard because of Delia... *God, poor Delia.*

I stared down at the plate that Nik put in front of me and took the fork he offered with a murmured, "Thanks."

He squeezed my knee under the table and I forced a smile and looked over my plate with much trepidation. I wasn't hungry at all. Whatever appetite I'd had had completely fled.

30

Z eb...

"Are you flinching?" Ghost asked her and she nodded. "Well, stop flinching," he said and she looked a bit taken aback, but I could see her think about it and by god, it worked. She wasn't flinching every time one of the guns cracked off. I smiled to myself and wished everything was that easy. If it were, I'd tell her point blank things like *well, stop being afraid,* and *stop being so hard on yourself.*

Right now, she was listening closely to what Ghost and Trig were telling her, and while they were at it, I was standing in line with Archer, Rush, and Nox, having a go at some target practice of our own. I didn't fancy getting shot again like I had last year. Right in my leg, trying to help Data and his girl. That had been one hell of a firefight, I tell you.

Tiffany's fingertips sometimes traced the scar as she lay across me, but she'd never asked about it. There were a lot of things she didn't ask about me and I didn't think it was disinterest so much as street smarts on her part. There just were some things you didn't ask about, but then again, I think she and I were past the awkward phase of our relationship. Still, I had to be careful with club business. Club business was just that, club business. Not girlfriend business and not even ol' lady business. Certain things you just kept to yourself, as much for your safety as the safety of your bros, not to mention the peace of mind of the girl you were with.

I know that Tiffany knew I was a man capable of violence, but I wasn't entirely sure she realized that she was, too. Everyone was, it just required the precise set of circumstances, like a lock-and-key setup. The circumstances had to be the right set of teeth to move the tumblers aside to unlock that potential in a person. Everyone had a lock, it just was a fraction of the population that ran into the right trigger or key to make things move and subsequently, things to happen.

"Good, job," Ghost said, squinting downrange.

"Did I hit it?"

"You sure did," Trigger said. "A decent shot, too. Now let's see you do it again so we can rule out luck."

"Okay."

She took aim and sighted and cracked off a shot, and though she hit the paper, she missed the black. Still, she managed to hit the target at all, which was an improvement in and of itself.

"To be fair, I don't think you'd be this far away from whatever you were shooting at," Ghost said.

"Probably not," Shelly agreed from behind us all. "I wasn't."

"No. No, you were not," Ghost grunted and shook his head.

"What do you mean?" Tiffany asked. "You shot someone?"

"Yeah, he attacked me in our kitchen. I was home alone. I got the gun out of the drawer Ghost kept it in and he was pretty much on top of me when I blew his head off." Tiffany blinked and Shelly gave her a sad smile, "It was him or me and I wasn't about to get raped a second time."

"Me, too," Tiffany said softly and sighed. I stood up a little straighter and focused on her.

"Silas, during our relationship. I didn't know it was really considered rape. You know, the old-fashioned backward ideas –"

"Oh, believe us. We know," Shelly said cutting her off. "You don't have to explain yourself, honey. It happened and we believe you."

Tiff nodded and explained anyways, "I didn't realize it until I started my schooling in social work. We have a series of classes about dealing with trauma and sexual assault was a big chunk of it. Reading other survivor's stories really clued me in."

"No shame in it," Ghost said and Tiffany made a face like he was an idiot and I tried not to laugh.

"I know that now," she said. "Took me a while to get there, but it happened and it's a part of me now, like so much else he did." The steel and determination were back in her voice, that iron will to not be a victim anymore.

"Sorry," Ghost said.

"Sorry I snapped," she apologized. "I'm still working on a lot of it."

"That's what matters, eh. That you're dealing with it," I said and she turned to me and nodded slightly.

"Enough of this heavy shit," Archer grated, and put out his cigarette. "I'm gonna go find something and kill it, anyone want to come?"

"Deer or wild pig?" Rush asked.

"Human," Archer answered, and stalked off with his bow. As a felon, he tried not to carry a gun anymore at all. He had two boys and Melody, now. Said the last thing he wanted was to let them down by getting picked up on a weapons charge and that sticking to his namesake unless shit was dire was good for him.

No one argued. We all knew just how proficient he was with that compound bow of his. A silent killer, nine times out of ten you never saw or heard Archer coming. He'd come by his road name honestly, that one.

"I'm in," Nox declared, his gaze lingering on the deep scar marring my girl's cheek.

"Not without me, you ain't," Rush declared.

"Check in with Dragon before you do anything," Trig called. Archer waved over his shoulder as he, Rush, and Nox trudged back down through the snow toward the back of the main clubhouse.

Tiffany starred off in the direction of the target she'd been shooting at and asked, "Do you really think they'll find him?"

"Yep," Trig said, loading a fresh magazine. "If Dragon and Reaver haven't already, or Data."

"What will they do when they find him? Just kill him? Just like that?"

"That's not for you to know, Sweetheart," Trig said.

Ghost went to Shelly, kissed her gently and said, "Come on," putting an arm around her bundled form and leading her back to the club.

"I have to see him," Tiffany said. "I need to confront him." She sounded almost desperate like the thought hadn't even occurred to her that this would just be done without any involvement on her part.

"I don't make the rules, Baby. I just enforce 'em," Trig said and sighed.

"Well, who does make the rules?" she demanded.

"Dragon," I told her. "Or rather, he proposes them and the club puts it to a vote. We make our own rules."

"What Zeb said," Trig agreed.

She looked upset but she was thinking, calculating, and finally let out an explosive breath.

"Do you know when he'll be back?" she asked bleakly.

"No, I do not," Trig said and handed her the gun. "One more time and then you need to go inside and warm up."

She sniffed, her nose running from the cold and nodded; she wasn't about to pass up any sort of practice when it came to anything that would keep her from being victimized again, but at the same time, I knew that look. The conversation about her participation wasn't done and I wasn't looking forward to being at odds with her on this.

I wanted her safe, but I also understood it was hard for her to trust. The fact that I had gained her trust as quickly as I had felt like a bit of a miracle, but at the same time I understood it. She was a lone canoe, cast adrift in a raging storm and she was being swallowed by a sea of emotions. Still, she was fighting to stay afloat harder than I'd seen anyone fight before and I admired her for that.

Her struggle was real, and I didn't want to be yet another thing she felt like she had to struggle against. Fuck me and the position I felt like I was in. My loyalties were being torn between my club and this fierce, wounded woman.

I watched her carefully take aim and really work on her aim and was proud of her. She finished the clip and squinted downrange.

Trigger nodded slowly and said, "Much better. All you need is focus. We'll work on some more tomorrow. Right now you need to take a rest and get warm. People don't realize that shooting takes a lot out of you. You've had about as much recoil as you should take for one day."

"Thank you," she said, and I could tell she was emotional by her tone.

"You're welcome, and I wouldn't worry about him anymore. Have a little faith. You got more people in your corner than you know."

"I'm realizing that," she said gently. "And I can't tell you how grateful I am for it."

"I get you," he said with a nod and then with a smile said, "Go get something warm to drink. Like to be freezing my balls off out here."

She smiled and confessed, "Can't really feel my fingers or toes anymore."

I was with her on that one. "Hot shower then?"

"Mm, maybe," she replied and took my hand. I let her lead me back towards the outbuilding that housed my room and even with the bone-deep cold, my dick started to get hard just thinking about her in my bed.

Once inside my bedroom, Max jumped off the bed and slunk under it. Tiff looked slightly hurt, but I lifted her coat off her shoulders and hung it up on the back of the door for her. I hung my jacket and cut up beside her coat and took her thick gray scarf. She rubbed her hands together and huddled in on herself slightly, and I sighed.

"Come here."

She came to me and I folded her into my arms, against my chest.

"I don't know what to do," she said.

"Me either," I confessed. "Stuck between a rock and a hard place on this one."

"How so?"

"Loyalty to the club and my love for you."

She leaned back sharply and stared me in the face, eyes wide and almost disbelieving before she said, "You really mean that."

"I do."

"Pretty sure that's rushing things," she said and I laughed but she cut it off by grabbing both sides of my face with her chilly fingers and smashing her mouth over mine, going up on her toes to do it.

I pulled her body close to mine, winding my arms around her lower back, my hands on the ass of her jeans urging her up. She gave a little leap and wrapped her legs around me and I strode over to the bed, laying her on it.

We kissed and shoved cold hands under clothes, jerking and laughing into one another's mouths as we tortured each other with icy touches until our hands warmed up. Clothing came off bit by bit and the look in her eyes when I peeled off her socks and braced her cold feet against my bare chest to warm her frozen toes was one of soft wonder. I covered them with my hands and rubbed the life back into them, and she just watched me, her eyes misting slightly.

"No one has ever taken care of me like you do," she said, her voice carefully steady.

"About time someone did, innit?" I asked, and she nodded slowly.

"I guess, I mean, I don't really know."

"I do, and it's way past time," I said and let her feet go, climbing up her body and laying over her, pressing my mouth to hers again.

We were down to our underthings and it was still far too many clothes. I needed her nude and writhing under me like a starved man needed food. I let my hands glide over her soft skin, learning her body by touch as well as sight, breathing deep her light scent like freshly fallen rain on new spring leaves. She was all things sunshine and warmth on these cold dreary days and I couldn't help but warm my soul by her.

"Nik," she said softly, voice a solemn plea as I kissed across her stomach. I glanced up at her and she was practically begging with her eyes for all that I could give her and I was more than happy to. I would give her the world if she asked it.

I skimmed her knickers down her long legs and kept her gaze locked on mine as I licked her from opening to clit. I plunged my middle finger carefully into her, her body wet and ready for it, hips arching; lightly rising and falling in an unconscious effort to fuck my hand.

I loved her reactions. I loved that she could let go with me and turn herself over to just feeling in the moment. I knelt by my bed, her legs practically wrapped around my head and did everything in my power to make the world shatter around her.

She moaned and rocked against my tongue, gripping the duvet in her fists, her pussy clamping around my fingers and I knew when she tightened up like that that she was close. I took a deep breath just before she snapped back like she'd been electrocuted. Her body went stiff, her pussy rippled and a stiff, choked-off cry escaped her lush mouth. She forgot to breathe when she came, and I thought it was fantastic. She always crashed back to earth and sucked in air like a drowning woman and I loved that I could make her drown in sensation so completely that she sometimes forgot the basics, like drawing air.

She went limp, her legs releasing me and twitching faintly with her little aftershocks as she gasped for air, chest heaving. I climbed her body, fisting and stroking my cock. We'd already fucked up and done it without a Frenchie once, but I couldn't really care about it, it'd been so amazing and worth it. Still, we agreed we needed to be more careful, so I swept one of the gold foil packets off the top of the mini-fridge by the bed. She watched me, eyes dark with lust and if darkness could glow, her eyes did it with a light of a completely different emotion.

My heart knew it without her ever having to say the words. She loved me, too.

I rolled the slick latex down my length and got between her legs. She reached for me and I introduced myself into her body slowly, so slowly it'd like to drive me insane and I didn't break eye contact as I did it. I wanted her to see, hear, feel, taste and hear just how much I loved her.

I wanted it to sink in, for her to understand that she was so much more than the scared, abused woman that I'd met weeks back.

She was stronger than she knew, braver than she knew, smarter than she knew, and she needed to own that. She needed to hold onto it and never let it go again.

31

T iffany...

My mind was a pleasant blank. He moved over me and inside me, staring intently, lovingly, into my eyes as he did it. I was so calm, so languid, so relieved that right in front of me was what I thought I would never have again. I wasn't alone, and I knew deep down in my soul that I never would be and it was such a beautiful agony.

I missed my friend, there would be no replacing her, the hole left in my heart from her murder would never heal. Right now, though, I clung to Nik and was just so grateful for him. I never wanted this to end. It was peaceful here in his arms, safe and sure. I didn't have to fight, I didn't have to be afraid; I could simply be who I was and even be happy if I wanted to. He was my refuge where I'd never had one before.

I wrapped my legs around him and palmed one firm globe of his ass and pulled him in deeper. He groaned and it was such a low-key yet ecstatic sound I couldn't help but smile. He buried his face in the side of my neck and kissed along the side of it until he found that spot that sent shivers all over my body and elicited a moan of my own out of me.

I loved that he could go for what seemed like forever, I loved that I could let everything fall away and just be with him. I loved him, and I wasn't afraid to admit that to myself. It was so freeing, I can't even explain it, and the deep well of emotion just went deeper and deeper just as he moved deep and deeper still inside of me like he touched my soul.

I pushed on him and he rolled onto his back, taking me with him. I rose up above him and the way he looked at me made me tighten around him. I rode him with a smooth rolling motion of my own hips, taking him deep and rising to the point I almost lost him before I plunged back over the top of him, riding him all the way down again.

Slow and sensual, I made love to him and I swear, I just couldn't get enough. It was like I was on the edge of something huge, the universe holding its collective breath around me and he was so good at keeping me there. *Right there*, on the very precipice and it felt so damn good, like butterflies kissed the insides of my walls with their wings setting off sparks alighting down my nerve endings, flaring bright and winking out, another spark flaring brightly where the first had died. It was a chain reaction that was magical, mystical, and I'd never felt anything like it.

I was surely hooked on it, though. It was better than any drunk or cannabis high I'd ever experienced and I vaguely wondered if this is what a harder drug might feel like. If it was, I could understand why the rate of addiction was so high.

To me, Nik had become my perfect drug. All of the benefits, none of the nasty side effects.

"Oh, baby, I'm going to come," he warned and I bit my bottom lip and frowned slightly. I wasn't ready for this to end. I wanted to stay here, like this, forever and even though I knew in the front of my mind that wasn't possible, I was happy living in my little fantasy world for the time being.

Nik reached between us, and that slow beautiful sparkling firefly effect seemed to fully ignite and before I could stop it, I was burning. Flashfire sweeping through me and over me, burning me to cinders, then burning me still, until nothing but fine ash remained and I was reborn, limp against his chest, held close, his lips playing against my forehead, his hands sweeping over my body in a light caress as he slowly went soft inside me.

"Holy shit," I gasped out between breaths, and Nik laughed beneath me, just as out of breath as I was. I closed my eyes and slid down his body some, laying my ear over his heart. He threaded his fingers through my hair and I loved it when he did that. He played with it, combing through it and trailing fingertips down my back and I shuddered and he cried out in reaction.

"Ah, God! That was almost too much," he said.

I sighed, asking lazily, "What was?"

"Whatever reaction that was just did some fantastic things for my cock, but I'm too sensitive, you know?"

"Mm, I do know." I sighed out, content, mind still quiet, and I swear, Nik was better than any of the Valiums Lia used to slide in my direction when the anxiety got too bad.

I physically started with how violently the thought crashed into my brain and Nik immediately asked, "What's wrong, eh?"

"I love you, too," I blurted. I pushed up off his chest so I could look him in the eyes. "I just realized I never said it back."

"Ah, to be fair, you were a bit busy showing me, eh?"

"You're not upset?" I asked.

He shook his head and lightly ran fingertips along the curves of my face as if committing my face to memory by touch as much as he was by sight.

"Could never be mad about what we just shared."

I bit my bottom lip and nodded when a light knock fell at the door. I sat up and Nik had me roll off to the side so he could get the quilt at the foot of the bed up over us.

"Come in!" He called and Dragon poked his head in. I held the quilt to my chest even though he'd seen me naked like a thousand times by now, and he smiled a knowing and glad smile.

"Party out at Point Nowhere, you coming?" he asked.

I froze and Nik and I exchanged a look. Before he could answer, I said quickly, "I want to go, too."

Silence hung between the three of us and Dragon let go of the doorknob he'd been resting his hand on with a clatter that was almost too loud to be believed. He shut the door behind him and crossed his arms over his chest.

"You gave this to us; technically its club business now," he said, and I dug my heels.

"Just because its club business now, doesn't mean it ever stopped being my business. I asked you for help, it's true, but I need this."

Dragon rose his eyebrows and Nik laid his palm on my lower back, kneading with his fingertips along either side of my spine, a silent urge to caution. It both calmed me and tempered my resolve into steel.

I'd done nothing but be cautious and self-centered about it, too. Now Zeke had been hurt and Delia had been killed and by God, I wouldn't let him get away with it. I would look this monster in the eyes. I would slay this dragon of mine and know, for a fact, that he would never hurt another person ever again. I had to, I needed to, and Delia needed someone to speak for her who loved her.

I said all of it, spilled my truth into the air and punctuated it by punching the mattress by my hip. Dragon stared at me, expression shuttered, and took a deep breath, letting it out in a rush.

"Now you really do remind me of my wife."

"Well, if your wife's answer to this particular problem would be to kick you in the balls and climb over your body to get to the motherfucker who killed her friend, then yeah. I'm with her."

He laughed, a rich, loud booming thing that bounced from the ceiling and dripped down the walls, coating the room with rich sound. He thumbed a tear out of the corner of his eye and nodded, "Yeah. That would have been Tilly's answer. She either went over me, under me or damn near through me if she wanted it bad enough. I gotta tell you, girl. This is the kind of thing you don't come back from. You should let us handle it, trust us that it's done, get on with yer life."

"If Lia were still here, that'd be an option, but not anymore."

"I don't see you trying to talk her out of this shit," he remarked to Nik, who was leaned up against the headboard behind me.

"She knows what she wants. I'm here for her. I honestly think she's right. I may not like it, but I get it."

It was less than a rousing endorsement but I'd take it. Dragon hung his head and sighed, looked up at Nik and said, "Well, ain't you stuck between the past and the future?"

"Just taking it minute by minute here, Boss… but yeah. Yeah, I am."

"Put some fuckin' clothes on, I'm goin' out to have a smoke and think about it."

He went out the door and closed it behind him. I let out a breath I hadn't known I'd been holding.

"Do you think -?"

Nik cut me off, "I don't know, but it's a good chance, eh. Find some clothes."

We dressed, quickly and for warmth, and headed out of the building. Dragon's old truck was idling on the track and he turned around, sucking on a cigarette.

"Get in the truck before I change my mind," he grated and I nodded and slid into the middle, feet on either side of the hump, my nerves on fire for a completely different reason now.

Dragon got behind the wheel and Nik got in beside me, taking my hand closest to him and rubbing it between his own. The gesture was both reassuring and appreciated as he worked out the chill in my fingers. I got cold so easily, I swear but the kind of cold I was now? Frozen down to my very soul? It wasn't a chill that could be rubbed away or cured with a blanket. No hot shower, no cup of tea was going to fix it, and I'm afraid it only grew worse, my stomach knotted with dread, the closer we got to the place Nik took me shooting the first time.

Why they called it Point Nowhere I didn't know and it didn't seem like a question I should ask. I'd learned in my line of work since Silas fucked up my face that ignorance really was bliss. That there were just certain things you didn't ask or talk about and that it really was better to just go with the flow. It was amazing what you learned when you kept your mouth shut and your ears and eyes open.

The snow was falling, and it was making it slow going. We made it up the long driveway to the lot outside the metal outbuilding with its rusting wrecks of cars, so blanketed with white they were unrecognizable, like hunkered hulking creatures poised to wake and leap out. Sleeping sentinels.

Dragon cut the engine and sighed. He looked over at me, the cold creeping in slowly, wafting in off the glass and said, "Last chance to spare yourself, Sweetheart. You don't have to go in. You can stay right here and just let us handle this for you."

I shook my head. "Not how it works," I replied simply and he nodded, his mouth set in a grim line. I wasn't sure how he got it, that I needed to do this, but he did, and I wasn't going to poke at it. I just needed to finish it. Suck it up, get my ass in there and throw the closet door wide, lift the proverbial blankets and confront the monster under my bed. Except this was a waking nightmare and all too real, and it was one I was sick and tired of living in. I understood now, it was him or me, and the police? Law enforcement? The system? It was a joke. An illusion. A construct to make people feel better but that didn't really do shit when it counted.

These guys had it right, forming their own society. If you wanted something done right, you had to do it yourself and they were just as sick and disillusioned with the lies as I was. I looked over at Nik and he hooked a hand behind my neck and dragged my forehead to his lips. My eyes dropped closed and I took the comfort. I felt grounded by the gesture and I was honestly as ready as I would ever be.

"Right, let's do this," Dragon said. "Get your closure or whatever and get this waste of fucking space out of yer life."

"Here, here," I murmured.

I followed Dragon out of the truck on his side and Nik slid over and out behind me. It was a better option than trudging around in the front of it in the damn near knee-deep drifts of snow that showed no sign of stopping.

"At least the weather is on our side, yeah?" Nik commented as we went past a black SUV with deeply tinted back windows.

"Ah, yeah," Dragon agreed.

I didn't ask, even though the question of what that was supposed to mean was on the tip of my tongue.

The side door to the building opened and Reaver stuck his head out. He spotted me and frowned, saying, "You don't honestly think this is a good idea, do you?"

"My call," Dragon said, and Reaver nodded like that was enough for him. I don't think I'd ever seen such unquestioning loyalty displayed before and it was a bit of food for thought.

We passed through the door, and Archer, Rush, and Nox looked up from where they were standing around an old fifty-five-gallon metal drum, flames licking over the rim.

"The fuck?" Archer scowled as he said it and the look was so menacing I took a half-step back into Nik, who'd come in at my back.

"Not our call," Reaver said with a shrug and looked over to Dragon.

"Last time we involved a female in club business, that one got shot." Rush jabbed a finger in Nik's direction and I looked up at him. I'd seen a few scars on his body, but I hadn't figured any of them for gunshot wounds.

He shrugged and told me with his eyes we'd talk about it later and I turned back to the men in front and to the left of us.

"She's here now, have it out later," Reaver said and it seemed to be the end of the discussion. He was standing off to the right of us and that's where my gaze landed, on him and the two hooded men hanging by their wrists from chains dangling from the ceiling. I tried not to let it show but I was pretty sure I paled.

"Time's up, fuckers," Reaver snarled and ripped the hoods from their faces. The first man, furthest from me, was Cooper, a strip of silver duct tape over his mouth. The second, blinking from the lights on stands in here, was Silas.

I shuddered slightly. He'd put on size while in prison. His shoulders were wider, chest much bigger and his arms and hands something I was glad were tied above his head. He glared at Reaver, who grinned back and ruffled his hair playfully. Silas jerked, his eyes dark with anger, and snarled from behind his own bit of tape. Except, when he jerked at his bonds it spun him and he spotted me and his eyes went from pissed-off to incendiary, with an edge of surprise.

Reaver ripped the tape off of Silas' mouth and I bit my bottom lip. I actually probably could have lived without that, but surprisingly, Silas didn't say anything. At least not right away.

I shook my head and stepped closer, but still stayed a goodly distance away. I mean, I wasn't about to get within distance of him lashing out with those shitkickers of his. I knew how much it hurt to take a shot to the ribs with the pointed toe of one of those boots.

"I didn't think you had it in you to pull something like this off," he snarled, and I shook my head.

"Learned quite a few things in the last few years," I said coolly and I was proud of myself. Nik hadn't left me, remaining at my back, within reach, but at the same time letting me stand on my own, here.

"Way Delia tells it, you learned the finer points of how to be a fucking whore. Only work you could get with a face like that?" he sneered.

"Fuck you, Silas," I snapped.

"Hey!" he barked, then said with barely suppressed rage through gritted teeth, "You say 'fuck you again,' when I get out of here, I'm coming to find you and that's just what I'll do. I'm going to fuck you, just like I fucked your slut fri–"

He didn't get to finish. Adrenaline surged through my veins and the rush of fear, anger, rage, and pain was immediate, hot, and fresh. It welled out of the center of my being, erupting like blood from a cut, and painted the inside of my vision in red. I reached out, snagged the gun I knew Nik had in the back of his waistband and I emptied it into Silas without a second thought.

I pulled the trigger over and over, and stopped only when it clicked empty. There was no missing at this range. There was no fear of hitting anyone else. There was just the white-hot desire to end him, to wipe the blight that was Silas-fucking-Grable off the face of the earth so there would be no more me's and there certainly wouldn't be any more Delia's.

"Awww, dammit!" Reaver cried. "You did that way too soon. You gotta make fuckers like him suffer. Put the fear of God into 'em a little." He stuck his lower lip out and pouted but I was staring past him at Cooper who was writhing at the end of his bonds like he couldn't get away from Silas fast enough, even though there was nowhere for him to go.

It suddenly clicked. Why they called this place Point *Nowhere.*

I shook my head at what Reaver had said, watching my ex, motionless and hanging, swinging slightly by virtue of inertia alone. The blood was falling from him in a wet spatter, seeping across the cement floor. I couldn't hear the patter of it, my ears still ringing from firing the gun in the enclosed space. The vibrations still echoed on the air, reverberating soundlessly from the steel walls, sightless, soundless, but still palpable. Well, maybe that was just me projecting the magnitude of what I'd just done into the physical space. A way to psychologically rationalize to myself that this was, indeed, huge. Life-altering on a scale that I'd yet to comprehend and wouldn't, until I had time to process.

"You don't fuck with a rabid dog and try to retrain it, you put it down," I said, and turned to Cooper whose eyes were too wide, nostrils flaring and contracting with every breath, screaming muffled behind the duct tape, and the rage and pain surged again.

My feet carried me across the cement floor but I don't remember putting any thought into walking. I pressed the barrel of the empty gun into his cheek and I knew it was hot, I knew it would burn. He screamed behind his gag and started to sob, and I hissed at him, "Judas," as I pressed the burning kiss of the barrel harder into his cheek.

"She was so hung up on you and you knew it. You used it."

He shuddered and shook, the chains holding him rattling as he sobbed and I backed off in revulsion and turned to Reaver.

"You can do whatever you want with this one," I said, and I knew deep down inside exactly what I was doing by telling him that. I saw the monster move behind his eyes. The darkness and crazy rise to the surface that I knew instinctively was there. *Psychopath, antisocial, sociopath,* pick your flavor of disenfranchised crazy and I was sure Reaver had it. He was too charming for it not to be. He was good at making people like him. Even me, but I was less than a quarter away from my practicum and I knew there was broken to him, that he held a severely-cracked psyche inside.

I dropped the gun back to my side and took two rushed steps back from Cooper Reese. I looked back to Reaver and told him, "Make him suffer like he made Delia suffer," and it was like he lit up like a fucking kid on Christmas morning.

"Fuck, I'm out of here," Nox declared from behind me and I startled. I'd forgotten they were even there.

"Me, too," Rush said. "I don't need nightmares for the rest of my life."

"I've had enough for one day, too," Archer said, tiredly.

"No way are you staying for what you just asked for," Dragon said.

"I don't need to," I replied and my voice was as cold as the falling snow outside. "I am so done."

32

Z eb...

I asked Nox to phone ahead to the club. We rode back to it in the back seat of the black Escalade the club kept for things like this. Archer drove, Rush sat shotgun, and Nox sat behind me and and Tiff in the third row of seats. Tiffany had retreated inside her own head and stared out the window on her side of the cage. I wanted to hold it together and wanted to hold her at the same time, but I knew the two were at odds with each other.

She'd shot Silas at a pretty close range and was probably covered in all sorts of forensic evidence. We needed to deal with it, and quickly, which is why I'd had Nox call ahead.

"Pull around back, eh?" I said to Archer when we got close to the club and he grunted. A wordless acknowledgment of what I'd said. That was just Archer, though. He was always a bit of a grump.

I dismissed it, rather than being a bit of a dag for once. I was more concerned with getting home and hosed with Tiff. The mission was only half done. No one ever stops to think about the cleanup efforts or the after-effects of your first time killing someone. I wouldn't be surprised at Tiff going bush for a while over this. I had my first time, but in the end, I was too much of an extrovert to stay away from people for too long. Tiff wasn't the same as me, though. I was afraid if she went bush, she wouldn't come back from it. I couldn't tell which way she'd go, though.

"Everybody out," Archer declared when we pulled up on the track. Off to one side, Blue, Thirteen, and Data stood warming their hands over a fire in the pit.

"Come on," I urged Tiffany out of the back seat and toward the flames.

"I don't really feel like being social," she said gently and Archer huffed a laugh.

"Ain't about being social, it's about covering your damn tracks. Do what he says." I frowned at him and made a motion behind Tiff like he should pump the brakes. He scowled back and walked away muttering some shit about amateur hour under his breath.

Nox and Rush looked on in our direction with twin looks of worry plastered on their twin, but very different, faces.

"She'll be right," I told 'em and Nox nodded, giving his twin's jacket sleeve a tug. They followed their older brother in the back of the club.

"There they are," Thirteen declared when we came 'round the cage, then cheerfully said to Tiffany, "Best get to doing what you do, girl."

"What?" she asked, and her face smoothed out into confusion that almost looked like surprise.

I worried about her. I think she was going into a bit of shock over what she'd done, but she was in good company. Wasn't a soul among my bros that would judge her poorly for killing that wally.

"Strip," Data explained to her. "All of it, in a pile, right there," he said and pointed to the snow beside her.

"What? Out here?"

"Don't need you tracking DNA up inside the club, Sweetheart. Git her done and Zeb'll get you into a hot shower in no time."

"Just trying to keep us all safe," Blue said gently and captured Tiff's eyes with his own. He had a way about him, calm-like, that tended to rub off on everyone else. Especially when the shit was flying.

Tiffany nodded and stripped bare, shivering in the frigid snowfall.

"Come on, quick," I said and she trotted across the snow making a beeline for the outbuilding.

She said through chattering teeth, "I hope there will never be one, but next time, remind me to murder someone in the summer."

I barked a laugh at her black humor and felt my shoulders loosen up with relief. If she were coping with dark humor, then she had the constitution for this. She would make it.

I turned on the hot in the washroom and told her, "I'll be back. Going to grab you a flannel and a couple towels."

She practically dove under the spray letting out a little "Ah, ah, ha!" at going from such an extreme cold to warm.

"You good?" I asked, making sure, and she nodded, letting the water soak her hair.

I made quick work of striding up the hall and keying my way back into my room. I went for the supplies in the top of my closet and took it as a sign that there were just enough of my towels left that I could shower with her. I stripped down fast and pulled on a pair of shorts to make my way back to her but when I entered the washroom, it wasn't how I'd left her.

She'd waited until I was gone but she'd finally cracked and now she sat on the shower floor, hugging her knees and sobbing. I set the things on the bench, locked the washroom's door, and got in there with her, going to the shower floor and pulling her into my lap. Holding her while she wept and just letting her go, letting her cry. She earned a good cry, I reckon.

~

Sometime later, we were laying in my bed, nude and wrapped in each other, but I hadn't tried to give my ferret a run. She didn't need that. She just needed contact and hadn't seemed to mind we were skin on skin. We'd lain there silent for the longest time and was almost dozed off when her voice startled me awake.

"Were you really shot?" she asked and I jolted. She raised her head from my chest and turned to look at me, her eyes wide.

"I'm sorry!"

"Don't be, eh. It's all good."

She studied my face for a long time and I felt my heart sink as she tried to sort through her tangled emotions. Seeing that asshole again had scrambled her but good. I patiently waited her out, waited for her to decide I really meant what I said and that it was okay to relax again. She settled, laying her head back down, fingertips playing along a scar on my stomach from a knifing when I was a teen.

"Got knifed there," I said and she stilled her fingers.

"Where were you shot?" she asked.

"My leg."

"Oh."

More silence, and I wished I could see her face and what she was thinking.

"And the scar on your back?"

"Glamorous tale that one," I said.

"I'm listening."

"Fell out of a tree when I was nine."

She laughed slightly and sighed. "The one on my ribs is where Silas kicked me with his damn cowboy boot. You know, the kind with the metal tip on the toe. Everyone thinks it's a surgical scar because of the dots on either side from the stitches, but nope."

"What excuse did you give them that time?" I asked.

"Kicked by a horse, fell into a barbed wire fence. They weren't buying it, but I wasn't about to tell them otherwise."

"Mm," I murmured and traced fingertips over her skin, idle patterns from my dusty memory back when I wanted to make my dad proud before cancer took him and I got angry at the world.

"I can't stop wondering how this changes things," she murmured.

"It doesn't. Not really. You're changed, and you know you've changed but it's not like you did anything in cold blood, eh. You did the world a favor."

"I don't think killing anyone is doing the world a favor," she said.

"This time," I said, tracing along the line of a scar on her side, "it was."

"I feel like I'm this awful person now," she confessed, and I laughed a bit at the notion.

"The fact you feel that way mean's you're not, eh. An awful person wouldn't care if they were awful."

She pushed herself up and looked at me, "That is both incredibly smart and incredibly profound," she said.

I smiled one-sided, "I have been known to be both on occasion, I reckon."

She looked wounded, "I didn't mean it like that!"

"Hush now, Wahine. I know you didn't." I pressed her back down over my heart where I carried her always, now.

She sighed out and asked, "You're sure this doesn't make me a monster?"

"Nah, Wahine. You're a monster-slayer if anything. You brought your friend justice, today."

She sniffed and I felt bad for bringing Lia up. She shuddered against me and I put my arms around her to hold her through this fresh storm of tears and man, I wished I could take her pain away.

33

T iff...

I'd done a lot of hard things in the last few days. Watched my best friend die, murdered her killers in a fit of righteous anger, wrestled with the feelings over that, but by far, worse than the second was telling Zeke, Alan, and the rest of the girls that Lia wouldn't be coming back.

I'd had to go back to work. I had to behave normally, and part of behaving normally when you were a stripper for a living was that the bills stopped for no one and nothing. So I was back at work, and staring at my reflection in the boudoir mirror, thinking I was looking at a ghost.

The girl in the mirror didn't exist anymore, did she? I mean, she looked the same as ever but – the things I'd seen, the things I'd done. I wasn't the same and I wasn't sure how I could keep pretending that I was. The lace mask wasn't all that effective anymore now that I wore a mask every day for completely different reasons. I had an alter-ego for real now. One of violence, baptized in blood. One of self-confidence that I had to hide behind a veneer of fragility and anxiety that I honestly didn't feel even half as much anymore.

There was something about killing the man that put you through hell that was a confidence boost like no other. If I could survive Silas Grable, I could survive just about anything.

I turned my head as Alan sat himself down in the chair that Delia had always dropped into to chatter at me from while I fixed my mask and makeup for the next set. Typically, she'd sat there waiting for her turn at the mirror. It hurt, a raw, burning, aching hole in the center of my chest that she would never sit in that chair again. Would never insist I watch her dumb Hallmark movies, or ask what flavor of ice cream sounded good for that night. Would never plan a shopping trip or insist we go out and try some new thing. Last time, it had been a wine and paint night. I'd told her no, I'd had a paper to write. Now I regretted saying no, at not taking the chance to create that memory when I'd had the chance.

"I know that look," Alan said, leaning in and speaking in a confiding tone.

"What look?" I asked, genuinely perplexed.

He gave a gusty sigh and said, "You can't stay here anymore, kid. You're too good for this place, for one, and two, if you tried to stay I'd be afraid of the toll it would take. Delia is too much a part of this place and everywhere you look, she's going to be there. Besides, your heart's not in this," he looked around and sighed heavily. "Which brings us back around to number one; you're too good for this place. It's time for you to move on. You've got options for that now."

I stared at him a little wide-eyed and didn't immediately know what to say, but what I knew not to do was argue because he spoke the truth. Everything he said had been doing lazy circles in my mind all night. My shift was almost up. Nik would be coming soon to pick me up and I straightened up a little and said, "It won't leave you too short? On dancers, I mean."

I mean, Lia wasn't coming back and if I left now… that was two; one girl had come up pregnant and was going to have to knock this shit off once she started to show, which was going to be sooner rather than later with how far along she was. Would have been nice if she'd 'fessed up to being knocked up sooner so Alan could have started looking sooner but that was how a lot of these bitches were… not exactly long on smarts, never thinking beyond their next payday.

"Not your place to worry about that, kid. I'm the boss, remember?"

"Yeah, yeah, yeah," I said and looked down. I opened my mouth to ask for something and closed it, shaking my head.

"Spill it," he ordered.

"You're not my boss now," I said and he grinned.

"I haven't fired you yet and you haven't said 'I quit' so let me milk it for the last few seconds I can, huh?"

I laughed a little and tried not to get teary. This was more painful than I expected it was going to be. The whole idea of leaving.

"I was, ah, wondering if I could save the last dance for someone special," I said.

"Depends, is that someone me, Zeke, or a certain tribal-tattooed motherfucker that quite frankly, scares the living daylights out of me?"

I smiled and laughed slightly. "It happens to be that last one," I said.

"Let me ask you something." I nodded, listening. "He takes real good care of you?"

"Words cannot describe," I told him. "It's everything it's supposed to be and more if that makes sense."

He nodded slowly and reached up, tipping my chin with light fingertips. He flicked the pad of his thumb along my jaw in a feather-light touch that was so barely there it might as well have never been at all. The weight of the moment felt very father-daughter like and I kind of held my breath, enjoying it for the moment. I guess, if I had to be honest, even though we weren't far apart in age enough for him to be my dad, Alan was the closest thing to one I'd ever really had. It added another unexpected layer of *ow* to the whole I-was-really-leaving thing.

"He treats you the way you deserve, so yeah. You can save the last dance. Just let me know when you want to go on and what song. I'll let Drake know." Drake was our DJ.

I nodded and said, "Thanks."

"Just get on out of here and do well with whatever you do with your life from here on out." He pushed himself to his feet. "Succeed. That's all I ask." He looked me over, his eyes roving over my face and he sighed. "While I'm sorry to see you go, I'm so happy you're leaving. I really mean it when I say you're one of the best and far too good to stay here."

"You make my mascara run, we're gonna have problems boss."

He smiled and said, "Not anymore. You're your own boss, now," and with that, he walked away, down the hall, carrying on straight before making the turn and the end and heading up the back stair to his office.

"Crap," I muttered, snagging tissues out of the box on the table and pressing them to my eyes.

There was nothing for it. I cried like a little bitch. At least these weren't tears of heartbreak, though. Bittersweet, but definitely not broken.

34

Z eb...

"Hey, bro," I said kindly, with a nod to Zeke.

"You don't have to stop up front, you know," he said.

"Ah, nah, yeah, I know. I wanted to. Wanted to see how you were doing." He gave a shrug and shook his head, mouth drawn and grim. I nodded and he moved the frayed rope aside.

"Since you're here, you might want to get in there. It's Francesca's last dance."

"Thanks, bro. I reckon I owe you a cold one some night."

"Maybe after the weather warms up," he said, but though it was meant to be humorous there was no humor in it. Delia being gone hit Zeke harder than anyone realized and it didn't take a genius to realize that he had been as secretly infatuated with her as she had been with that Cooper bloke.

I wish I could have given Zeke the cold satisfaction of knowing what'd been done with Cooper but I wasn't about to put any of my bros in the club in any danger of word getting to the cops around here, not over some guy I barely knew and his feelings for a girl I knew even less. That was just madness and would be me begging to be put out bad. I'd walked that path once, even if it had been for honorable intentions. I wouldn't be trying it again.

I went into the club's dimly-lit interior and Alan, Tiffany's boss straightened up at the bar. He gave me a chin lift and I went over.

"A drink, on me. What will you have?"

"Gizza a beer," I said to the bartender and he gave me a nod with a quizzical look.

"I'm going to assume that meant 'give me' somehow," Alan said with a smile and I grinned.

"Ah, yeah, I do it without thinking, I reckon. Use things like that from back home."

"I figured."

"How're things?" I asked.

"Could be better. From a business stand-point, not too bad, from the standpoint of being worried about my girls and the rest of my employees..." He trailed off and shook his head, bowing it and grabbing the back of his neck.

I made a decision. "If I told you 'No worries, bro', would you believe me?" I asked.

He eyed me skeptically for a second and then a spark of recognition ignited in his eyes and he nodded slowly. "The reputation of your club proceeds you when it comes to believing. Your jacket definitely buys you some trust in this matter."

The bartender returned and set a bottle of beer on one of those paper coasters in front of me. I picked it up and took a swig.

"Francesca is about to perform her last dance; I saved you a seat by the stage," Alan said and gestured out that way with one hand.

"Thanks," I said and he led me over to a chair by a small round table just enough to hold my beer, an ashtray, and a pack of smokes if I had the latter. I wished I could fire up a blunt to mellow out some, but that would have to be later.

"Thank you for looking out for her," he said and clapped me on the shoulder. I nodded and with a smile, he was gone.

I settled in and took another swig of my beer. It was one of them good ones, not the cheap kind to scull to get down so you didn't have to taste it.

The dancer on the stage was just finishing up and the announcer came over the sound system.

"Alright, thank you, Candy! Let's give Candy a round of applause."

There was a smattering of clapping and an enthusiastic whistle and the music transitioned to some bass-heavy 80's music.

"Please welcome to the stage for her last dance, everybody, it's your very own queen of the night – let's give it up for *Francesca!*"

The music blared heavier and that hard-hitting voice that made you want to rise out of your seat declared she had everything I needed and more. I felt my lips curve into an appreciative smile as Tiffany burst from the curtains, striding along the stage one foot in front of the other, hands on her hips like she owned the night.

She made it to the pole and went around once, putting her back to it, sliding down, her knees parted and gloved hands, those fancy black satin ones that went to her elbow, tracing a line between her breasts over her stomach, tantalizingly to the waistband of the barely there scrap of panties covering her sex.

She had it. She knew just what she did to me, her eyes sparkling behind the black lace mask covering the one side of her face. The bass hit and she stood and did some really amazing shit around that pole that had every man around the stage panting for her, except I'd be the only one who got to lick, and I would until she came writhing underneath me as soon as I got her back to my flat.

She moved like fluid fire around that damn brass pole and along the black lacquered stage and there was something different about her. An unbridled joy to her dancing that I'd never seen before and I realized that she was performing her heart out up there and she was both beautiful and so fierce it squeezed my damn heart.

She made her way down the steps rather than do her seductive crawl like the first time I'd seen her dance, and made her way along the tables and chairs, drifting fingers teasingly over shoulders, giving one guy a playful shove against his forehead, until she came to me. She straddled my legs and bowed swiftly, coming up with her tits practically in my face and I couldn't say there was a complaint to be had about that. She turned around and gave me a spectacular view of her ass, and it was everything in me to keep my hands to myself as per the house rules.

She leaned back against me and I got an equally spectacular view over her shoulder, down between the valley of her breasts, her ass pressed lightly over my dick which was straining at the inside of my fly. She undulated against me, rubbing lightly against my crotch and I just about died and went to heaven.

She eased her bra off and held it off to one side, dropping it delicately, turning around again and sitting full on my lap, topless and alluring, her arms around my neck as she looked me in the eyes and with a wicked little smile, she kissed me. I lost what little self-control I had for a second and gripped her ass, pulling her hard up against me. The only thing between me and her and getting it on right there pretty much just my jeans.

She came up for air and, certain I had her, she bent all the way back, her hands kneading her breasts, her hips writhing over mine and I couldn't wait to recreate this without the damn clothes back at my place.

She came up slowly, passion in her eyes and I let her go when she stood. She took me by the hand and I stood with her. A little pirouette beneath my arm, she took a bow for the men, collected her cash from the floor around us and blew kisses, then took my hand again and with a little wave over her shoulder, led me to the back.

The *way* back, before she turned around and kissed me fiercely again. We broke the kiss, both of us breathing hard and I asked, "What the fuck was that?"

She smiled a little smile and said, "I saved the last dance for you."

"I see!" I exclaimed.

She smiled a little secretive smile and asked, "You park out front?"

"Yeah, I'll pull it around."

She shook her head and said, "I walked in the front door of this club the first time I ever came here, I think it's fitting I walk out the front when I leave."

I blinked, the gravity of what she was saying hit me.

"You quit?" I asked.

She nodded. "Alan and I talked. It's time."

I pulled her to me, an unexpected relief flooding through me, the tension draining out of me. I kissed her with a ferocity I'd never really dared try with her before, but I needed to. This was a kiss that said, *you're mine* and she stepped into it, pressing tightly up against me, her perfect tits molding to the front of my leathers, her hands finding my ass and pulling me closer.

"God, I need you to fuck me," she breathed and I realized what was different about that last dance. She was as turned on as I was, dancing for me, and she'd let herself go for real. Let herself feel the music, the vibe, just everything about it.

"Here? Now?" I asked.

She shook her head, "Never here. Not with you. Let me throw my clothes on and my shit together and take me home."

I grinned and said, "Sounds good to me," except I could never do that. Never take her home, because, for me, home was halfway across the world in New Zealand.

35

Tiffany...

We didn't make it into his apartment, which was the closest of the three locations we could have gone. He fetched me up hard against the wall outside its door in the hallway. Our mouths crashed together in a fit of passion that scaled higher and higher until I found my legs wrapped around his hips and the hard length of his cock pressing, scalding, against his jeans. Two layers of denim, a scrap of lace and depending on if he were wearing a pair of boxers or not, a thin layer of cotton was all that separated us from our heart's desire and it was way too much clothing.

He fumbled with his keys blindly, trying to get them into the lock and I loved how his hips thrust against me. How he dry-humped me like a horny teenager as he worked desperately to get us inside. I didn't care. I'd let him do me right here, in the hall, against the cracked and paint-chipped wall.

He shoved the door open with a triumphant grunt into my mouth that was swallowed by the laugh that came from mine. I held onto him, clung to him with arms and legs and he strode into the place, kicking the door shut behind us.

The mattress was where he'd left it, in front of the cold hearth, and I wistfully wished for a fire, but at the same time I didn't want to stop what we were doing for him to build one so I said nothing.

"Mm, down," he ordered. "Down, down, down, down, down!" he said rapid-fire against my mouth when I didn't immediately comply. I got down and he shrugged out of his coat and gave me a look like I wasn't getting naked fast enough. I laughed and stripped down twice as fast as he did. Of course, I had years of practice getting my clothes off – him not so much.

My panties were kicked off to the side in a soggy heap and he reached for me as soon as he was naked, too. I gladly went into his arms and we kissed for far too short of a time before he turned me around and shoved me onto my knees on the rumpled bed. I crawled up a ways to give him some mattress to kneel on and spare his knees from the hardwood and he gave my ass a playful slap in thanks.

It was that kind of a mood and the light sting made me bow lower to the covers, my ass up, hips pushed back offering the opening to my cunt to him and he didn't waste any time. He pressed the pad of his thumb and lightly teased my asshole which both surprised me and felt right in the moment. He didn't try to breach it, which I appreciated; he was just going for some down and dirty sex, and I was so looking forward to that.

I gave a low moan when he slicked the head of his cock up and down my slit from opening to clit and back. He teased me, thrusting between my legs, his dick hard and hot, running the slick head of it against my clit, teasing these high gasping little moans from me.

"Please," I begged, voice breathy and he slapped me on the ass again. A deep, wanting ache had taken up residence in my pussy and I just wanted him inside me so damn bad. I thrust my hips back lightly and tried to capture him as he played his body against mine and I heard him give a dark chuckle.

He stopped playing when I gave a whining little groan and shoved into me hard and fast, going balls-deep, but my body had been ready for him since the club and all he did was fit me like a lock and key.

He ground against me, pulling back on my hips and doing that thing he did that drove me nuts. Just something about him being all the way inside me and him pulling me down on him harder, grinding up and down touched off a chain reaction inside me that had me on the verge of orgasm in no time and fuck he was an expert at keeping me there, drawing out my pleasure for what felt like forever until I slid into an altered state of mind, a place where everything felt warm and the world took on this hazy quality that blurred around the edges.

"Touch your clit, make yourself come on that dick," he ordered roughly, and I was happy to comply.

I face planted into his bed so I could reach between my thighs and tease that delicate and sensitive bundle of nerve.

"Aw, God that's it, yeah!" he sucked in a breath between his teeth as I tightened up my pussy around him and that warm, golden glow, began to suffuse me from the inside out.

I rocked back to meet his every forward thrust, voice forced from me in an even cadence to match our rocking. I panted, gasping faster and faster, the fuller the feeling got as if I were a cup holding a steady stream of pleasure. I was on the brink, the pleasure barely held from spilling over by surface tension alone. I held my breath and with a cry, spilled out of my skin, up my throat in an ecstasy filled cry that rushed across the hardwood floor and flooded the apartment with pure, unbridled joy.

I found myself back in my body, gasping, satisfied, and floating on a sea of warm afterglow, lying on my stomach with Nik stretched out beside me. He lay on his side, head propped on his hand and fingertips lightly tracing patterns on my back. I blinked and focused on him and he smiled and said, "Never fucked a woman into losing it so completely before."

"Never been fucked so well," I said and smiled, stretching like a cat and moving over so I could cuddle him and be cuddled by him in return.

He rolled onto his back and pulled me against his chest. I sighed, a content and happy sound and he sighed too.

"I have no idea what I'm going to do now," I said.

"Part of the adventure isn't it?"

"I suppose so," I said softly.

"One day at a time, I reckon."

"That sounds good, although I like to have a plan."

"You plan to graduate, yeah?"

"Yeah, I have to do my practicum, that's coming up next quarter."

We talked about what that meant and how I needed to go about completing everything. We were quiet for a time and then he ventured with, "You know I only pay peanuts for this place a month, you probably pay more for your flat. I reckon to save money it might make sense to move in together, yeah?"

I liked the sound of that. I know Silas was gone, I'd seen to that, but my apartment wasn't in the safest part of town and I didn't exactly have a job now. It would also let me divert yet more money into other things.

"You mean that?" I asked softly.

"Of course I do."

"You honestly think you could live with me and my crazy cat?"

"Who, Max? She's not so bad."

I smiled, "I love that you love my cat."

"I love you," he said.

I cuddled closer to him and closed my eyes.

"I love you, too."

EPILOGUE

Zeb...

It had to be around three in the morning, but the party was still going hard. I lay in a hammock with my girl and we listened to the laughter around the campfire on the lakeshore. We were resting, it'd been a great day hanging with my bros while Tiffany had taught some pole dancing moves to Everett where the tetherball court was, in the back of the main cabin.

All in all, it was another successful spring lake run in the books. We'd been living together for a few months now. She'd been doing her practicum during the day, working out of a battered-women's shelter, and had been working some night shifts part-time at Hayley's family's diner to fill in. Waitressing didn't pay nearly as much as dancing had, but she was happy and to me, that was priceless.

"Mmm, answer it," she murmured lazily from where she rested against my chest. I frowned and did the math in my head as I pulled my phone out of the inside pocket of my cut.

"This is Zeb," I answered.

"Nikau, it's your auntie, Bubs," a familiar voice crackled over the line. I sat up and Tiffany struggled up with me.

"I know who it is," I said and I could hear the weeping, like singing, of my mother in the background. I wondered if it was my grandmother and forced out, "What's wrong?"

"It's your sister," she said and I felt my heart sink.

"What's happened to her, auntie?"

"Nikau, it's time to come home," she declared and I felt a grim resignation take hold.

"Be there as soon as I can."

We exchanged a few more words; she wouldn't tell me exactly what was going on until she saw me, but that was just the way of my people. Some things just shouldn't be said over the phone.

"You have your passport?" I asked Tiff.

"Yeah, yeah I do, actually. Never thought I would use it, though."

"Could be dangerous," I warned and she gave me a level look.

"I go where you go," she said softly, and I nodded.

It was going to be a long trip, but I was finally going home.

GLOSSARY

The following is a glossary of Kiwi terms used throughout the book that may be unfamiliar to readers in other parts of the world. Special thanks to Susan Brock for all your help with the Kiwi-isms and better Kiwi-fying this book.

Bloke – the American version of this would be 'Dude.'

Bonnet – Hood of a car or truck.

Boot – Trunk of a car.

Brassed Off – Pissed off. Angry. To take off angry.

Bro & Cuz – Pretty much means what it says but rarely refers to an actual blood relative.

Carked – Died.

Chur – Sweet. Awesome. Yeah. Good. Cool. Cheers. It means all of those things.

Choice – Cool. Sweet. Thanks. Depends on context.

Cuppa – as in a cup of coffee or cup of tea.

Eh – this slang word can be added to just about every sentence in just about every way. It's just a way of speaking, eh.

Facecloth – Washcloth.

Flannel – Washcloth.

Flash – Looks brand new or really good.

Flat – Apartment.

French Letter or Frenchie – A condom.

Gidday – Hello.

Give Your Ferret A Run – Have sex.

Gizza – Short for 'give me.'

Good As Gold – Everything is awesome.

Hiding – Fight or beating. "Wanna hiding, bro?" means "Wanna beating, bro?"

Home 'n' Hosed – Safe. Everything completed successfully.

Hoon – A hooligan but also refers to the nature of people's driving.

Knackered - Tired as fuck.

Knickers – Underwear.

Maori – Indigenous New Zealand people.

Mate – Buddy or friend.

Mean As – Referring to something being great, awesome, or good.

Metal Road – a country road with a gravel surface.

Munted – When something is broken or someone is fucked up on booze.

Nek Minute – Basically means 'next minute.'

Packing A Sad – Throwing a tantrum.

Piece of Piss – Same as when something is a piece of cake, or easy to do.

Piss Up – Party. Alcohol is usually referred to as piss. So 'pissed' depending on context could mean drunk or angry.

Scull – Drink beer rapidly. (America: Chug! Chug! Chug! In New Zealand, it's 'Scull! Scull! Scull!')

She'll Be Right – When something is going to be okay. "That leg looks infected." "Nah, she'll be right." Alternatively, 'she'll come right' or 'we'll see you right.'

Skux – To look cool, trendy, or hot.

Stink one – An expression of disappointment.

Stubbies – Short shorts.

Sus – When someone looks suspect or something is a bit suspicious.

Sweet As – Extraordinarily good.

Ta – Thanks.

Too Much – Awesome or good.

Wops – A place in the middle of nowhere.

ALSO BY A.J. DOWNEY

Indigo Knights

1. Her Thin Blue Lifeline

2. His Cold Blue Command

3. A Low Blue Flame

4. His Wild Blue Rose

5. Her Pained Blue Silence

6. A Cold Blue Call

7. Her Reluctant Blue Cavalier

8. Forged Under Fire

9. Under A Blue Moon

10. Sound of Blue Thunder

Sacred Hearts MC Pacific Northwest

1. Over the High Side

2. Wind Therapy

3. Apex of the Curve

4. Low Sided

5. Eating Asphalt

6. Hammer Down

7. Only Fool Riding

The Voodoo Bastards MC

1. Bourbon & Blood

2. Whiskey Shivers

3. Moonshine Lullabies

4. Cognac Secrets

5. Tequila Damnation

Iron Wraiths MC

1. Original Syn

2. Love & Fear

3. The Hangman's Rope

Royal Bastard MC: St. Augustine Chapter

1. Iron Hearts

Paranormal Romance (with Ryan Kells)

1. I Am The Alpha

2. Omega's Run

3. Hunter's End

Indigo City Darker (with Jared KingPacal Lain)

1. Triple Threat

2. Double Shot

Standalones

Synchronicity

ABOUT A.J. DOWNEY

A.J. Downey is a Pacific Northwest girl living in an East Tennessee world who finds inspiration from her surroundings, through the people she meets, and likely as a byproduct of way too much caffeine. She specializes in real and relatable romance stories featuring that real-life kind of love that everyone craves.

Stalker Information:

Website
www.ajdowney.com